ROAD
to
REDEMPTiON

ROAD
to
REDEMPT*i*ON

TOM FITZGERALD

PUBLISHING

Road to Redemption
Copyright © 2025 by Tom Fitzgerald.
All rights reserved.

Reasonable excerpts from this book may be photocopied or reproduced without explicit permission from the publisher provided these excerpts are to be used in published reviews or for sharing a particular idea or concept with someone who might personally benefit from exposure to it. Reasonable in this context is meant to constitute no more material than you would want copied or reproduced free of charge if you were the author and depended on sales of this work and others for your livelihood.

80/20 Publishing, LLC
1073 Oberland Drive
Midway, UT 84049
www.8020books.com

Distributed in the United States and Canada by Simon & Schuster

Library of Congress Control Number: 2024926886
ISBN 979-8-9892569-8-3 print
ISBN 979-8-9892569-9-0 ebook

Cover and interior design by Vicki Hopewell
Cover illustration: Francesco Bongiorni / Rapp Art

O the pain, the pain that comes upon me!
Let me be, let me be, you wretches!
May death the healer come for me at last!
You kill me ten times over with this pain.
O for a spear with a keen cutting edge to
shear me apart—and give me my last sleep!
Father, your deadly curse!

—EURIPIDES, *HIPPOLYTUS*

The human spirit is virtually indestructible,
and its ability to rise from the ashes remains
as long as the body draws breath.

—ALICE MILLER, *FOR YOUR OWN GOOD*

Contents

1. Renegade Race 1
2. Boston 3
3. Holy Crusade 15
4. A Natural Rhythm 33
5. Boxed In 71
6. No Tomorrow 77
7. In Too Deep 105
8. 8-Mile Mark 109
9. Second Fall 129
10. Overheating 133
11. Uncharted Territory 147
12. Out of Reach 155
13. Halfway There 173
14. Inner Turmoil 185
15. Challenge Accepted 195
16. New Resolve 201
17. Not Alone 209
18. This Is a Test 215
19. Collision Course 221
20. Heartbreak Hill 225
21. Extreme Duress 239
22. Survival of the Fittest 245
23. Citgo or Bust 259
24. Daffodil Dreams 263
25. Awakening 265
26. Making Peace 267
27. Unchained Melody 275

Acknowledgments 277
About the Author 279

1

Renegade Race

APRIL 19, 1983, 1:01 A.M.

Cooper was crouched behind a roadside berm of sand and debris not far from his home in Madbury, New Hampshire. A van, barely visible in the dark, stopped a few yards away. He remained a few moments longer, then emerged from his hiding place and, looking in the direction from which the van had just come, searched for headlights.

Nothing.

Cooper opened the rear doors of the van and, cringing to a metallic squeak, tossed a backpack into the rear compartment of the van, atop a deflated air mattress. The overhead lights revealed a sleeping bag and a boat potty—but no cooler.

Cooper spoke in little more than a whisper. "Cooler?"

"Up here."

"OK."

Cooper closed the rear doors of the van, then opened the sliding door on the passenger side and climbed onto a bench seat located just forward of his makeshift sleeping quarters. He tried to fasten his seat belt, but his fingers would not sufficiently cooperate. He struggled for a moment longer, then gave up. What difference did it make?

"All set," he said. "Giddyup!"

Cooper took a deep breath. By the time Tessa and the boys found his note, he would be in Hopkinton, hopefully sound asleep.

"Thanks for being on time," Cooper said.

"No problem. Thanks for the hire. We don't get many private hauls anymore. C&J's gets them all."

"Bummer."

As the van eased into motion, Cooper strained to look down the shadowy void that was Garrison Lane and felt a sting at the back of his throat. For a fleeting moment, he could hear the sound of children playing street hockey, with Whiskers, the neighborhood cat, serving as goalie.

The van abruptly stopped.

A deer stood in the road not more than ten yards in front of the van. It wasn't alone. The high beams revealed two companions positioned a little farther down Pudding Hill Road. All three deer stood perfectly still, eyes aglow, then suddenly leaped away.

2

Boston

Cooper's stomach felt as if it had turned itself inside out and had begun to digest his liver. He was standing on Main Street in Hopkinton, Massachusetts, about 9,000 runners back from the starting line. Cooper wore the same bright-red T-shirt he raced in at the Danville 5 Miler two weeks ago, which had "The Little Engine That Could" imprinted on the front and an illustration of a diminutive engine sitting atop a mountain on the back.

In addition to his running paraphernalia, Cooper was wearing a hockey helmet, kneepads, elbow pads, and bicycle gloves. He had almost left these accessories in Zeke's van. Each item was, in fact, essential to his having any chance of crossing the finish line. Furthermore, this was the Boston Marathon, and soon enough he would be surrounded by a large number of celebratory back-of-the-packers dressed in some kind of costume. Truth be told, nobody was going to give him a second look.

Cooper witnessed a few more seconds tick by on his watch—11:47:34, 11:47:35, 11:47:36—then bounced a few more times on the balls of his feet and again shook his arms limply at his sides. He was still feeling a little stiff from sleeping in the back of Zeke's van.

There was still time, he reminded himself, not for the first time, to call the whole thing off. He might even be able to get home in time for dinner!

There would be no shame. He could watch the *NBC Monday Movie* and eat Coffee Toffy Thunder out of the tub.

Bending forward, Cooper stared at his size-16 Nike's and grinned. Following a quick survey of the immediate area to see if he could catch anybody staring at him, he massaged his calves.

Despite being lathered with Ben-Gay, they felt a little tight.

No cramps! he said sternly.

Cooper smiled, remembering how talking to his muscles became commonplace not long after noticing the twitching in his hands and calves. If the brain can make a thumb flex simply by ordering it to flex, surely he could order his thumb to stop twitching.

Cooper drew in the deepest breath he could manage, held it a moment, then let it out of its own weight—which was noticeably less than what he had been able to manage two weeks ago.

Even though his last checkup confirmed he was continuing to lose lung function, he was losing it at a slower rate than expected.

In other words, he was still in the game.

His goal for the Danville 5 Miler two weeks ago had been to finish in 45 minutes or less. His neurologist had tried to talk him out of it, as had just about everyone else in his inexorably shrinking circle. They had all agreed that the likelihood of a fall—indeed, of multiple falls—was just too great. He had met his time goal by 30 seconds and finished the race having suffered only one fall, the effects of which had been mitigated by his protective paraphernalia. More importantly, he had demonstrated to himself that he was capable of running more than 5 miles. Maybe even *a lot* more! In fact, if he could run 5 miles, then he could run 6. And if he could run 6, he could run 7. And if he could run 7, he could run 8—all the way up to 26! What were comebacks for if not his very situation? They can't be even close to easy, right?

The last forecast Cooper had gotten, from Zeke, called for the sky to remain overcast and the air temperature to hold steady in the low to mid-50s through most of the afternoon. A warm front was expected to come through the area in the late afternoon or early evening and bring with it higher temperatures, more humid air, and, of all things, the possibility of a thunderstorm.

Bottom line: The temperature should stay in his favor, at least until he was able to get across the finish line. Essentially, he had dodged a bullet. A temperature of 60 degrees or greater would likely have brought him to his knees well before the midway point of the race.

A young woman in front of him turned and looked past him—to the right, then to the left—as if looking for someone. She didn't seem to notice Cooper's full-contact fashion statement. She was no older than 25, likely weighed little more than 100 pounds, and was wearing purple shorts and a white singlet trimmed in the same shade of purple. A gold crucifix was hanging from a delicate gold chain clasped around her neck.

The words from your golden lips
Do not speak to me;
They fall upon the humus of my soul—
But they do not take root there.

Cooper basked in a moment of comfort knowing his sons would have his journals as a means of knowing at least a little about who their father was and what he thought about things. How different things might have been had Cooper's own father shared with his sons at least a little of who *he* was and what *he* thought about various things.

Hearing a distinctive staccato sound, Cooper looked up at a dull sky and watched a canary-yellow helicopter pass overhead.

Navy SEAL Test

APRIL 1967

Cooper stood in formation on Coronado's Silver Strand facing the eternal expanse of the Pacific Ocean with the other trainees who had managed to survive the first two weeks of Underwater Demolition Team (UDT) / SEAL training. At least a quarter of those remaining, everyone well knew, would be gone before the end of the third week. Statistics ruled.

He was in trouble. The blisters on both of his feet, but especially those on his right foot, had gotten markedly worse over the past three days. His hammertoes were raw and throbbed unrelentingly.

Wearing jump boots a size too small would likely have been no big deal for a few days—maybe even for a week—but for two weeks?

"They's the largest we got, sir. Take 'em or leave 'em."

Cooper had placed a special order for size-16 boots at the Exchange almost two weeks ago now, but they still hadn't come in. "Any day now," he had been assured, over and over.

Surely they would come in this weekend!

Being able to stand in place for a few minutes allowed Cooper to favor his right foot, however briefly, fostering the illusion of it feeling better.

Lieutenant Knowles was standing in front of them in khaki cutoffs strategically tailored to flatter his NFL physique. He seemed to be on the verge of throwing a tantrum over being drowned out by the rumble of an Orion sub hunter taking off from the North Island.

The lieutenant's polished black boots were neatly trimmed at the top with the overflow of woolen socks worn only by Navy SEALs. Half his face was hidden behind a pair of mirrored aviators, epitomizing the manner and stance of one who can tolerate not so much as a glimpse of a rival anywhere in his proximity—chin slightly uplifted, feet slightly spread, hips tilted forward—in a posture intended to hint at the ferocity of the dragon that dwelled within.

The lieutenant was holding a clipboard in his left hand, levered against the inside of his forearm.

Cooper watched the Orion sub hunter bear toward the whaleback promontory of Point Loma and recalled a dream he'd had a few times in his 23 years. He would pump his arms at his sides and feel himself lift from the ground and slowly ascend. He would have to keep pumping his arms, though, or he would plunge downward.

If he could choose, he would come back as a bird. Not a big or raucous one. A chickadee maybe.

Chicka dee dee dee—

The drone of the Orion sub hunter abated as it began to dissolve into the haze generated by the frigid waters of the Coastal Pacific.

"OK, listen up!" the lieutenant bellowed, reclaiming his sovereignty. "Here's the deal. This evolution is a timed run. You hack it, you get to embarrass yourself in Hell Week; you wimp out, you get to go back to the fleet—where most of you belong."

The lieutenant gestured down-beach with his clipboard. "The course is a total of 4 miles—down to the dunes, *around* the Jeep, and back here.

"Any puke don't go *around* the Jeep is automatically disqualified. Comprende?"

A chorus of 123 voices sang out "Yes sir!" in perfect unison.

"You got 30 minutes—by my watch." The lieutenant glowered. "Any questions?"

Silence.

"Any questions!"

"No sir!"

"OK, you pukes better believe what I just said. Any o' ya can't hack this piddly little stroll on the beach, it's sayonara so goddamn fast, you won't have time t'pack your pantyhose."

Cooper could hear snickers from three young beach bunnies sitting on a berm behind Cooper, to his right. One of them, Cooper was pretty sure, was the lieutenant's girlfriend—artificially blond, deeply tanned, loosely haltered. Cooper had seen her lolling in the background a few times previously.

The lieutenant gestured in the general direction of the Navy Yard, to the east, where one would find a dozen or so gray-hulled Navy vessels moored at any given time, several of which would be nondescript support ships, more than likely the same ones that had been moored in the same berths seemingly forever, as if they had become mired in the sludge that was gradually filling the bay.

"I will personally recommend you for duty on an oiler. Is that clear?"

"Yes sir!"

"Jesus Fuckin' Christ! Is that the best you pukes can do?"

Although their collective volume had surely been as great as it had been back when their number had included 64 additional voices, it was *never* loud enough for Lieutenant Knowles, especially with a female audience bearing witness to his manifest manliness.

"Yes sir!"

"It *is?*"

"No sir!"

"OK—when I say 'fall out,' I wanna see a hundert twenty-three funky bodies standing behind the starting line."

The lieutenant stared as he might at an English teacher half his size who had just given him an F on a book report the day before the big game.

Why were there so many bullies in the world? Wasn't it the meek who were supposed to inherit the Earth?

"Faaaaall—in!"

Cooper charged toward the line Officer Stovers had drawn in the sand between two Day-Glo flags. Then it struck him—Cooper shifted himself into reverse, but it was too late.

"Everyone that moved, drop and give me 50!"

Fifty? It was always just 20! Why 50 now? So this fucking egomaniac could demonstrate his dominance to his worshipful gallery?

Cooper assumed the position and winced as the hot sand burned the sores on his palms. Every time he wasn't able to do the required number of pull-ups at morning physical training (PT), he was ordered to climb a rope to a height of about 20 feet and hang on until he had slid to the ground, abrading—burning—his palms the entire distance.

Unfortunately, Cooper had never been able to develop the kind of upper-body strength most of his peers seemed to have been born with. Hence—at 6 foot, 2 inches and 212 pounds—he *never* really had a chance of meeting the daily quota of pull-ups.

Cooper pumped out his push-ups with his usual exactitude—keeping his back straight, going all the way down, all the way up—knowing full well that almost everybody else was cheating to one degree or another.

Down—25. Down—26. Down—27. Down—

If he stuck to his principles, though, Cooper made himself believe, and refused to compromise, sooner or later even the more sadistic of his instructors would take notice of the difference between his efforts and those of the cheaters and would extend him a badly needed break now and then. Justice would prevail.

Down 49. Down—Cooper's arms trembled. His face burned. 50! Two more and he would have collapsed. He had taken a needless risk. *Why? Am I actually* looking *for a way out?*

"Re-cover!"

Cooper rose to his feet—in company with several other overeager "pukes"—and felt the blood drain from his brain, his knees buckle. He braced himself, hands on knees, to lower his center of gravity, and took a few deep breaths.

If Lieutenants Knowles or Richardson detected the slightest weakness, they would pounce on him. They would make him do squat thrusts or eight-count bodybuilders until he passed out.

His right foot felt hot—swollen. Nauseous and dizzy, this "puke" was about to puke—another show of weakness! He pictured a rubber band stretched to its breaking point. He could feel the tension in it. He visualized the rubber band contracting. He could feel the tension lessen. He willed the rubber band to contract a little farther. He could feel a further lessening of tension—

"Faaall—*out!*"

Boston

Cooper hesitated a fraction of a second, then sprang into motion.

"Last one gets 30 seconds added to his time!"

Cooper winced with each footfall. *Mind over matter*, he told himself.

Reaching a freshly drawn starting line, Cooper looked over his shoulder to assure himself he wasn't going to be the recipient of the penalty and watched one of the enlisted trainees, Hustveldt, join the pack at the very rear. Hustveldt was one of those perennial fuck-ups you wanted to have close to you to serve as sort of a lightning rod for unwanted attention—but not *too* close.

Cooper searched for the Jeep marking the turnaround point. He could make out a few people strolling near the surf line and a couple of civilian runners off in the distance, but nothing more. He didn't trust that the Jeep would be where Lieutenant Knowles said it would be. Stationing it farther down-beach, in fact—say, at the 3-mile mark—was just the kind of stunt Dickhead Knowles would pull to break the spirit of anyone just hanging on by the skin of their teeth.

Reality #1: Just about everybody else in the program was at least 30 pounds lighter than he was.

Reality #2: There wasn't a pair of boots on the planet large enough to accommodate his grievously blistered feet.

So what am I doing here? Cooper took a deep breath.

It didn't matter. He would make it, or he would die trying.

Hell Week

FALL 1961

Cooper was standing with his fellow pledges inside a two-stall garage attached to the Phi Delta Omicron (FIDO) house. They all looked on as the fraternity president, Stone Phillips, tied Sammy Kahn's hands behind his back and blindfolded him.

Two of the other brothers, Tony Calabrese and Bob Kneeland, their monogrammed Phi Delta Omicron beer mugs clutched in one hand, climbed a ladder leading to the loft above.

Another brother, Gerry LeCompte, removed the ladder from the loft entry, then he and Tony Defedele laid Sammy out on an old mattress and positioned his head directly beneath the opening in the loft floor.

Sammy began to shake his head back and forth—half pleading, half wailing.

Stone told Sammy that if he didn't stop moving his head, he would be depledged. He would be dropped off at the dorms, and that would be the end of his welcome at FIDO. Being a brother, Sammy was reminded, meant doing what one was told and being loyal to one's brothers no matter what.

Cooper knew Sammy would do whatever was demanded of him. Phi Delta Omicron was the only fraternity on campus that a Sammy Kahn had a prayer of getting into. The big men of Delta Upsilon took no Sammy Kahns. The jocks of Theta Chi took no Sammy Kahns. The animals of Sigma Delta took no Sammy Kahns. The Boy Scouts of O-Pi-O took no Sammy Kahns. Even the dweebs of Theta Xi took no Sammy Kahns.

Sammy held his head steady.

"Open wide."

Sammy hesitated, then, tears welling up in his eyes, opened his mouth.

"All the way!" Stone commanded.

A glob of raw egg splattered on Sammy's forehead as he attempted to stifle a yelp.

Boos erupted from the brothers, several of whom had arrived within the last few minutes in their black-and-gold FIDO jackets just in time for the show.

The next glob struck Sammy on the blindfold, almost directly over his left eye. Sammy put in a plea for it to stop while holding his head motionless.

The third glob disappeared en masse into Sammy's mouth.

In an instant, Cooper's mind hurtled back ten years, to the Royal Republic of Brainia and the Grand Humiliator. "This is bullshit!" he yelled. "Fuck you guys! Fuck you!" Cooper stormed out of the garage and did not stop running until he had reached his dorm.

In Denial

APRIL 1967

Lieutenant Knowles looked toward Stovers, who was standing beside the Jeep that would be used to collect the quitters.

"Ready?"

Stovers was holding a stopwatch. One cheek was bulging with the usual chaw of tobacco.

"Ready—sir."

Cooper could tell by the way Stovers said "sir"—always a beat late, with just a smidge of gratuitous emphasis—that he disliked the lieutenant every bit as much as the trainees did. He could tell also, by the lieutenant's lack of reaction, that he never got the message.

"Get set...go!"

Cooper squinted, tracking the stark-white T-shirts on the lead runners that rhythmically moved down the beach like tails on a herd of galloping deer.

The two specks of Day-Glo orange Cooper had caught a glimpse of a few minutes ago seemed no closer—as if Lieutenant Knowles was already moving the turnaround farther away with every step Cooper took toward it.

Cooper winced to a sharp pain in his right foot. *Who knew stepping on a kelp bladder could be like stepping on a nail?*

He should have *forced* himself to report to the corpsman. To show the corpsman the swelling in his right foot. The red streaks running up his right leg.

He should have *forced* himself to admit the truth: What he was afflicted with was *not* a bad case of blistering; it was a bad case of cellulitis! *Life threatening if left untreated.*

The bay was polluted, and open sores, as from constant blistering, were an invitation to infection. The same thing had washed Lieutenants Carothers and Savich out of the program, as well as several of the enlisted trainees. But instead of doing the right thing, Cooper had done what he always did when confronted with a reality he didn't want to deal with—he had pushed it out of his mind.

Logic 101: *If you refuse to look at something, if you refuse to acknowledge its existence, it can't possibly exist.*

3

Holy Crusade

Motion ahead. Shouts and whistles. *This was it—sink or swim!*

At first, the great mass of runners moved so slowly, Cooper could only shuffle. Then it began to oscillate between pulling him into a jog and forcing him back into a shuffle. A few times he had to stop altogether.

"Just like commuting!" Cooper shouted to the runner on his right, but the black-bearded man made no response.

Shuffling past Hayden Rowe, Cooper checked his watch: 12:04:34. The elite runners would already be a mile downstream. Toggling back to his stopwatch, he quickly confirmed the display read all zeros. The starting stripe would appear without warning. He had to be ready.

Fifty yards or so ahead, the roadway was spanned by a platform attached to a cherry picker—the kind used by utility companies to work on power lines. He knew the official starting line would be just ahead of the platform.

A man wearing a headset was pointing a TV camera at the crowd below.

Several runners were waving at the camera, shouting and whistling, and wasting a lot of precious energy—which likely was not an issue for them.

As he approached the village green on the right, Cooper placed a thumb on the Start/Stop button on his watch, which, of course, was ridiculous. If the only thing that mattered was crossing the stripe at the Prudential

Center—crawling across it if he had to—why did he need a watch? To create unrealistic expectations? He could *not* allow that to happen. But wasn't that, in fact, exactly what he was doing? Wasn't this the kind of thing that running addicts did?

No sooner had Cooper fixed his eyes on the heels of the runner immediately ahead of him than he stepped on the blue-and-yellow starting strip. He pressed the Start button on his watch.

"This is it!" he heard someone say.

"This is it," he heard himself echo. "There's no tomorrow."

He watched a few seconds flash by on his watch, then looked ahead at a rivulet of color and costume. Only 26 miles, 385 yards to go!

Where would he find the strength? He might have had it two months ago—maybe even one month ago—but now? He should have listened to Tessa. To George. To himself! He was setting himself up for what could only be another failure.

Looking to his right, Cooper scanned the spectators standing several deep on an embankment overlooking the roadway. They were cheering with great gusto, as if seeing off an army of foot soldiers embarking on a holy crusade.

Holy *crusade? Is this an oxymoron I see before me?*

Unfortunately, it would be out of mind before he could write it down.

Looking to his left, Cooper noticed several people observing the passing pageantry from the upstairs windows on an old colonial cape.

Saving the World

MAY 1964

Cooper was standing behind a lectern in the grand ballroom at the Château Laurier in Ottawa. He had been president of his class since his sophomore year, and the senior ball was to be his crowning achievement, despite the fact he would not be graduating with his classmates a few days hence.

He had flunked German, a required course for all math majors.

In the past, senior balls had been unremarkable affairs held within the unremarkable environs of Potsdam, New York—but not this one! This event was being held a stone's throw from Canada's parliament buildings and had involved, so far, busing the entire class of 1964, along with their dates and several guests, from Potsdam to Brockville, Ontario, and then transporting everybody from there, on a chartered, booze-laden train, to the CN station in city-center Ottawa.

There was grandiosity here, which, if it were grand enough, would surely be noticed.

Among the twenty-one other people at the head table were the president of Clarkson, his wife, and the US ambassador to Canada and his wife.

Cooper had just finished reading another of several "telegrams" sent by a variety of celebrities offering words of wisdom and/or congratulations to the graduates, most of whom were dangerously under the influence of a cocktail "hour" that had begun in Brockville and ended at the Château. The more inebriated of the arrivers included Walter Jaynes, the "village drunk," who had joined the assembly in the grand ballroom only after being detained for two hours by the Royal Canadian Mounted Police for urinating in the tunnel connecting the CN station with the hotel's main lobby. It had taken a whisper from Cooper in the US ambassador's ear to finally spring them loose.

For some reason, Canadians were very forgiving toward American excesses, which Cooper suspected had something to do with the superior upbringing of Canadians.

Of course, there were exceptions. Cooper's great-grandfather, Horace Spafford, a druggist by trade, had been born in Canada but had ended up a raging drunk.

Cooper had failed German yet again, having neglected to attend class. For his penance, he was going to have to spend the first half of the summer taking German for a third time, at the University of Rochester, or else he would not be able to matriculate at the Cornell Law School come September.

Which, actually, might not be a bad thing.

Did he really *want* to be a lawyer? Or was the degree just a means to a different end?

Cooper picked up another "telegram" from the lectern.

"This one," he announced, "comes to us from the very shadow of the Berlin Wall." Cooper stiffened and clicked his heels to raucous laughter. "Ach–tung! Ich bin ein Klarksohner! Herr Villy Brandt."

Everyone at Clarkson—students and faculty alike—was aware of Cooper Haynes's troubled history with the German language.

The previous autumn, William Louis Willson had crowned himself president of Clarkson and lord of the realm and had feted himself with a lavish, tuition-funded coronation that had included importing a troupe of bagpipers from Canada to lead a grand procession around the perimeter of the hockey rink. In the nine months since, Dr. Willson had employed an autocratic style to alienate both the student body and the faculty, save for a few bootlickers.

Turning now, with martial precision, to face Dr. Willson, who was seated next to the ambassador's bejeweled wife, Cooper cried out, "Vive el presidente!" resulting in pandemonium.

Hours later, on the train ride home, a much beloved but circumspect math professor would tell Cooper, "No one at Clarkson would have had the balls to do what you just did. Thank you."

Waiting for the tumult to subside—savoring it but wishing for it to stop—Cooper looked above the archipelago of circular, linen-draped tables and noticed a man braced against the balcony railing overlooking the cavernous ballroom. Dressed in the hotel waitstaff attire, his gaze was fixed on several young ladies, dressed in stylishly low-cut gowns, sitting with their dates at the tables below.

Cupping his hands around his mouth, Cooper megaphoned, "Sir? You up there!" The man stiffened. "Yes—you!" The man appeared simultaneously self-conscious and apologetic, like a boy nabbed with his hand in the proverbial cookie jar. "Sorry—no photographs from up there, please, if you don't mind."

A few hundred pairs of eyes turned as if following a blistering forehand shot at Wimbledon and arrested en masse on the bewildered man standing on the balcony.

Silence.

One of the female guests strategically tucked her cloth napkin into her bosom.

Tentative murmuring gave way to sporadic laughter, followed by a collective roar. Even the venerable honorables at the head table began to laugh—including the Honorable Mister Ambassador and even the Honorable Über Alles.

A man at one of the tables jumped to his feet and began clapping and whistling. More people stood until everyone in the room was standing.

"Danke schön!" Cooper shouted as he bowed, then continued, "If I may, I would like to leave you with two interrogatives: What right did Lincoln have to prevent the Southern states from seceding from the Union? Was it the same right George III had to prevent the colonies from seceding from the British Empire? And what likely would have happened had JFK famously quipped, 'Ashk not what your country can do for you. Ashk *not* what you can do for your country. Ashk, friend, what we can do for each other.'"

Morning Light

SEPTEMBER 1982

Cooper's right thumb was throbbing. Tessa was shaking him. As he gained wakefulness, he could see the shade above her desk framed in early morning light.

"Bad dream?"

"Cramp," he replied, slapping his hand in quick succession.

He had read a while back about a man who couldn't stop hiccuping, and the cure only came when he was given an electric shock in a higher dose with each successive hiccup. Lucky man—he either was going to stop hiccuping or was going to die.

"Can I kiss it better?"

Cooper offered his hand to Tessa.

She kissed it several times. "All better."

"You're a powerful woman."

"I know."

"I'd better keep you then, eh?"

"You'd better."

Cooper shook his hand. "It's gone. Thanks."

"See? What did the slapping get you?" After a pause, Tessa pressed, "I'm concerned, Cooper, about the pressure you're under. Remember back in Iowa when you came down with that persistent rash all over your body?"

Of course he remembered. For more than two years, he looked like a leper. In addition to taking a full load of courses in order to qualify for the maximum VA benefit, he had also been teaching a section of freshman composition and spending several hours a week in the writing clinic disabusing an endless stream of verbally impaired freshmen of the notion that appositives were funny-looking animals that lived in trees. And there were the writing workshops held in schools across the State of Iowa, which required him to miss up to a week of classes at a time, but he found himself unable to permit himself to turn down a single gig because of the hefty $100 a day it paid. Meanwhile, to fulfill his thesis requirement, he'd been writing a contrived, unforgivably self-conscious "literary" novel, *A Voice from Heaven*, in lieu of following the lead of his successful literary fable titled *Gabriel: King of Hearts*, about a squirrel who loses his way.

Tessa patted Cooper on the leg. "Look at what your present self is doing," Tessa said as she began enumerating her case against him on her fingers. "You're holding down a full-time job—one you absolutely hate and that requires you to commute over a hundred miles a day. You're doing work on the side for that company in Newmarket. You're keeping a journal. You're growing a garden as if our very lives depended upon it. And you're—what? There's something else. Oh yeah, you're tutoring that friend of yours."

Tessa moved on to the pinky finger of her other hand, stating, "And now—as if all that weren't enough—you're about to take on a teaching job at Rivier." She patted him on the leg again. "Could it be, Cooper, that all that twitching and cramping you're experiencing is a message, just like that body rash back in Iowa?"

Cooper took a deep breath.

Until now, he had privately feared his twitching and cramping might be a harbinger of a creeping arthritis that would eventually leave him unable to use his right hand. Arthritis often follows in the wake of a traumatic injury. Once again, by dwelling on some little fear, some little possibility, he had blown it all out of proportion—magnified a harmless dust devil into a swirling vortex.

"Your body told you back then that enough was enough, so wouldn't it make sense, given everything you've got going now...it might just be doing the same thing—trying to get your attention? Remember that back problem you had when you were teaching in Watertown while trying to run your father's marina for your mother, and the doctor couldn't find anything wrong? And then it just went away, on its own, once you stopped teaching and got rid of the marina job?" Tessa again patted Cooper on the leg. "Enough already?"

Cooper drew in another deep breath, more slowly this time, as if to draw in the lingering aroma of Tessa's reasonableness.

"Figures, doesn't it? Finally, I get a chance to teach creative writing, and it turns out to be the proverbial straw that breaks the camel's back."

Tessa's gaze was fixed on him. "I know. But do you really want a broken back?"

He had some thinking to do. He didn't want any more broken anythings. He would go for a walk at noontime, climb a mental mountaintop, and take a good, hard look at where he was and where he was going. He would make some decisions—not the kind that merely rearranged the same furniture in the same room. There comes a time to throw out all the old stuff and start over.

Hearing a rumble of shod feet on the stairs, Cooper squinted at the alarm clock on Tessa's nightstand: 6:21.

"Guess we might as well get up too, eh?"

"Yeah—I guess so," she replied.

The inertia in Tessa's voice triggered a pang of guilt in Cooper. A dreamer by his own admission, he had led Tessa and the boys down a path that had, inch by inch, trapped Tessa in an all-consuming sinkhole of a job that deprived three full-time boys a full-time mom. He would make it up to them. He would find a way.

Neither Cooper nor Tessa moved.

"You first," Cooper finally said.

"I'm always first. *You* this time."

Taking a deep breath that read like a sigh, Cooper peeled the covers back and, swinging his legs over the edge of the bed, held them elevated to give Tessa time to touch her feet on the floor first. Leaning backward, Cooper strained against a noticeable weakness in his legs.

Clearly, he could *not* put it off any longer. He simply had to start doing *something* to get back into shape. A few calisthenics maybe. Every morning before he started his day. He hadn't done a single sit-up since washing out of SEAL training almost fifteen years ago.

Starting tomorrow, he would roll out of bed and directly onto the floor and do some flutter kicks and push-ups. He would pretend Richardson was standing over him. *Down—1. Down—2...*

When Cooper felt Tessa's weight lift from the mattress, he allowed his feet to touch the floor.

"Never trust a man with his pants off," Cooper quipped.

"Never trust a man *period*," Tessa corrected.

"Thank you for the pep talk."

Cooper spotted the spiral notebook he kept on his nightstand; he remembered having written in it before drifting off to sleep. He felt a little rush of excitement. As was often the case, he wasn't able to recall what he wrote down—which, of course, was the reason he kept the notebook in the first place.

How many times had he spent an entire commute going through the alphabet, over and over, desperately trying to set aglow an ember that had gone too cold to be revived?

Notebook in hand, he opened it to find two partially overlapping scrawls that looked as if they were written by a nondominant hand. Picking up the pencil, Cooper retraced the two words, turning his scribbles into legible print—

truth

pols

Cooper set his notebook out where he would be sure to remember to take it to work and found himself wishing it were Wednesday instead of only Tuesday. Wednesday was his day to work at home—in his loft office— where he could toil on his own stuff as much as he wanted without feeling a need to be wary of corporate spies.

Not that anybody would care one whit. Andy, his boss, certainly wouldn't.

It was just that it wouldn't look good. It would look like he was favoring working on self-stuff over company stuff, which, of course, is exactly what he would be doing!

Cooper pulled on a pair of briefs, raised the shades, and waited for Tessa to finish arguing with the bathroom scale. He grinned as he heard her step on, mutter to herself, step off, test the zero—step on, mutter to herself, step off, test the zero—

She appeared in the bathroom doorway. He was about to ask her who had won the battle of the bulge today but decided against it. Never having had sisters of his own, it had taken him a while to learn that it was always a high-risk venture to create anything resembling a joke around a woman's weight.

They touched hands as they passed by each other.

Someday—sooner rather than later—he would be able to swoop her onto his white horse and carry her off to the life she deserved but would never ask for. He could do it. Getting *Gabriel* published—albeit an impetus of thirteen years and counting—had given him the confidence.

He just needed to be persistent...tenacious. If obstacles got in the way, there was always a way around them. He only needed to find it.

As he waited for the water to run hot, Cooper turned to the window and pulled the lower sash up as far as it would go, having to summon, he noticed, a little more effort than usual.

He would do 10 push-ups and 25 flutter kicks every morning starting tomorrow. He grinned.

Never promise to do t'marry
what you've been able to put off so-farry.

He turned off the water and, resting his forearms on the window sill, pressed his head against the screen and slowly drew in a deep breath.

Although it was not yet autumn by the calendar, the morning air was of that crisp, nostril-tingling sort that Cooper had long associated with mid-September—when the days would start out cool and dewy, downright chilly sometimes, then warm up into tranquil, 70-degree afternoons hosting flock upon flock of white puffy clouds scudding across a bottomlessly blue sky.

It was a time of transition—of finally emerging from under the tyranny of summer's oppressive heat and once again feeling fully alive; of getting stocked up with wood for the stove and foodstuffs for the pantry; of taking solitary walks down paths shaded by trees beginning to blush in shades of red and orange; of frenzied squirrels scrambling to gather acorns against the urgent tickings of their ancient clocks; of soft, slanted sunlight lacquering everything it touched in hues of amber and gold; of renewing old resolves yet unfulfilled and embracing new ones. Ah, yes—

Cooper pictured himself carrying a mug of coffee to his office; sharpening a half dozen or so no. 2 Ticonderoga pencils, pulling a legal-size tablet out of the bottom left-hand drawer of his desk, listening to the muse for a pregnant moment, then writing the first line of the Big One—

It was a dark and stormy night.

He grinned. Yet—who knew? It just might work! It all depended on what came next.

Olivia was at her wit's end.

Why did no one believe her? Had she a history of deception, other than, of course, that one time, when she had invented all those transgressions against God His Own Self so she would have something to confess for her First Communion?

He'd give it some thought. Why not? He had nothing but blue skies ahead of him. In half a lifetime, he would come up with as many ideas as he could and give some thought to each one. He wouldn't come back from his noontime walk until he had gotten a good start.

He just needed to make more money. Between them, he and Tessa earned just enough each month to pay their bills. The downpayment on their house was borrowed from his mother. Not a penny of their own to put toward it, let alone savings or an emergency fund.

Other than keeping a journal and capturing his own Thoreauisms as they popped into his head, Cooper hadn't done any "real" writing in years. There had never been enough time to get a momentum going—nor, truth be told, had there been enough energy.

Holy Crusade

Cooper watched a chickadee flutter to one of his backyard feeders, where it searched in vain for a sunflower seed and then fluttered away, uttering a single forlorn *cheep.*

He had too many things to remember, too many chores, too many obligations, too many responsibilities!

Code: His hand on his car door handle would serve as a reminder, "Fill the feeders!"

Turning back to the sink, he turned the hot water back on, pulled the stopper lever up, and stared at the stranger in the mirror. *Who the hell are you?*

The dark hairs beside his nose needed pulling. His part was too low. Bending over the sink bowl, he plunged both hands into the water and immediately withdrew them. He had forgotten that the plumber had set the new thermostat at a higher temperature. He had gone so far as to tell everyone and put notices up in all three bathrooms but had neglected to heed his own warning. He hadn't reset the new thermostat yet because it would mean pulling part of the insulation off the tank and then taking the face plate off, and then—

He shook his head. He added some cold water to the sink and then, skittishly testing the temperature, settled on a little more cold water. Cupping the water with his hands, Cooper splashed it onto his 40-going-on-65 face.

He would reset the thermostat when he got home from work. More code: Grasping the doorknob would mean "Reset the thermostat."

Now hurried, Cooper shaved with just enough caution but managed to cut himself anyway. After rinsing the whiskers from the sink bowl, he staunched his wounds with wisps of toilet paper and, returning to the bedroom, stared at the same old shit in the closet.

The same old shit stared back at him.

After giving consideration to each pair of pants, Cooper finally decided on the same pair of stretch jeans he had worn the day before. To avoid repeating himself entirely, he decided on a different shirt—a red-and-green plaid that he hadn't worn in a long time. Truth be told, he didn't really like it.

Tossing his selections onto an unmade bed, he paused for a moment. He still had time to fix his part and to pluck those ugly hairs.

No. What difference did it make in the Grand Scheme of Things, for God's sake, whether or not he combed his hair and plucked those hairs today, tomorrow, a week from tomorrow—or never?

He zipped his fly, buckled his belt, and noted the shabby condition of his belt that had seen his college days. He simply *had* to get a new one. Maybe this weekend...Sunday.

Most of Saturday he would need to prepare for his first class at Rivier. He smiled.

Every bit as much as he loved to write, Cooper loved to teach. But should he *really* be trying to do both at the same time? Tessa was right. His body was sending him a message. The chronic fatigue, the generalized weakness, the cramps, the twitching—it was all a part of the same phenomenon.

The Rivier gig was simply too much! Once again, he'd be burning the candle at both ends, saddling himself with even more fatigue. He would just teach this coming semester—he had already committed himself. Then he would use part of his stipend to get Tessa the amethyst pendant he had been wanting to buy her for her 40th birthday—and, of course, a pair of matching earrings. He imagined the look on Tessa's face when she reached the bottom of a Cracker Jack box and came up with a purple prize.

Unrequited Valentines

FEBRUARY 1953

Cooper opened the bottom drawer in his dresser and pulled a white envelope out from under a couple of sweaters. He hated sweaters for making him feel even fatter than he was. The three ink-smudged letters on the

Holy Crusade

envelope—*MOM*—looked even stupider now than they had when he first made them, two days ago, with a leaky fountain pen.

For one thing, he should *not* have made all three letters capitals—just the first one. Why did he think he had to use all capital letters?

Sitting down at his desk, Cooper located a box of crayons in the center drawer and pulled the reddest red from the top row. Holding his breath, he traced *MOM* with surgical care.

He drew a heart around *MOM*. It looked even worse! Cooper tried to smooth out the curved lines forming the heart, but the more he tried, the heavier, and smudgier, and more uneven they became. Why was he always trying to make everything perfect?

Springing to his feet, Cooper threw the reddest-red crayon against the door to his closet, leaving behind a garish wound, and tore open the envelope. Pulling the card out, he tore the envelope into shreds, tossed them into his wastebasket, and rearranged its contents until not even a shred of the envelope was visible.

He didn't have enough money to buy another card. The clock on his nightstand read 8:36. The school bell would ring in 24 minutes.

Cooper considered trying to find a large enough envelope in his mother's secretary, what looked to him like a marriage between a desk and a bookcase, but there wasn't enough time. He would have to run all the way to school as it was. And his mother would be mad if she got any more calls from the school nurse about him being late.

Next time, his mother said, she was going to let his father deal with him.

He should have just gotten a regular-size card instead of the biggest one they had in the store. Why was he always doing stuff like that? Why couldn't he just be like everybody else? Like Stephen, who never did *anything* wrong and knew everything there was to know about everything.

Cooper picked the card up from his desk, together with the bag holding the 29 cutout Valentines he had made for his classmates, and descended the stairs two at a time, holding the oversized card behind his back as he hurried into the kitchen.

His mother was sitting alone at the table, meaning his father wasn't up yet after working late at his grocery store. Stephen and Davey had obviously already left for school.

The kitchen smelled of burnt toast and hot radiators. Cooper's mother looked at him, then at the clock on the wall above the stove.

"You're going to be late again."

"No, I won't. I'll run the whole way."

Cooper felt his mother's eyes take notice of the bulge around his middle. He would eat only half his sandwich at lunch. He would not eat any snacks after school.

Barely able to hold back a cat-got-your-tongue grin, Cooper pulled the card from behind his back and held it toward his mother.

"What's this?" His mother's expression held steady.

It's the biggest Valentine's card they had in the whole store, Cooper wanted to say, but of course did not. *It cost a whole dollar!* he wanted to say.

His mother took the card and looked intently at the ribbons. She opened the card.

He should have gotten one just like everybody else's. It had to be the stupidest thing in the whole world to give somebody a card without an envelope. He should have waited. He should have taken the time to look for another envelope. He should have gotten another card. If he could steal boxes of matches from Aubrey's, he could steal one lousy Valentine's card from Horton's. Why was he always charging ahead when he should be patient? Why couldn't he do things the way everybody else did them?

"You shouldn't have gotten such an expensive one."

Cooper's gaze was fixed on the grotesquely oversized card.

"Hadn't you better hurry?"

He took a quick glance at the clock above the stove, grabbed a powdered donut off the table, and jammed it into his mouth. Taking his jacket from the closet, he gathered up his *Davy Crockett* lunch box and his bag of Valentines and fled out the door.

He ran past the snow fort that his brother Stephen and his fellow Brainians had made in the backyard and ducked through the hole in the back fence.

He would hide his bag of cutout Valentines in the bushes behind Otis's house. After school, he would retrieve the bag and return to his Mr. Peanut bank the shiny new penny he had placed inside each card.

Jefferson County Mental Health Clinic
J. COOPER HAYNES

3/30/53 Mrs. McKenzie called upon the recommendation of Dr. MacAskill and the public health nurse. Patient is "down on everyone" and unmanageable, is gaining too much weight. Appointment made for April 20th, 10:00 a.m.
BVL

4/20/53 Mr. & Mrs. H and Cooper in. Cooper was seen by Mrs. Ackerman. Mr. H is a large, attractive-looking man. He let Mrs. H do most of the talking. When he would interject something, it was with a smile. He seemed much less disturbed about the situation than Mrs. H, possibly because most of the day-to-day responsibility of guiding and disciplining the boy falls on her. Mr. H owns and manages a village grocery store, spends from 8:00 a.m. to 9:00 p.m., six days a week there. He grew up in Cape Vincent, one of two children, was a great wrestler and boxer in his school days. Mrs. H is a thin, rather tense woman. She started right off talking about Cooper as a problem. He has always had ear infections; a year ago, was hospitalized with a mastoid infection; this past fall seemed deaf although he would not admit he could not hear. Dr. MacAskill found the tubes filled with scar tissue and gave him three radium treatments. Since then, he has gained weight; now weighs 102 pounds and has been much harder to discipline.

Cooper is no problem at school. He has always been an average student, but this past term made the honor roll.

There are 16 months between Stephen and Barry, 14 between Barry and Cooper. Stephen and Barry share a bedroom and have always been close. Cooper has a room alone. He was prepared for Benjamin's arrival, was very interested and affectionate with him when he was a baby. Now his behavior is so unpredictable, Mrs. H is afraid to leave him alone with Benjamin.

Cooper loves animals and is very kind to them. Has two turtles and a pet beagle dog named Tex; he takes very good care of them. He is tender with plants and flowers also but has no friends. He flies off the handle, has temper tantrums, can be an angel one minute then "possessed with demons" the next. He is stronger than the two older boys, wrestles with them for a while, then cries, says they are picking on him, and wants his mother to take his side. He thinks all the family is against him, tells Mrs. H she is always scolding him. He resents the other children in the neighborhood coming in the house to look at TV, comes home from school saying he beat up several boys. He beats up his pillow at night. Wants to stay and look at TV after his brothers have gone to bed, so there is a scene every night and he goes to bed crying and mad.

Holy Crusade

Mrs. H is so upset over Cooper's behavior that she dreads holidays and to see him come home from school. She and Mr. H have not been away from the children for two years. She is an only child and her mother was always willing to keep the children, so she could get a rest, but Cooper is too much for her. We talked about how Cooper's behavior seems to point toward his great need for an extra amount of love and attention. When I asked if Mr. H thought he could spend a little extra time with him, Mrs. H immediately said that Mr. H is so busy at the store that he has very little time for any of them.

Mrs. H needed to be reassured several times that his gain in weight and more difficult behavior had not been caused by the radium treatments. We talked of his spending more time out of doors and less time inside looking at TV. He likes to play cowboy and guns, is wrestling in a school exhibition next week. I suggested a punching bag as a good way to release hostility. I believe both Mr. & Mrs. H have insight and can be worked with. Certainly, they both seem genuinely interested in the children and in giving them a good home. Mrs. H seems pretty worn out right now with the daily conflict with Cooper.

Explained that Mrs. Ackerman would want to see Cooper a few times and then, we would send them an appointment to come in again.
JRS:bl

4

A Natural Rhythm

Ashland, already? Could it be?

Was he running too fast?

Cooper looked at his watch: 17:42:19. Actually, he was only doing—half of 17 equals 8.5; half of 42 equals 21; 21 and 30 equals 51—he was doing 8 minutes and 51 seconds per mile.

Which was just about right—unless his watch wasn't working properly. He should have put in a fresh battery—just to be safe.

Rule #1: Anticipate!

He watched a few seconds flash by to be assured his watch was working... 8:51 per mile. If he could maintain this pace over the first half of the course, he would only have to do—what? 51 from 60 equals 9—just 9:09 per mile over the second half of the course to make it to the finish line in four hours. *Less than* four hours, actually. Wow, if—

Dammit! He was doing it *again*! Setting his sights a little higher, and a little higher, and a little higher—until there was no way in hell he could succeed!

He began to replay the advice George's friend Gary, a member of the Rochester Runners Club, had shared with him about distance running: "What you want to do is get yourself into your natural rhythm just as soon as the pack starts to thin out a bit—and then stay in it—no matter what. In other words, don't let yourself get snookered by all those juiced-up colts. Ever been out running and had a young thing pass you by, leave you in the dust, and you just can't stand letting her do that to you, so you pick up the pace a little, but you're still falling behind, so you pick up the pace a little more, and then 3 or 4 miles down the road, you're out of gas and practically on your hands and knees? Well, that's what I'm talking about. Somebody else's rhythm isn't necessarily your rhythm. And almost never is. That's the mistake almost every first-time distance runner makes. Everybody's all juiced up on adrenaline, and they're jumpin' up and down 'cause they gotta nervous-pee again—third time probably in the last five minutes—and when the gun goes off, they take off like a bunch o' month-old stallions feelin' their oats. It takes discipline, though, to hold back. More 'n you might think—especially at the beginning, where, as I say, it's *real* easy to get snookered into a pace that'll prove disastrous for you later on."

For once in his life, he was *not* going to give in to grandiosity. He was going to be patient.

Family Ritual

SEPTEMBER 1982

Finished with his push-ups and flutter kicks, Cooper fumbled with the buttons on the front of his shirt. Buttons had always presented a challenge, but lately, they had become an even greater challenge.

He was trying not to think about the noise he had heard driving home last night from Rivier. He had even resorted to gradually pressing his foot on the accelerator so as not to trigger the sound he did not want to hear. If he couldn't hear it, it couldn't possibly exist. If it didn't exist, then there couldn't be a problem. The noise had continued, though, until finally Cooper had had to admit to himself he was going to need to get the front axle on his piece-o'-shit Le Car replaced—for the third time in as many years.

Sitting down in the dressing chair, Cooper pulled on a pair of socks and took a deep breath. What this meant, of course—if in fact he did need to replace the front axle on his piece-o'-shit Le Car—was he would not be able to get his car fixed and buy Tessa that amethyst pendant.

Why had he allowed himself to get talked into buying a French car? He knew better—

*When shopping for the family stallion,
never buy French, British, or Italian.*

He took a deep breath.

Pulling on his shoes, Cooper was reminded he had not yet gotten around to polishing them. They were a mess. Returning to his closet, Cooper lifted his shoe-shining kit from his Navy days off the shelf and dropped it on the floor where his shoes would inevitably be returning.

He went downstairs, where he found Noah, Luke, and Zak sitting at the kitchen table, leaning intently, territorially, over bowls of cereal in various states of consumption.

Smiling, Cooper imagined a *Mondo Cane*–inspired scene in which three growling dogs were snarfing up bowls of raw meat, their wary eyes shifting from neighbor to neighbor. While *Mondo Cane* was one of Cooper's all-time favorite movies, right up there with *Casablanca* and *Forbidden Planet*, he had never met another movie enthusiast who had even heard of it.

Amazed by the amount of food being consumed by one 14-year-old, one 11-year-old, and one 10-year-old in concert, Cooper recalled that they were having trouble making it through the week on their current budget. Tessa had assured him she could make do for now; she just didn't want to hit him with any surprises.

The options, Cooper had to acknowledge, were few. Near term, he could channel part of his teaching stipend into the food budget. Longer term, he could teach a course in the spring semester. He had already told Paul he wouldn't be able to teach in the spring, but he was pretty sure Paul had not yet found someone to take his place.

Or he could try to get more hours at Fastek, the start-up he was doing work for on the side, although things had been pretty slow there for the past month or so. In fact, Cooper had been wondering if the company might be in the process of shutting down.

He could certainly postpone replacing any of his same-old-shit clothes, including his same-old-shit belt. The truth was, if he spent a bunch of money to replace his old shit, he would no sooner have the new shit hanging in his closet only to have it start looking like the old shit it replaced. So what did it really matter?

Besides, the *last* thing he wanted to be doing on a precious weekend was trying on new clothes in a department store.

Hell isn't an eternity of being deep-fried in the hot grease of one's sins; hell is an eternity of standing in a little fluorescent-lit torture chamber surrounded by mirrors you could not get away from.

Tessa was at the stove dredging poached eggs out of a pot. The air smelled faintly of vinegar.

"Bonjour, Papa," Noah greeted. "Comment vas-tu?"

"Guten morgen," Cooper replied, showcasing his best German.

Smiles all around. The boys were well acquainted with their father's history with the German language.

Cooper sat down at the table and looked into the backyard as best he could through the glass of the sliding door, with its smears and smudges of various origins. He noticed a female cardinal perched on one of his feeders. The male would not be far away.

Noah was reading the side panel on a box of Crispix. Zak was half hidden behind a semicircle of cereal boxes. There would be no morning greetings from Zak—in French, German, English, or Swahili. The usual halo of sugar crystals surrounded Luke's bowl.

"I finished another poem, Pop," Luke announced between mouthfuls of Raisin Bran. The nearby box claimed to contain "Twice the Raisins."

"'Twice' relative to what?" Cooper had long wanted to ask the manufacturer.

Tessa set a plate of poached eggs and dry toast on the table in front of him.

"Thank you," he said to Tessa. "Good," he replied to Luke. "When can I read it?"

Luke hurried another spoonful of cereal into his mouth and started to get up from his chair.

"Just set it on top of my tote when you're done eating. I'll take it to work with me."

Luke settled back into his chair. "Thanks, Pop."

"Which kind of jam would you like?" Tessa was standing in front of the refrigerator, holding the door open.

"You didn't, by any chance, get more strawberry, did you?"

Tessa smiled and set an unopened jar of Smucker's Strawberry Preserves on the table.

Cooper noticed the dark circles under her eyes. If he had pursued a *real* career, one that paid *real* money, instead of continuing to follow a dream he likely would never be able to catch, they wouldn't be living two paychecks to two paychecks. He would make it up to her.

"Thank you."

"You're welcome."

"How many poems does that make?" Cooper asked Luke, shaking a red pill from an amber vial.

"Thirty-three. Do you think that's enough?"

Cooper added a vitamin pill, a calcium pill, and a magnesium pill to the little red pill and looked at Luke. "Thirty-three sounds like a good number."

Cooper popped all four pills into his mouth, swallowed them with a gulp of orange juice, and picked up the jam.

A Natural Rhythm

"I think I'll do seven more," Luke said. "Then I'll have 40. Forty's almost halfway to 100."

Cooper strained to unscrew the lid from the Smucker's jar. He strained harder. Finally releasing his grip, Cooper struck the bottom of the jar twice with the heel of his left hand and tried the recalcitrant lid again.

All three boys were grinning—even Zak, who, eyes still puffy with sleep, had come out from behind his fortress of cereal boxes. The boys knew that their father was carrying on a tradition his own father had started 2 gazillion years ago.

Cooper again struck the bottom of the jar and tried to twist the lid loose, using first his left hand, then his right, each time pressing the jar against one thigh or the other for better leverage.

"Dammit," he finally grumped, shaking one arm and then the other.

"I'll do it," Noah said.

"I'm not kidding," Cooper snapped. "I really can't get it off!"

"Let me run hot water on it," Tessa intervened. "It's probably stuck."

"I know it's stuck," he growled.

Now the boys were no longer grinning.

Cooper struck the bottom of the jar again, hard, and tried again to loosen the lid, until his arm began to tremble. He released his grip too quickly, wincing at the feeling of his arm being wrenched from his shoulder. As water cascaded into the sink, Cooper watched his right hand twitching at the base of his thumb joint.

The boys returned to their bowls.

Cooper took a deep breath. He would *not* call Paul and tell him he'd changed his mind and would be willing to teach a course in the spring. He simply *had* to make some changes. He took another deep breath.

"I'm sorry I snapped at you guys."

Nods and grunts. Tessa smiled.

If he backed out now, though, he'd never get another chance. Paul would find someone else, a *real* writer, and that would be the end of that.

And then there was the food budget—he would make a final decision during his noontime walk. He had to cut *something* out, that was for sure.

Tessa handed him the jar; it felt warm. "Try it now," she said. Tentative, the boys looked up from their bowls.

Cooper searched for a twinkle in Tessa's eyes, wondering if she had loosened the lid on the sly. He cocked his arm and again torqued the lid—but *still* it would not yield. He relaxed a moment, took a deep breath, and as if springing a sneak attack, he torqued the jar with a burst of resolve. Relieved, he felt it start to ease!

Sometimes lids get stuck. It wasn't a big deal. Sugar sometimes acts like glue. Life is like that. In fact, wasn't life a succession of one stuck lid after another? What mattered was not whether you got all those lids unstuck but whether you made a complete ass of yourself in the attempt. Cooper held his grimace a moment longer, as if he were still losing the battle, then released his grip.

"I give up," he said, offering the jar to Noah. "You try it."

"I dunno," Noah said, shaking his head. "I'll give it a try." Noah cocked his arm and strained mightily. "I can't get it," he lamented, handing the jar across the table to Luke. "You try it."

Luke cocked his arm and strained mightily. Finally giving up, Luke handed the jar over to Zak. "You try it."

Zak made a muscle with one arm, and then the other. Gripping the lid with only the tips of his fingers, he unscrewed it with perfect ease, as everyone else, including Tessa, now sitting at the far end of the table, cheered and applauded.

The ritual was complete.

Cooper worked the yokes of his eggs into his toast and out of the corner of one eye watched Zak douse a fresh mound of cereal with milk. History held true, as at least half of what was intended for Zak's bowl had a 25 percent chance of finding its way onto the floor.

Cooper wished Noah good luck on his geometry exam. "Are you all set?"

Noah hesitated before nodding—meaning, of course, he wasn't.

A Natural Rhythm

Noah seemed to have the same relationship with math that Cooper had with language. Try as they might, the mystery remained. Alas, Noah had taught himself to write computer programs in two languages, Basic and Pascal, with virtually no help—and on a PDG (pretty darn good) supermini, one of the most advanced computing systems in the world. Here was a kid who could do all that—without flying into a rage—yet he wasn't able to do better than a C in geometry. It just didn't make any sense.

If Cooper could just get Noah to trust in his ability to perceive the logical flow of a proof, how one step led *logically* to the next, versus relying on memorization, he'd be fine.

"Go where the logic leads you!" he had recently reminded Noah.

"I'll try, Pop."

"That's all anyone can do."

Noah smiled.

Luke rose from his chair. "I'll go get my poem, Pop."

Cooper looked on as residual orange juice dripped from Luke's glass onto the floor.

Biting his tongue, counting to 10, Cooper reminded himself that in just a few years, they would be gone, leaving a void that would never again be filled, except maybe on holidays, but not then, really, either. Knowing the romantic in himself, he would probably resort to spilling all manner of grime on the kitchen floor himself, just to resurrect this world.

...7, 8, 9, 10.

"Are you going to enter Fosters' writing contest again this year?" Cooper asked Luke. "The deadline must be pretty soon now."

"I might."

OK, enough said. He's been reminded. If he enters, fine. If he doesn't, no harm done. It's gotta come from him.

Luke headed for the stairs. Tessa called after him: "Don't forget your lunch money!"

Noah and Zak finally stowed their cereal bowls in the dishwasher and headed for the stairs: Zak to get dressed as pokily as possible, Cooper mused, so he could make it to the bus stop no sooner than just as the driver was closing the door; Noah to get dressed as quickly as possible so he could spend a few minutes in his father's office logged on to the mainframe at Digitronics—to write a program, Cooper could well imagine, to tap into the computer at school and change his geometry grade.

Holding his coffee mug in both hands, Cooper looked across the table at Tessa.

"Sorry I snapped at you."

Tessa smiled. "How was the jam?"

"The best. Thank you."

"You had to work hard for it." She paused. "Is today the day you call the doctor?"

"If I don't hear anything by noon, I'll call."

"Good boy."

"Do I get a reward?"

"You do indeed."

Despite the dark circles around her eyes and the creeping crow's-feet, Tessa was a beautiful sight to behold. Not in that superficial, "Sunday Styles" sort of way, but in the way of an indomitable spirit.

A Farm for Five

APRIL 1972

Their 13-acre farm in Oswego, New York, consisted of a ramshackle house, a no-babbling brook, a few scrawny apple trees, and a nest of garter snakes under the front steps.

Zak had made his debut into the world only two weeks earlier, blessing Cooper with a fifth mouth to feed. In subsequent years, Zak would take a certain pride in having been a "welfare baby." He was also counted as the first of the "Lamaze babies," in the Oswego hospital, thanks to Tessa, who had issued an ultimatum: If the hospital overlords refused to allow her husband to be in the delivery room with her, she would have her baby in the hospital lobby. Tessa took up station in the hospital lobby at the beginning of her labor, and shortly thereafter, a set of scrubs was delivered to Cooper by a disapproving nurse.

The family income at the time came almost entirely from substitute teaching. Being tall and male made Cooper very popular in three school districts, in every subject from social studies to fifth-grade health; algebra to French; girls' phys ed to special ed. But no German! When he wasn't subbing, Cooper was squirreled away in the unheated upstairs bedroom writing a novel (*Chocolate Charlie*) and trying to snag a publisher for a novel titled *The Mother, the Daughter, and the Holy Cow* and a fable titled *Gabriel: King of Hearts.* The idea was to get plenty of bait in the water as soon as possible.

Tessa was spending almost every waking moment tending to three babies 4 years old and under—feeding them, dressing them, changing them, rocking them, shopping for them, singing to them, playing with them, reading to them, cleaning up after them—and emptying a diaper pail into a washing machine whose ancient belts and gears seemed to announce that each load of ammonia-reeking diapers might be the last.

In hindsight, Cooper knew most outside observers likely noticed a certain amount of arrogance in his choices. How could they not? His dream of being a writer defied good sense. "Keep your day job," they might have warned. For Cooper, however, wielding a pen and mining the moral, ethical, and material imaginations was not a hobby, a vocation, or even an addiction; it was a matter of life or death.

*Live a life of purpose and passion
or watch your soul wither and die.*

As it turned out, his pursuit almost cost him all prospects of future happiness. The sound of Tessa tumbling down the stairs in the middle of the night with a two-week-old infant clutched in her arms was one he could never forget. He had never been able to figure out exactly how Tessa had managed to avoid serious injury to either herself or Zak.

She had lost her footing, she explained, because she wasn't able to see; and she wasn't able to see, she explained, because she hadn't turned on a light; and she hadn't turned on a light, she explained, because she didn't want to wake anybody...referring, of course, to Cooper—the light sleeper—the delusional dreamer.

A few days later, Cooper received an offer from Sequoia Books in San Francisco to publish *Gabriel*. The offer included an advance of $500: $250 upon signing, $250 upon publication. Too little, too late.

Date Night

SEPTEMBER 1982

Tessa looked up from her steaming mug and smiled quizzically at Cooper. "What are you thinking about?"

"Nothing."

"That's not fair. You're always asking me what *I'm* thinking."

"And do you always tell me?"

"Yes."

"I was wondering what you'd like to do this weekend."

"That's what you're thinking *now*."

"I was wondering what quarks are made of. And whatever that might be, what *that* is made of. And whatever that is, what *that is* made of," he conceded.

Tessa gestured defeat. "What would *you* like to do this weekend?"

"I'd like to be alone with you."

Tessa nodded.

A Natural Rhythm

"I don't mean that. Though, of course"—Cooper flexed his eyebrows Groucho style. "I mean just you and me—by ourselves. No schedules. No obligations. No noise. No kids. No nothin'."

Tessa smiled. "I'd like that. Can we afford a dinner out?"

"No—but would you like to do it anyway?"

"Sure."

"Where would you like to go?"

"Well, I don't know," Tessa demurred. "Where would *you* like to go?"

"Where can we *afford* to go, do you mean?"

Tessa smiled.

"Well, anyplace but the Oracle House, I guess," Cooper said. "Or the Blue Strawberry. Or the Dolphin Striker. Or the Library. Or the Oar House. Or the Al Dente. Or the Seventy-Two," he said, followed by a grin. "How often do we go out? Maybe once every two months? Let's not decide on the basis of cost. That's what we always do."

He could easily let the front axle on his car go for a couple of weeks. Nothing would happen, he knew from experience, other than that unnerving noise worsening. Or he could put $150 toward their credit card balance this month instead of the $200 he had budgeted toward paying it off before Christmas.

He would go ahead with teaching at Rivier in the spring. That would solve a whole bunch of problems. And he loved to teach, so what's the problem?

"We haven't been to Michael's in a while," Tessa noted.

Cooper stymied a grimace. The last time they had eaten at Michael's three anniversaries ago—or was it four?—it had been so noisy where they ended up sitting that Cooper had had to lean halfway across the table to hear anything Tessa said. And the portions had barely been large enough to satisfy a 9-pound cat, much less a 206-pound man whose blood sugar had dipped into the red zone two hours earlier.

They had had trouble finding the place, which looked like just another beach house on scenic Route 1A, so they ended up being a few minutes late. But because they were five minutes late, they had been bumped from the reservations list. It had been at least an hour before they finally got a table—squeezed in between two other tables—a level of intimacy that had drawn Tessa into whispering when shouting was necessary.

They would not have been bumped, though, it had become abundantly clear, had they been regulars from one of the château-like "cottages" that fronted the ocean along 1A and whose tables the proprietor conspicuously visited to dispense generous portions of fawning familiarity.

"Micheal's sounds good," Cooper lied.

Digitronics

SEPTEMBER 1982

Cooper eased his foot off the accelerator and allowed the distance between his canary-yellow Le Car and the silver Continental directly ahead to increase slightly—from what looked like about a yard and a half, at most, to perhaps a Le Car length.

The thumpity-thump from his front axle ceased.

"C'mon, dickhead!" Cooper shouted. "*Move* that thing! There are actually people in this world who are not on your schedule!"

There was no traffic coming from the Digitronics parking lots ahead, as one would expect in the early morning. He would pass the sonuvabitch—swerve around him in a punishing George Carlin sort of way. *Zip, zip, zip, zip, done.*

No, he would not do that. He was almost there, for Christ's sake. It would be exactly the kind of stupid thing Tessa warned him against every morning.

"Drive carefully," she would say, which essentially meant *Don't be stupid.* She knew him.

Cooper took a deep breath and forced himself to hang back two car lengths. The silver Continental turned ponderously onto Tara Boulevard and began to creep to the right to enter the driveway leading up to the fortresslike facade of the Sheraton Tara.

Edging closer, in hungry anticipation, Cooper slammed the accelerator to the floor and swerved triumphantly around the Continental, allowing his body to sway in dramatic fashion to each jerk of the wheel.

"Pretentious asshole!"

The thumpity-thump had returned.

Cooper shook his head with exaggeration, hoping to register at least some measure of disgust should the driver happen to glance his way, and teetered on the brink of giving the sonuvabitch the finger, toward adding insult to injury (or would it be injury to insult?) but thought better of it. He had remonstrated quite enough. He smiled.

What oversized putt-putt is not a prosthesis for an undersized pee-pee?

Holding the steering wheel with one hand, Cooper used the other to scribble a short mnemonic—*pp*—on the Post-it pad he kept in the caddy over the steering column. A familiar voice told him he should pull off to the side of the road to do this, but he needed to pee too badly to be that circumspect. He tossed the pad onto the passenger's seat, where he would be sure to notice it before bolting for the men's room.

Sensing a spasm coming on in his right hand, Cooper ordered his thumb muscles to relax. The technique hadn't worked in the past, not even once, and it didn't work now, not even in part, but Cooper had decided he had to keep trying anyway.

As he had told Tessa earlier, if he hadn't heard anything from Dr. Lewis Weiss's office by noon, he would call and ask to speak to the doctor directly.

This was getting ridiculous. It had been almost two weeks now, for God's sake, since he and Tessa had driven down to Mas General so Cooper could undergo a few "routine tests" to rule out "the bad stuff."

"Like what?"

"Parkinson's. Myositis. Multiple sclerosis. Autoimmune."

Cooper took a deep breath. No news was, in fact, good news, he reminded himself.

He sensed it would be warm enough to eat his lunch on the embankment overlooking Route 3. He'd do a little thinking about how to lessen his load. And, of course, he'd check out the clumping on Route 3.

Cooper had come to suspect that the clumping he observed on multilane highways was due to some as yet unheralded law of nature. He sensed a common thread running through clumping cars, clumping raindrops, clumping stars, clumping galaxies, clumping of nearly everything that involved movement of some kind. Nothing, it seemed, was evenly distributed, until such time as the number of its elements reached a certain threshold—as in the example of traffic jams. But why?

As he passed the entrance to Lot A, Cooper recognized an overweight, balding jogger trudging toward him, on the left shoulder. He had encountered the same man dressed in clashing colors over the past several mornings, his eyes fixed on the pavement directly in front of him.

Cooper hoped the man would look his way so he could give him a thumbs-up—but no such luck.

Next time, he told himself, he would give the man a little toot of the horn to get his attention. No, he would not do that. The guy was probably staring at the road in order to avoid just such an intrusion.

Sixteen years? Had it really been that long since he last went for a run? No wonder his muscles were getting weak and twitchy!

He needed to get back to it. It was time. The truth was, of course, that running—even just a mile or two a day—would do him far more good than

10 push-ups and 25 flutter kicks every morning. Of course, if he were to take up running again, he would need to buy himself a pair of running shoes, which would run—so to speak—at least $50, especially in size 16.

He shook his head. He was doing it again! Pushing the grandiosity button!

He could always take up running *later*. After he had figured things out. After he had made some decisions. First things first.

He was like the guy in *The Pit and the Pendulum* who, trapped in a shrinking room, could find no way out. The longer he dithered—the longer he held on to the devil he knew—the harder it was going to be. In just ten years he was going to be 50. And in just ten years after that—60! In just the time he had been out of college—twenty years—it was going to be pretty much over. And what did he have to show for it?

So, what do you do, Mr. Haynes?

I'm a technical writer—like the guy who wrote Zen and the Art of Motorcycle Maintenance—*only I don't have a motorcycle.*

How interesting. Oh, look who's here! I must go over and say hello.

At lunch he would not just watch cars clump; he would do a little visualizing. He would visualize himself in certain contexts—doing certain things. Like getting himself on the management track at Digitronics. Or going back to law school. He would imagine himself in new territory, boldly going wherever his imagination might take him! He would come up with several possibilities, then weave an aspiration—a "dream"—around each one. Like becoming a kickass trial lawyer.

Why not? No more screwing around.

Turning into Lot C, Cooper parked in the usual area. The needle in his bladder was well into the red zone.

Grabbing his Post-it pad off the passenger seat, Cooper stuffed it into his shirt pocket and, lunging from his car, snatched his tote from the back seat. He was tempted not to bother locking up, but the last time he had left his car unlocked, some asshole had relieved him of his only pair of sunglasses—in broad daylight, no less.

Setting his tote down on the pavement, Cooper pushed firmly against the driver's-side door, which was closed but hadn't latched.

Knowing full well slamming the door wouldn't work—it would merely bounce—he stepped back and thrust the heel of his shoe against it, striking it just to the right of the keyhole, and heard the latch click.

Fumbling with his keys, Cooper tried to gain quick dominion over the correct one, his fingers feeling almost numb, as if he had just awakened from sleeping on them—all the while sensing he was in serious danger of wetting his pants.

Yanking the key out of the lock, Cooper picked up his tote and began to double-time toward the second of two two-story buildings that housed Digitronics' software development organization. He could tell by his location in the parking lot that he was a few minutes later than usual—the extra time it had taken him to fill his bird feeders and stop for gas.

He was glad he had made the effort to fill the feeders. Since witnessing a squirrel work the lid on the seed can until the rock holding it in place dropped off, Cooper had made no further attempts to deny an obviously superior intelligence unrestricted access to the bird food.

As Cooper hurried toward the nearer of the two buildings, he glanced at his watch: 8:37.

Taking a deep breath, Cooper looked ahead at a tier of dark-tinted windows looking out from a grove of third-growth oaks. As he approached the slope leading to the entrance to the nearer facility, he could feel the same old bag of powdered cement begin to weigh him down.

One thing he would think about over lunch was the possibility of resurrecting one of his old projects. *A Voice from Heaven* maybe, which he had partially written in grad school. Or one of his children's stories—one that didn't need a whole lot done to it.

Or he might dig out *The Mother, the Daughter, and the Holy Cow*: a depressed, disillusioned, emotionally constipated priest finds himself the lightning rod of an angry, disillusioned, emotionally volcanic archfeminist.

Cooper felt an old ember glow anew. Maybe now—with the benefit of a little distance, a little maturation, a little hard-earned wisdom—maybe he could make it work, write it the way it needed to be written instead of the way he had needed to write it at the time or was able to write it at the time.

That had to be *the* single most difficult lesson about writing—how to keep one's ego on a tight leash and allow the characters and their context to run the show.

The good writers are artists,
the best, midwives.

The second most difficult-to-learn lesson had to be letting go of one's little darlings—those self-satisfying turns of phrase that, on the surface, are oh-so-very clever or oh-so-very pretty but do not belong where they presently reside, or anywhere else, truth be told.

Maybe he was going about this all wrong.

Even before he reached the heavy glass doors to his building, Cooper decided not to show his badge. He was already on the verge of peeing his pants, so no way was he going to take the time to go through all the mechanics of digging his wallet out of his pocket, pulling his badge out without spilling everything else in his wallet on the floor, and flashing an ID badge that didn't even have his picture on it at a somnolent guard who almost never bothered to look.

Cooper wished to Christ whoever the asshole was who was pulling down probably 90 grand to head up corporate security would make up his mind one way or the other—either everybody was absolutely required to show his or her badge or everybody was absolutely *not* required to show his or her badge. Period. No more of this sometimes-yes, sometimes-no crap—depending, it seemed, on which side of the bed the guard on duty happened to have gotten up on that morning.

The guard looked Cooper's way. Cooper did not recognize him. A newbie?

Directing a perfunctory nod toward the unfamiliar guard, Cooper kept moving, expecting any moment to feel something warm running down his leg.

"Sir, can I see your badge, please?" The voice was just insistent enough to be authoritative.

Cooper emitted an audible sigh and planted his tote on the floor near the guard station.

If he didn't make it to the men's room in exactly 3.2 seconds, it was going to be too late! Cooper slapped his keys down on the guard station counter, dug his wallet out of his rear pocket, managed to catch his Visa card before it could escape to the floor, considered flashing his driver's license instead of his company badge, nodded curtly in response to the guard's "Thank you," noticed he had three or more teeth missing, stuffed his wallet back into his rear pocket, picked up his keys and his tote, and, turning away, hurried onward, feeling an impulse to shake his head with disgust but resisting it. After all, it wasn't the guard's fault. He had only gotten up on the wrong side of the bed. It was some perfectly coiffed MBA's fault.

Crashing through the men's room door, Cooper dropped his tote and had his fly unzipped by the time he had cozied up to the leftmost of three urinals.

Full stream ahead!

Recalling his all-time record—2 minutes, 19 seconds—recorded in the same venue, Cooper checked his watch. If ever he was to set a new record, this would seem to be the time.

Cooper shuddered.

Gooseflesh prickled down his spine.

He smiled at an image—mirror image?—of Zak barely making it to the bus on time. Father and son, forever joined in brinksmanship by genetic imperative.

Closing his eyes, Cooper relished a rapidly deepening sense of relief. Resting his head against the wall above the urinal, he imagined what it would be like the day he walked out of this building for the last time, knowing he would never again be required, by the practicalities of life, to imprison himself in an eight-by-eight cell for lack of money in the bank to bail himself out.

Finished, Cooper checked his watch—2 minutes, 13 seconds. Add a few seconds to make up for being late in reading the start time and call it a tie.

Claiming a sink, Cooper recognized a pallid-faced man, late 20s to early 30s, who had just emerged from one of the stalls. Cooper had seen him in the same general area a few times but did not know anything about him. They nodded to each other.

Beyond his group of technical writers, Cooper did not know much about anybody in the building—even the engineers he worked with.

The man left the room without washing his hands.

Cooper smiled. Kitchen help!

Exiting the men's room, Cooper bore left, then left again, and entered the low-ceilinged, sound-dampened, artificially lit, climate-controlled space that hosted his writing group.

It would be noontime before he saw daylight again.

Though he knew he would find nothing in it, Cooper stopped off at his mail slot anyway. Even the smallest chance of some kind of good news finding its way to him either at work or at home was worth the risk of another pinch of disappointment.

After a glimpse of his empty mail slot, Cooper made his way through a maze of look-alike cubicles that made up the Technical Communications section and paused at the cubicle labeled "J. Cooper Haynes." Instead of entering, though, he peeked into a cubicle across the aisle labeled "Dana B. Hill."

Dana's tote was not on her visitor's chair, and her desk lamp was dark. Apparently she had opted to drive to work in lieu of taking the company van up from Boston; otherwise, she would have been in her office by now.

Cooper recalled the first time he had discovered Dana stretched out under her desk, all 6-feet, 1-inch of her, taking a nap. Dana had to have her rest. And her telephone time. As a '60s flower child and daughter of a Methodist minister, Dana pushed the boundaries of the establishment without ever crossing them.

Cooper entered his cubicle, removed his lunch from his tote, and set it next to his terminal. The wrinkled brown bag reminded him of the face of a wizened old peasant. He could smell the tuna fish. There was a cafeteria in his building, shared by both buildings, upper and lower, but Cooper had bought food there maybe four times in the past three years.

Turning back to his tote, Cooper took out Luke's poem, as well as his bedside notebook, and set these items on his desk. Reminded of his most recent note, he slipped the Post-it pad from his shirt pocket, tore off the top sheet, and then slid it back into the pocket, hopefully to be returned to his car for future use.

Peering hungrily at the assortment of "confections" on his desk, Cooper felt a little flutter of anticipation. He would read Luke's poem first, then nibble away at the rest of his serendipitous confections—letting his musings lead him where they might, for however long they might. Then he would pop over and chat with Dana, who would surely have arrived by then. By the time he and Dana got through chatting, it would be too close to 11:30 to start anything major, especially if Dana was particularly wound up, as she almost always was following her Monday afternoon sessions with her shrink, so he would just diddle around until it *was* 11:30—or maybe 11:31— then he would carry his soggy tuna fish sandwich off to the embankment overlooking Route 3 and turn himself over to all available and willing muses.

He *did* have to do some real work today, though—to forestall adding any more guilt to an ever-burgeoning pile of it, if for no other reason. Last Wednesday, his most recent work-at-home day, he had spent most of the day freezing vegetables from his garden. He couldn't remember what he had done last Thursday—or even last Friday.

He smiled. One thing he *had* done: He had sent a note to his mother-in-law and included a few of his little ditties, which she loved, or at least pretended to, which, of course, was the same thing.

A Natural Rhythm

The family joke was that because the Caldwells had adopted Cooper as their own, Cooper had ended up married to his sister.

Cooper took a deep breath.

He would absolutely, positively force himself to do some company work just as soon as he got back from his tuna picnic—and some more tomorrow. Once he got a momentum going—once he got the pump primed—it would get easier. There wouldn't be so high a bar to climb over every day.

He simply *had* to start pulling himself out of what was beginning to feel like a giant sinkhole. The deeper he found himself, it seemed, the faster he sank.

The muscle relaxant Dr. Weiss had prescribed had not helped him in that regard—or in any other regard, as far as Cooper could tell. And what about those tests? He would call Dr. Weiss's office just as soon as he got back from his walk.

At the very least, he would do just enough work each day, from now on, to justify using two or three hours of his Wednesdays-at-home time to begin putting into motion whatever plan he decided to focus on—like taking a fresh look at *The Mother, the Daughter, and the Holy Cow*—the concept, at least. Or trying his hand at writing a screenplay. Or—why not?—*all* the above!

Dana might know a screenwriter, or *of* one, because of her literary connections. If he asked her, though, he would have to explain what he was up to, and he wasn't sure he wanted to confide in anybody just yet.

Reaching behind his terminal, Cooper flipped the power switch and waited for the screen to awaken. He hit Return and typed HAYNES and NUTS4NMM into the Username and Password prompts, respectively. He hit Return. The response bell sounded, and a message flashed onto the screen:

You have three new messages.

Cooper typed DIGIMAIL at the prompt and hit Return.

The first message was from AZURE::TRUDY.

The next lecture in the LVx-1100 lecture series will be held this
Friday at 10:00 in the auditorium.

Cooper hit D and Return in rapid succession. The message disappeared
from the screen.

The next message was from LOBO::THOMPSON.

Those of you planning to attend Loye Samson's get-together this
Saturday needing directions should see me tomorrow. I'll get a
map to his place and make copies. Let me know if you need one.

Cooper edited the text down to three lines from four. He couldn't resist:

If you need a map to Loye Samson's Saturday get-together,
please let me know.

The next message was from COSMOS::DODD.

Friday's Pascal lecture will cover compiler data structures.
Everyone who is attending should have a listing of the definitions
available. The listings are (note that the file types are not _.LIS]:
COSMOS::PAS$:[DODD:DIGUS]PASLIB.LST,PASTREE.LST,
UTILITIES.LST

Say what?
Cooper hit D and Return twice: NO MORE MESSAGES
Thank God!

Feeling a spasm coming on in his right calf, Cooper squeezed the muscle
until the feeling dissipated. Rising, he did a few stretches, fingers pointed
at toes, knees slightly bent, then grabbed his mug and, exiting his cube,
checked Dana's.

No sign of life.

When he reached the coffee alcove, Cooper opened the drawer beneath the countertop and dropped two dimes and a nickel into the money cup. There was just enough coffee left in the brown-handled "regular" pot that would fill a mug and a half. Normally, when this occurred, Cooper would return to his cube, wait ten minutes, then return to the coffee alcove, where—voilà—there would almost invariably be a fresh pot.

In the three years Cooper had been a resident of that building, he had avoided learning how to use the company-provided, state-of-the-art coffee-maker that was dedicated to his Technical Languages team. He hated gadgets of all kinds. And when they were needlessly obtuse in design and/or usage, he loathed them.

Instead of returning to his cubicle to wait, Cooper poured his mug a little over half full, returned the near-empty pot back to the warmer, and, pulling a half gallon of milk from a minifridge, added as much milk to his mug as he dared without risking spillage.

Turning to leave the alcove, Cooper almost ran into three men, two of whom were wearing suits—a mode of dress rarely seen in a Digitronics engineering facility. Each man was holding a company-branded mug. Feeling a twinge of cop-in-the-mirror anxiety, Cooper avoided eye contact and, setting himself into motion, tried to accelerate without being obvious about it.

More power, Scotty!

"Sir? Excuse me!"

Cooper's impulse was to keep going. Giving into it, though, he knew, would only make the situation worse. He stopped and turned halfway around. All three men were staring at him—Father, Son, Holy Ghost.

Bless me, Father.

The shortest of the three men—a strawberry blond bearing a generous salting of freckles—continued, "I believe it's the custom here to brew a fresh pot when you finish one."

How could he even begin to explain?

I'm so very sorry. I just couldn't face it. I hate gizmos, you see. Actually, I hate just being here. Nothing is real. Nothing has any meaning. I don't belong here any more than I belonged in my undergraduate school or in law school. I keep looking for a way out, but I haven't been able to find one. I wasted ten precious years of my life writing a bunch of amateur horseshit when I should've been building a real career, like everybody else. And even worse, I tried to do it full time, instead of being realistic about it. I thought I could do any goddamn thing I set my mind to. All I had to do was just focus myself—all that energy I had at my disposal.

I'm a fish out of water here. I can't breathe. I die a little more with each desperate flapping of my gills—

If not for a look of imperial disdain on the redhead's face, Cooper would likely have made a little "Ah shit, ya got me" joke out of the situation and begun an effort to brew a fresh pot of coffee, which would have demonstrated his lack of familiarity with the instructions. Instead, he shook his head and uttered "No Anglish" with a phony accent. Turning away, he continued toward his eight-by-eight cube, spilling coffee on his shoes, wishing to Christ he had not just done what he was always condemning the rest of humanity for doing—being a complete jerk.

Cooper passed by his cubicle and peeked into Dana's—still dark. He checked his watch: 9:03.

Maybe she had to change her shrink appointment from yesterday afternoon to this morning. She had had to do that at least once before, after getting all the way down to Cambridge, only to find out that her shrink had been unexpectedly called away from her office.

If Dana had had to do that, though, Cooper was sure, she would have sent him an email from home.

Cooper blotted coffee from the bottom of his mug—and from the toe of his right shoe—then took a sip. The coffee was life-threateningly strong. He should have gone without. If he had invested the few minutes it would have

A Natural Rhythm

taken him to learn how to use that damnable coffee machine, he wouldn't be sitting in his eight-by-eight world right then soaking in a puddle of piss-warm regret.

Maybe *he* should see a shrink. Then again...Dana had been seeing hers for fifteen years now, and to what end? All she seemed to be getting for 75 bucks a pop was a pair of bought-and-paid-for ears for 50 minutes a week. Nobody had listened to her when she was a kid, so finally she was getting her due.

In Cooper's mind, something terribly untoward had happened to the healing arts since the days when the village doctor was paid in plucked chickens and darned socks. Cooper suspected it hadn't even occurred to Dr. Weiss that keeping a patient completely in the dark for two weeks was not only insensitive; it was inhumane!

Still, if anything truly dire had shown up on any of those tests, the Mass General people would have gotten in touch with Dr. Weiss *immediately*. That's the way things worked. Right? If you were a bona fide basket case, you got noticed. If you were not, you were just another unheard sound in the forest.

One of these days, he was going to learn how to relax instead of allowing himself to get all worked up over every little thing—like right now!

Cooper took another sip of coffee, grimaced, picked up Luke's poem and a no. 2 pencil—just in case—and began to read.

Sports

Hockey is rough, you can get killed
Or dumped or kicked or scratched or spilled.
Tennis is tough, you might be hit in the face,
or at least trip over your own shoelace.
Football is brutal, you could get whacked in the chin
or scrunched or tackled, but you must to win.
Boxing is the worst of 'em all.
You could be punched right through a wall.

And if you stop to tie your shoe,
your opponent's gonna beat on you.
Baseball is a really bad sport.
How could they play anything of the sort?
With bats and balls flying at you,
the safest thing's the gum they chew.
But now I must stop this sporting blame
'Cause I'm already late for my football game.

Cooper was on his feet. "Holy shit!" he wanted to shout.

"Already a poet laureate at 11!" Cooper wanted to boast to Dana. To *someone*—anyone!

Cooper drew a smiley face at the bottom of Luke's poem, then a single strand of hair on top, and added a bow to the single strand of hair. He immediately regretted having tried to draw something he was not capable of drawing. He should have left well enough alone!

Rising again, Cooper searched for any sign of Dana. He saw a few heads moving along aisles but no sign of Dana's, and at six one, she was sure to stand out. He sat back down. She *had* to be at her shrink's. Either that or her frisky Dodge Colt had bucked her out of the saddle.

Then he remembered! She would be getting her car serviced in the morning and working at home the rest of the day. She had told him the previous Friday.

Feeling a rush of relief, Cooper typed BOOKS into his terminal, pressed Return, typed EDIT MUSE.TXT, and pressed Return.

The screen filled with text headed by "Food 4 Thought."

Cooper located a section titled Truth and moved the cursor below the bottom entry:

Politicians rarely tell us the truth
because we rarely want them to.

He opened a blank line, typed in .sp 2, and, beginning on the next line, typed,

The truth of ourselves is like a bathroom mirror.
We all look at it, but few of us see what's actually there.

Was it worth keeping? Time would tell. Wisdom, the expression of it, as in the case of fine wine, is best not hurried.

Sensing a presence behind him, Cooper turned expecting to find Dana— and felt his stomach tighten.

Andy. Authority figure. Possessor of all the power.

Cooper's reflex was to clear his screen before Andy could see what was on it, but his rational self told him to behave as if he had nothing to hide.

Everybody took liberties. They were, in fact, tacitly condoned. Within limits, of course. One needed to be discreet versus flagrant.

"How's it going?" Andy asked.

"Great!" came the reply, a bit too declarative.

"Got a minute?"

Cooper was suddenly barely able to breathe, much less speak. "Sure."

"Let's grab a conference room."

They had gotten into his files! They had seen everything! It had quickly become obvious to them he hadn't been doing nearly enough company work to offset all the self-work he had been doing. He would be blacklisted! He would never be able to get another job in technical writing! What would he say to Tessa? The boys?

Rising from his chair, a little too quickly, Cooper felt the blood drain from his brain. He staggered a step and gripped the back of his chair just long enough. Grabbing a pad and a pen, he followed Andy to a corridor lined on the left with conference rooms of varying sizes. These rooms, Cooper knew, were generally occupied morning to night. Digitronics used a matrix style of management, centered on getting people together fairly frequently to talk things through and make group decisions.

They weren't actually going to fire him. His performance evaluations were just too strong for that—all 5s except one or two 4s. All they were going to do was read him the riot act. He would confine his writing strictly to his own time from now on. No more taking liberties.

Cooper followed Andy into the Rutherford Room. Every conference room in the building was named after a pioneer in science or technology. Only the conference rooms had windows—the dark-tinted kind.

He waited for Andy to sit down—at the near end of an oval table—before sitting down himself, directly opposite.

Andy set his clipboard down on the table and glanced at his watch. "I haven't got much time, so I'll get right to it."

Cooper forced himself to breathe.

"As you know," Andy began, sitting back in his chair, "we've been getting a lot of new work lately because of the new platforms being foisted on us." Andy shook his head. "They keep stuff under wraps, then they expect us to come up with complete docsets in whatever amount of time there happens to be between official announcement and first ship." Andy bowed his head and massaged his forehead with his fingertips. Puffy dark crescents under his eyes made him look older than his thirtyish years.

"At the moment, we've got you working on the LUX-11 Pascal docs..."

Cooper told himself he was going to get back to work on that project *today*, come hell or high water!

"And we've got Dana working on the LUX-11 FORTRAN docs. Fortunately, we were able to get Engineering to push the COBOL docs back a bit. I say 'fortunate' because I just learned"—Andy glanced at his watch—"not 30 minutes ago that we're going to have to produce for the Micro/VFP the same docs we're producing for the LUX-11." Andy ran a finger down his clipboard. "'Complete user and installation guides for both Pascal and FORTRAN.' I told them these docs would have to be quick-and-dirty massages of the VFP-28 guides because there just isn't time or resources to do anything else."

Andy looked again at his clipboard, rattling off a series of additional software requiring instruction manuals, marketing pieces, and white papers.

Andy held up a hand. "*And*, on top of all that, and I just found *this* out, too, if they don't slip again"—Andy smiled—"let's pray for at least a four-month slip—we're going to be getting a complete docset for the Micro/LVX dropped on us. Same drill: user and installation guides for each language, including Ada, at least eventually."

Cooper savored a hot-fudgy sort of euphoria. The truth of the matter was that neither Andy nor Armen, Andy's boss, likely gave a shit if people worked on their own stuff on company time as long as they continued to meet all their company obligations.

Andy glanced at his watch. "Finally—this is looking down the pike a ways but probably not all that far—once we get all this new-release stuff out the door, they want us to start coming up with all-new docsets for the new platforms. These would be essentially from scratch, with everything geared more toward this 'naive user' we've been hearing so much about lately." His bewilderment shifted to a smirk. "Apparently Marketing thinks our manuals should contain at least one cartoon for every five words—I always knew I'd end up in the comic book business."

"Sign of the times," Cooper managed nonsensically.

Andy blinked as if to flush his eyes of a lingering irritant.

He continued, "Now, what all this means for me, in the near term, is about fifty more meetings a week and no time to do what I'm really supposed to be doing around here. I've been a supervisor for, what?" Andy furrowed his brow. "Nearly eight months now—or is it eight years? Anyway, I've been so busy putting out brush fires, I haven't had a chance to do much else—*anything* else, actually.

"To make a long story longer, Armen and I have decided what we need at this critical juncture is someone to step in and build a fence around this onslaught of microrelated business and claim it as their own. As I said to Armen, 'I just haven't got any more fences in me. I'm all fenced out—or is it "in"?' Anyway, that's what we've decided to do—turn the whole thing, all the coordinating with Engineering and Marketing and so on, attending all the meetings, the whole shebang, over to someone we know can handle it." Andy smiled. "And in case you haven't guessed—you're it."

Cooper didn't react. If he said anything, it would be a mistake.

"As far as Armen and I are concerned, you're a perfect fit for it. You know Pascal..."

Know Pascal? Jesus Christ, just because I worked on a couple of Pascal manuals doesn't mean I know Pascal. I don't know Pascal, and I never want to know Pascal!

"You've worked with VFP-28s..."

He hadn't turned on one of the mothers, much less "worked" with one.

"And you have the people skills. Your sense of humor is known far and wide. And you certainly have the work ethic. Your performance evaluations have been consistently exceptional. And you certainly have the writing skills—straight 5s across the board."

Cooper felt a flush of pride despite himself.

"OK—let me anticipate your questions," Andy continued. "The way this would work—at least in the near term—is you would probably have to do quite a bit of the writing on the 'need-it-yesterday' projects yourself in addition to coordinating with Engineering and Marketing. At the moment, there's just no way around this. Armen doesn't have the budget to bring on any new hires. Even if he did, though, it wouldn't do us much good at this point, because of the learning curve. And you know as well as I do that the chance of our finding someone who could jump in and start swimming is essentially zero, especially given the time frame. But what Armen sees happening, once we get past putting out all the brush fires, is this thing very rapidly evolving into a full-fledged supervisor position—probably in no more than nine months to a year. In fact, it's got to happen before we take on any of those from-scratch docsets because no way is Armen going to take any of those on without a full team in place—a full team meaning four or five dedicated writers and yourself."

Cooper knew he should be sitting on the edge of his chair, tail wagging, tongue hanging out, but he simply could not find the wherewithal to do it. He had faked it too many times in the past—*saying* all the right things, *doing* all the right things, *pretending* all the right things.

"The writing you'd have to do in the near term shouldn't be all that much of a burden, because, as I said, all we're going to do—and I spelled this out to Engineering and Marketing in no uncertain terms—is a little massaging of the existing manuals, just enough to get by."

So there it was. Instead of getting reamed out, he was being offered one last chance to begin a belated climb up the corporate ladder. All he had to do was allow himself to be exploited for a year or so, and he would get his reward. One had to pay one's dues to get into the brotherhood. If he turned this chance down, that would pretty much be it. At least at Digitronics, and probably everywhere else.

"Of course," Andy continued, "because of the number of meetings that are going to be involved with this—and the general crisis nature of it—you would probably have to plan on being on-site on a fairly consistent basis. More like five days a week. Seven days a week, actually." He grinned. "Well, not quite that bad, but it's not something you could do on the day-at-home schedule you're on now, as I'm sure you can appreciate."

Cooper knew he should just tell Andy straight out, *Thanks but no thanks.* He was *not* the right person for the job. He would have to fake it—the whole damn thing. The interest. The energy. The enthusiasm. The comradery. The diligence. The lingo.

He just couldn't do it. It was all he could do just to keep the boulder he had been rolling uphill for the past several years from rolling back down, flattening him in the process.

Andy was waiting for an enthusiastic "When can I start?" but the most Cooper could offer was a phony "Wow."

"Think it over," Andy added, "and let me know. No hurry, but the sooner we can get things settled, the better. OK?"

Cooper nodded, feeling painfully awkward, thinking Andy had to sense it. "OK—will do."

Feeling obliged to add something suggesting at least tentative interest, Cooper almost said "I've got to talk it over with my wife" but decided against it, just in the nick of time.

Andy rolled his chair back and stood. "Yesterday I had three meetings, including an all-morning marathon at Tewksbury. Today I've already had one—two, counting this one—and"—he glanced again at his watch—"as of two minutes ago, a third."

His eyes widened. "See why we need you?" He headed for the door. "Think it over. Ping me if you have any questions. OK?"

"OK, thanks."

Andy bore left.

Cooper bore right—relieved to be returning to his quiet little space instead of to another meeting.

If God had called a meeting,
the universe would still be in committee.

Could he actually make it work? For Tessa's sake? For the kids' sake? He had done it before. Corning, Bache, Americana, Wang.

Well, not exactly. He had survived several fish-out-of-water experiences, but the leopard still had its spots, the peg still was square.

Cooper entered his cube, sat down, and leaned back in his chair, staring at his coffee mug. He couldn't remember the last time he had washed it. He felt a lump form at the back of his throat. He needed to find a "home"—a place to be, a square hole.

Feeling lightheaded, Cooper took another deep breath, then left his cube, mug in hand. The coffee alcove was empty. The pot resting beneath the brewer was still about a third full. Moving this pot to one of the upper-level warmers, next to a pot half full of plain water, Cooper filled an empty pot with cold water, up to a white line near the top, and turned to the instructions taped to the wall. He (1) ground a full measure of coffee beans in the grinder, (2) stuffed a fresh filter snugly into the filter holder, (3) poured the coffee grounds into the filter, (4) emptied the pot of cold water into the reservoir at the top of the brewing mechanism, and (5) placed the emptied pot onto the warmer directly beneath the brewer. Piece o' cake!

While waiting for the proverbial pot to boil, Cooper used a food-infested scouring pad on the coffee stain from the inside of his mug. Making little progress, he added dish soap to the equation. He was tempted to toss his mug into the trash and start afresh but decided against it. The mug's sorry condition was not, after all, its fault. He would take it home and use it as a pencil holder.

When steaming dark liquid began to trickle from the brewer, Cooper left the alcove, his partially cleansed mug in hand, and smiled at a young man afflicted with what appeared to be a permanent case of bedhead. A super-sized mug was dangling from two fingers at one side.

Was it kosher to use so large a mug? Should this young man be reprimanded? Cooper was disappointed the young man wasn't a freckle-faced strawberry blond.

Arriving in his cube, Cooper checked his email to see if Dana had sent him a message from home. She hadn't.

Dana was living proof one could find the family he never had but desperately needed, and Tessa's parents only further proved the point.

Cooper was struck suddenly by how barren his cube was—what little of himself he had invested in it. He would put up some posters. In particular, he would try to find the one he had seen recently that consisted of a bouquet of hot-air balloons at various stages of lofting.

He vowed he would think only positive thoughts for the rest of the day. He vowed he would do some company work.

Resuming control of his keyboard, Cooper moved out of BOOKS and, opening TK_PASCAL file, typed the commands and searched for the 33333 he used to mark where he had left off. Deleting it, he read through a cumbersome paragraph on data types that Janis Crawley, an English teacher turned technical writer, had written before Andy turned the PRO Pascal project over to him.

Cooper noted each bump in the road, each pothole, each missing road sign. Finally, he stood up and pulled from the shelf directly over his desk the bulky three-ring binder that contained one of the other Pascal manuals he had worked on. There wasn't enough room adjacent to his terminal, so he had to open it on an auxiliary space located several feet away.

He made a few notes on a Post-it, returned to his chair, and began to type. When finished, he printed his output:

Scalar Data Types

LUX–11 Pascal provides four standard and two nonstandard scalar data types:

Standard Scalar Data Types

INTEGER Used to designate data items that can hold any integer in the range –32,768 through +32,767

REAL Used to designate data items that can hold any real number (in the range –0.29E–38~ through +1.7E38) that can be expressed to a precision of *seven* decimal places

BOOLEAN Used to designate data items that can hold the value TRUE or FALSE

CHAR Used to designate data items that can hold any character in the LUX–11 Pascal character set

Nonstandard Scalar Data Types

SINGLE   Same as type REAL

DOUBLE   Used to designate data items that can hold any real
          number (in the range −0.29E−38 through +1.7E38)
          that can be expressed to a precision of 16 decimal
          places

Note: Throughout the remainder of this manual, the term "real type" refers collectively to types REAL, SINGLE, and DOUBLE.

Cooper took a deep breath. He felt better.

Tessa was right. He needed to stop approaching *everything* on an all-or-nothing basis. There was always a middle ground.

From now on, he would spend every morning on company stuff and then an hour or so every afternoon on his own stuff. To avoid any awkward moments, he would write on a legal pad with his back toward the entry to his cube. No one would be able to see what he was doing.

He would transcribe his scribblings to his computer account as time and opportunity allowed—most likely on weekends—as well as Wednesday afternoons if he didn't accept that goddamn "opportunity"!

An hour or two a day would be plenty! Even if he were able to write only a few lines a day, if he kept at it—if he was consistently consistent—over the long haul, he would end up with something other than a shitload of regret. What it all came down to was allowing himself to derive satisfaction from the means—the process—rather than from the ends. Which meant he had to stop thinking in terms of being on the cusp of running out of time.

He had *plenty* of time! He was only 40 years old!

In addition to putting a few colorful posters up in his cube, he would put up a few portraits of people like Grandma Moses and Golda Meir and Johnny Kelly and George Burns, so that no matter where he chose to direct his eyes, he would be looking one of these longevity superstars in the eye.

He saved his file and exited.

A message appeared—

New Mail on node AZURE:: from Trudy

He had missed it earlier. He typed READ and pressed Return—

Dr. Weiss's office called. Please return asap
603-742-3753

Cooper felt the floor drop.

5

Boxed In

On nearing Framingham, he was overheating. How could he feel so good at mile 2 and now so shitty at 5? His highly perishable self wanted him to walk a bit—just a few steps—but it was way too early for that.

How could he have allowed himself to even *think* about making it to the finish line in less than four hours? This was *exactly* the kind of self-sabotaging he had been doing his entire life—always raising the ante one notch more, then one more, until it was a fait accompli that he would fall flat on his face.

Just being in the Boston Marathon was self-sabotage enough—never mind trying to run it in less than four hours! Any moron with two eyes and half a brain could see that it was. All he had to do was let himself actually *see* what was staring him right in the eye.

What he should have done, of course, was let the Danville 5 Miler he had run two weeks ago be success enough. That's what George had wanted for him and what Cooper had tried so hard to make him want for himself.

Now it was too late. He had boxed himself in. He had set himself up for one, last, colossal failure. If he quit, he failed. If he didn't quit, he would eventually fail anyway. Already his body was insisting, *You don't have it. There's no way you can make it to the finish line. Stop now!*

Ring the Bell

APRIL 1967

Most of the other trainees on the Silver Strand had already rounded the Jeep and were on their way back to the start line. Cooper, on the other hand, was falling farther and farther behind. Even Hustveldt was ahead of him. Those ill-fitting boots had spelled his doom before he even started.

If he quit, though, they'd cart him off the beach right in front of everybody. They would banish him to the fleet. He would spend the rest of his life waking up every morning to the sting of unrelenting regret.

He *had* to finish! But he hadn't made it to the halfway point yet.

He would pass Hustveldt if it killed him!

He needed to face reality. He had cellulitis in that foot! He had been denying it, as one does when they come face-to-face with something unpleasant. It wasn't just a couple of infected blisters that would eventually respond to the Bacitracin he'd been dabbing on them—

No one could possibly finish this run in his condition. He would be lucky if they didn't have to amputate his right leg just below the knee. Wake up!

No! Only losers quit. None of the instructors would ever quit. Richardson would crawl the entire distance on his hands and knees if he had to. Lieutenant Knowles would not quit as long as there was someone to impress.

But they all belong here. Look at them, for God's sake. This is the toughest physical conditioning program in the world—remember? The world! *Hardly the place for a 232-pound amoeba suffering from delusions of grandeur.*

And how many of these guys do you suppose played midwife in their youth to breach-birth daffodils unable to push their way through a stubborn residue of winter debris? Face it. You do not *belong here. And not in a million years would you* ever *belong here. This is yet another example of your chronic capacity to lose touch with reality. Grandiosity is thine middle name. You should* never *have volunteered for this macho sneak-and-peek bullshit, and you goddamn well know it. You should have jumped at that "critical skills" deferment Corning Glass all but begged you to accept. So what if your "critical skills" consisted mostly of doing crossword puzzles at your desk?*

Remember Cornell Law? You were going to become a lawyer as a first step toward holding high office and saving the world from itself—even though the world had absolutely no interest in being saved from itself, by you or any other self-appointed seer into the moral night. You didn't belong there either, did you?

Isn't that exactly what's going on here? Aren't you just denying the terrible weight of another reality that's about to come crashing down on you? And even if you do manage to finish this run, what then? That infection in your foot is not going to miraculously disappear the moment you cross the finish line.

Give it up! So what if they all think you're a quitter? You will know you're not. You will know the truth, and isn't that really all that matters?

Freefall

SPRING 1964

He was in a small airplane—a two-seater. He grabbed the pilot by the collar— or was it someone else who grabbed the pilot by the collar?

No—it was him!

He pulled the pilot over his lap and pushed him out the door. He watched the pilot plummet toward the ground—limbs flailing. He could feel the pilot falling.

He could feel himself falling! It was him! He was the pilot! He was the one falling!

His eyes suddenly popped open—the translucent window curtains were ablaze with late-morning sunlight. The room was stifling despite the windows being cracked open. He was wet with sweat and smelled of it. He sat up and looked toward the opposite side of the room.

Jason's bed was made up of hospital corners. Earlier he had heard Jason getting ready to make the mile-long trek to the lower campus. How much sense did it make for Clarkson College to locate the residence halls a mile

Boxed In

from the academic buildings—in a climate where subzero temperatures during the winter months were the norm?

Reaching overhead, Cooper found his alarm clock and checked the time: 11:06. He had missed all his morning classes again—every class, in fact, so far this week! He had to get back on track, get some momentum going. Tomorrow, he had advanced calc at 8:00, ortho at 10:00, and American lit at 2:00. He would prepare for those classes and would force himself to attend every one of them. Friday he had thermo at 9 a.m. and Deutsch at 11 a.m. He would study for those classes tomorrow and attend both of them on Friday. That would give him momentum to ride into the weekend.

He would move his alarm clock back to his bureau so he would have to get out of bed to shut it off.

If he missed any more German classes, he was going to be in deep trouble. He would never be able to catch up before finals. It would be so much easier, though, if Frau Rollins didn't make everybody read out loud in class. It was supposed to be a course in *scientific* German, not *conversational* German.

Cooper took a deep breath. Going into the final with a D average meant that if he flunked it, that would be it—he wouldn't be able to graduate with his class, and he wouldn't be able to enter law school in the fall. He would be completely without an option, other than moving back home, which he would *never* do.

Off the Back

APRIL 1967

He had to get off that foot—even if for just a minute, 60 seconds, just long enough to count to 10...15 at the most. But that could be the end of it. He might not be able to get going again. A timid momentum is all he had going for him.

If he stopped, his legs would lock up like overheated pistons. He *had* to keep going.

Cooper snapped his eyes open the moment his head hit the hot sand. He scrambled to get up but was restrained.

"You're done," someone said. Was that Richardson?

Stovers gave Cooper water and helped him onto the back of the Jeep where he found himself sitting next to Hustveldt. The throbbing in Cooper's right foot had abated, leaving only a dull, defused ache—the kind anybody could endure for however long.

Jamie Brierton was doing push-ups in front of the formation, being honored, along with George Greene and two of the enlisted types—Carlson and Pugh, it seemed. They had been the first three to cross the finish line and were being inducted into the Fraternity of "Real Men," in the only way someone like Lieutenant Knowles could ever honor anybody.

"Eighteen, 19, 20. Hooyah, Lieutenant Knowles!"

"Re-cover!"

Springing to their feet, the three honorees scurried back to their places in the formation.

"*Mister* Thompson!"

"Sir!"

"Get your funky body out here and give us a song."

"Yes sir!" Pete Thompson jogged to the front of the formation and, using his index fingers as batons, began to lead the timed-run survivors in the song he had taught them the first week of training, following a 2-mile swim in 57-degree water.

> *How 'bout them moose goosers*
> *Ain't they recluse?*
> *Down in the boondocks a'goosin' them moose*
> *A'goosin' them big*
> *A'goosin' them tiny*
> *A'goosin' them snoozy moose*
> *Right in the heinie!*

The truck jerked into motion as an Orion sub hunter, ascending from the North Island Air Station, passed raucously overhead. Bearing left, it lofted over the shimmering Pacific. The haze previously hanging over Point Loma had burned off under the relentless glare of a Southern California sun.

Cooper imagined himself standing in the doorway near the tail, the prop wash like a stream of cool water flooding over his burning face.

He imagined letting go. Falling—

6

No Tomorrow

On reaching the outskirts of Framingham, Cooper knew he needed water. He was sure he had not passed the 7-mile mark. There would have been water there. He would have remembered.

Then again, since he crossed the starting line, his focus had been within, not without.

Lifting his eyes from the pavement, Cooper noticed runners veering right in order to slap the hand of a man sitting in a wheelchair. He felt a strong need to do the same, but to make it happen he would have to break his rhythm and momentum—he would have to make a special effort. He would have to do something more than what he was barely able to do as it was.

If he was to have any chance of making it to the finish line, he needed to conserve every ounce of strength he had left, every fraction of a fraction of an ounce.

Cooper saw that these hand-slappers could afford to squander whatever amount of energy they might wish to spend—for whatever reason. If they ran out of gas, no big deal. There was always tomorrow.

Test Results

SEPTEMBER 1982

Cooper recognized the receptionist in Dr. Weiss's Danville office: mid-20s, medium-brown hair, a bit wide of girth, reflexively smiley. There was a slight discoloration on her left cheek.

"Cooper Haynes to see Dr. Weiss."

The woman didn't recognize him. How could she? He hadn't been there in almost two weeks!

"Oh, yes. Mr. Haynes. The doctor's expecting you. Have a seat and I'll let him know you're here."

Cooper's stomach felt as if a herd of wildebeest had just stampeded through it, kicking up a dust storm. Cooper scanned the woman's eyes for any hint of why he had been summoned to his doctor's office so late in the afternoon.

Relax, he commanded himself. *Everything's fine.* If there was a problem, they would have notified him days ago. He just needed to let go of a few things, get himself back in shape, stop worrying about everything, stop trying to control everything.

He should not have lied to Tessa. She should be there with him. Truth be told, though, if she was here with him, it would make everything he didn't want to be real all the more real.

Cooper sat down on a plum-and-raspberry chair that faced the receptionist's window, noting that he was the only person in the waiting room. Not a good sign. He scanned the magazines in a vertical rack attached to the wall to his left. Seeing nothing of compelling interest, Cooper found himself drawn to a gold-framed print hanging on the wall to his right.

It was distinctly impressionistic. He had not noticed it on his previous visit, and now he couldn't take his eyes off it.

What he wouldn't give to be able to do with words what the creator of this painting, whoever it was—Renoir? Monet?—had done with color and texture. If he could create just one thing of such beauty, he could rest content.

Success enough. Just one.

It felt strange to be sitting in a doctor's waiting room alone. How many empty waiting rooms indeed had he ever seen in his forty years on Earth? Under normal circumstances, he would have relished such an anomaly, but not now—not at almost six o'clock in the evening when he should be home with Tessa and the boys.

He tried to ward off another stampede of wildebeest. If there wasn't a problem, he wouldn't be here right now. There would be no reason for him to be. The doctor would simply have given him the test results over the phone: *Mister Haynes, this is Dr. Weiss. I'm very happy to report that everything came through negative. You're fine. Go home and hug your wife and kids. Take tomorrow off. Spend the day reminding yourself what really matters in this world.*

Cooper took a breath. His breathing was out of sync.

He tried to assure himself that Dr. Weiss was just making a special effort to get the results to him at the earliest possible opportunity. He was attempting to make up for the delay on Dr. Parag's end as best he could. He hadn't done it by phone because he was too busy attending to other patients to make phone calls, and he wasn't about to have his nurse do that sort of thing. That would be unprofessional, good news or bad.

Number two, doctors just couldn't afford to do that sort of thing anymore—as with house calls. If they started, they would end up spending all their time on the phone and not be able to collect a dime for their trouble. Reason enough, for sure.

The receptionist reappeared.

"The doctor will see you in just a moment, Mr. Haynes."

The receptionist was smiling with what seemed to Cooper like a note of sympathy.

"OK, thanks."

He didn't recognize his own voice, which now sounded at least an octave too high.

No Tomorrow

Cooper pictured Dr. Weiss sitting in his office, door closed, feet propped up on his desk, talking to his broker, getting the good news about how much he had made on pork bellies that day.

He caught himself picking at the corners of his thumb cuticles—cannibalizing himself. He desisted. He took another deep breath.

He rested his eyes on some magazines resting haphazardly on a table that separated two sections of plum-and-raspberry chairs. It was all he could do not to rearrange them into a neat pile or put them back into the wall rack. A disorderly—chaotic—world was somehow an ominous one. Cooper took another deep breath.

If he had just managed to stay in law school—had just managed to hang in there—he would be talking to his own broker right now. He would be sitting in a spacious office—leaning back in a padded swivel chair, his size-16 shoes propped on a massive wooden desk, luxuriating in a soul-deep sense of security and well-being.

He didn't need millions—he wouldn't accept them even if they were offered by Harold A. Lipton himself. Excess wealth allowed one to imagine needs where in fact there were none.

All he wanted—all he *needed*—was enough metaphorical cordwood stacked in the backyard to last a lifetime. Enough so Tessa could quit her job and take up her guitar again—make music again. Cooper swallowed.

"The doctor will see you now, Mr. Haynes."

His stomach felt as if it were being sucked into a vacuum hose. He should *not* have lied to Tessa! This was no time to be alone. He was an idiot!

Rising to his feet, Cooper paused to a head rush, then followed the receptionist into the inner sanctum he had visited twice previously. Not one thing looked familiar.

The receptionist led Cooper past two empty examining rooms on the left, stood in front of an open doorway, and gestured for him to enter the surprisingly small office.

Dr. Weiss was in his mid-50s with semi-intact dark hair, deep-set eyes, and a graying beard. He was seated behind a wooden desk with his back to a pair of matching windows. Several tiers of intimidating and simultaneously reassuring books filled shelves to Cooper's right; a collage of glass-encased shingles and certificates hung on the wall to Cooper's left.

The doctor stood and shook Cooper's hand. "Thank you for coming in on such short notice. Please have a seat." His eyes seemed avoidant. Not good.

Cooper sat down in the closer of two lushly upholstered chairs to forestall any chance of his tripping over the first chair and landing in the second.

Dr. Weiss looked to the receptionist. "Thanks, Marge. You can head out now. I'll close up."

"I can stay."

"No, that's OK. See you in the morning."

"OK—good night then."

"Good night."

The receptionist closed the door.

Why the hell was she closing the door? There wasn't another soul in the place. Not good.

A file folder showing a red tab and a green tab was lying on the doctor's desk. Cooper fought to keep control of his breathing. He wasn't winning the battle.

He crossed his legs, careful not to kick the front panel on the doctor's desk, which, although smallish, was strikingly beautiful—a work of art in addition to being an article of practicality.

His own desk at home, in his loft office, consisted of an $18.95 hollow door stained dark walnut, resting on two bright-red Sears & Roebuck file cabinets.

That he be allowed time enough to create just *one* thing of true beauty—that's all he asked.

"First, Mr. Haynes, I want to apologize for it taking so long to get your results to you."

No Tomorrow

81

Cooper couldn't breathe. His brain began to buzz with a sort of static.

"I didn't realize it had been quite so long until I got your file out this morning. I'm sure you've been quite anxious." The doctor paused for a moment as if to gauge his patient's state of mind. "Again, I apologize."

Cooper was unable to recall a single word of the righteous diatribe he had been rehearsing in his head for the phone call he was going to make to Dr. Weiss's office.

Dr. Weiss opened the red- and green-tabbed folder.

"Apparently there was some delay in getting the final report back on the tissue biopsy. And then Dr. Parag was out of the country for a period, vacationing in her native India, I believe. We just received her report this morning."

If he didn't get in control of his breathing pretty soon, he was going to pass out. He was sweating.

"Mr. Haynes, you strike me as a rather solid sort, so I'm going to be completely upfront with you."

Cooper was standing on a high wire, 40,000 feet in the air, wobbling to and fro, beginning to lose his balance, desperate for something—*anything*—to hang on to.

"I'm afraid the news is not good."

Cooper's vision tunneled. He swallowed.

Brain tumor! I have a brain tumor! That's the reason for all the spasms, the chronic weakness. I'm going to need surgery—chemotherapy. My hair will fall out.

I'll fight it—wrestle it to the ground and beat the living shit out of it. No way am I going to fail on this one!

"It's Dr. Parag's impression—" The doctor cleared his throat. "Excuse me. It's Dr. Parag's impression, Mr. Haynes, based on the results from the tests she ordered for you—she wanted to be definitive, that's why she did so many—that you have a comparatively rare disease known as amyotrophic lateral sclerosis, or ALS."

Dr. Weiss held Cooper's eyes with his own for a moment, as if waiting for a reaction. "You may have heard it referred to as Lou Gehrig's disease."

He had seen the movie—a long time ago—but only because his father had once owned a baseball autographed by Gehrig. Unfortunately, Cooper and his brothers had used this same ball to play catch in the backyard of their Point Street home. The signature had become hardly discernible. They had not known any better. The ball had long since been unaccounted for.

Dr. Weiss slid a few stapled sheets across the glass plate protecting the top of the doctor's desk.

It was time to wake up!

This could not be happening!

"This is a copy of Dr. Parag's report. I've got some other materials here for you also, which I'll get to in a moment."

Cooper slid the sheets off the glass and stared at the typescript, but his eyes could not—would not?—lift the words from the paper.

"I assume, Mr. Haynes, that you have a few things—personal goals, that sort of thing—you would like to accomplish before...while you still can. We all have a dream or a good intention or two we keep putting off, it seems." The doctor showed an uncertain smile. "I know I do."

Cooper could feel his brain shutting down.

His lungs.

He tried to take measured breaths.

"Anyway, the bottom line here is—there's just no good way to put this—I'm afraid you're going to have to move your schedule of personal pursuits up a bit." The doctor paused. "Probably by quite a bit. To date, I'm sorry to say, there is no cure. Extensive research is ongoing even as we speak, and a breakthrough could come at any time—any moment, actually. Incredible discoveries are being made in medical science almost as a matter of course these days. Dr. Parag is herself heading up a large research effort at Mass General. So there's always hope."

No Tomorrow

The doctor's voice seemed to move away from Cooper—or he from it—just like the time, all those years ago, when Dr. Peckham gave him gas before setting the bones in his wrist.

"How did this happen, young man?"

"I fell out of a tree fort."

"Well, you're going to have to be a little more careful in the future, aren't you? OK, breathe deeply and start counting backward from 100."

"One hundred, 99, 98—"

"In fact, the literature I have here for you"—the doctor slid another few sheets toward him—"will give you some idea of the kind of research that's going on. Some of this material is a little on the technical side, but at least it will give you some...Well, as I say, there is *always* reason to hope. I've also got some materials here I had Marge copy from one of my medical journals. Unfortunately, this material is also a little on the technical side, but I think you will find it useful, especially in regard to helping you understand your disease and what it means for you and your family. You will want to share these things with your wife. I apologize for not having more appropriate materials for you, but, as I mentioned, this is a comparatively rare disease, and we just don't see much of it here. I've had Marge include the address and phone number of the ALS Foundation. I'm sure they can provide you with materials you will find much more appropriate for your needs."

He was going to wake up any moment now!

Dr. Weiss lowered his eyes, then again held them on Cooper's. "What you are facing here, Mr. Haynes, is a degenerative motor-neuron disorder that begins in the extremities—notably the hands, arms, and legs, where you've already experienced atrophy. Over time, it will affect your entire body and progressively disable all your voluntary motor functions, including swallowing and breathing. The speed at which this will occur can vary, but—" The doctor paused and continued to hold his eyes on Cooper's. "It would appear, judging from the speed of progression to date, that you are afflicted with one of the more virulent forms of this disease. You've got no fewer than six months but likely no more than two years—three at the most. I'm so very sorry."

Cooper bowed his head.

Summoned

SEPTEMBER 1967

Cooper was composing a letter to Tessa in his head. He would transcribe it to paper later. There was no hurry. His unit was stationed off the southern coast of Vietnam, and it could be days, even weeks, before the *Cook*, a World War II vintage destroyer escort, met up with an opportunity to offload mail for eventual transport to the mainland. He was sharing his opinion of Nathaniel Hawthorne's *The House of the Seven Gables*—how hard he was finding it to stay with it for more than a few overwrought pages at a time. The same had been true of *The Scarlet Letter*. He had managed to get through it, but only just barely. Once he discovered that the first fifty pages were essentially a gratuitous display of the author's powers of description, he found it increasingly difficult to overcome a growing skepticism over this "classic" being worth the effort. Mostly it was not. Had Hawthorne access to an editor when he wrote it?

Earlier, Cooper had tried to force himself into reading another ten pages of *Seven Gables*, ensconced in his favorite reading nook, near the bow of a ship that was older than he was, but mostly he had amused himself standing lookout for flying fish and sea snakes. An occasional sighting of either creature was by far the better bargain.

It had been six months now since Cooper had been discharged from the San Diego Medical Center and billeted to the *Cook*, which was serving, ironically enough, as a platform for UDT/SEAL teams operating off the coast of Vietnam.

He had caught up with the *Cook* at Subic Bay. There were worse billets Cooper could think of, but not many.

Following a brief anchorage off Vung Tau, just long enough to exchange mail and take on a new SEAL team, they were presently steaming at breakneck speed toward the Con Son Islands. Cooper suspected the CO was hellbent on running down an oiler and a new batch of movies before another ship could beat him to it. The CO had to have his mail and his movies. To everyone's benefit!

The bunk room, illuminated by the glow from a single red lamp, reeked of diesel fumes. The relentless throb of the ancient engines, dominant even over the steady drone of the only fan in the room, was rapidly becoming Chinese water torture.

Cooper needed to get some fresh air, but even more, he needed to avoid bumping into the two enlisted sailors he had recognized from his SEAL class. He couldn't face them.

From the moment he had gotten his orders, Cooper knew this kind of meeting would happen and had been dreading it. Just enough time had elapsed for new graduates to have filtered into the teams.

"Oh, hello, sir! Fancy meeting you here!"

Cooper had been relieved to the extent he had recognized only two faces—both enlisted types.

In truth, he didn't have the energy to go back outside, much less try to read another ten pages of *Seven Gables*.

Here he was, having spent almost his entire adult life feeling guilty for having not read all those books one simply *had* to have read in order to be a member of the club, only to discover that a goodly number of them were largely unreadable!

So he had decided at this point that instead of forcing himself to finish *Seven Gables*, he would take the XO up on his offer to lend him some of his books—at least a few of which, presumably, would not force him to wade through page upon page of gratuitous description.

All he *really* wanted to do was gallop into town on a white horse, sweep Tessa onto the horse's back, and ride off to someplace he could try his hand at writing—even though his parents would disapprove of him not opting for a "real job."

They would be proud of him in the end, though, when complete strangers began coming up to them and telling them how much they loved reading their son's books.

Probing under his pillow, Cooper pulled out one of the pale-blue envelopes he had received while the Cook was anchored off Vung Tau. Thank God the CO had to have his mail!

Touching the envelope to his nose, Cooper inhaled the lingering scent of *Somewhere*. He closed his eyes. If he focused hard enough, he told himself, he would be able to transmit his thoughts to Tessa. She would be able to sense them. Einstein was wrong. There was at least one thing in the universe that could travel faster than the speed of light.

Cooper startled to a burst of daylight from the bulkhead doorway.

"Mister Haynes, sir?"

He recognized Resniak's voice.

"I'm here."

"Sorry, sir. I knocked, but I don't think you heard me. The XO wants to see you in his quarters A-SAP."

Cooper felt his gut tighten. He had fucked up—forgotten to log something. There were just too many ways to screw up on watch—especially since he was comparatively new.

"I'll be right up."

"Aye-aye."

The bulkhead door closed.

Swinging his feet to the floor, Cooper waited for his eyes to readjust to the ambient reddish glow, then rising to his feet, pulled a can of Right Guard from his shaving kit and sprayed the underarms of his damp shirt—inside then outside.

One of these days he was going to have to give some serious thought to getting his laundry done. He kept procrastinating because at least in part

No Tomorrow

he didn't like the practice of using Filipinos as de facto slaves. Everybody benefited, but that didn't make it morally defensible.

Maybe he would slip the laundry help a couple of bucks each time they did his laundry. No one would know. The beneficiaries certainly wouldn't tell anybody. Of course, he *should* do his laundry himself, right in front of everybody, down in the stifling laundry hold. All that would be required on his part was the balls. He'd think about it.

Pulling his shirt on, Cooper aligned a slightly tarnished belt buckle to his gig line, rubbed the toes of his shoes with a pair of skivvies pulled from his ditty bag, and squared his hat two fingers above his eyebrows. He swung the heavy bulkhead door open and stepped into what felt like the equivalent of a steam bath.

Finding the door to the XO's quarters open, Cooper removed his hat and rapped his knuckles against the steel door, just hard enough to be heard over the whir of a solitary fan.

Commander Schneider, turning from his desk, pulled a dormant pipe from his mouth. "Come in." A strained look in his chestnut-brown eyes conflicted with the tone of his voice. "You'd better"—he gestured toward the door—"if you don't mind."

Cooper closed the door. He *had* done something wrong! But what? It had been just another uneventful night. They hadn't come across so much as a single junk. Cooper's stomach felt as if it were being hacked into small pieces for a stir fry.

They were going to transfer him to an oiler, make him ship over for another tour! He wouldn't see Tessa again for several months, maybe a year—he would not be able to survive that!

"Have a seat."

Half rising from his chair, the XO removed a pile of books from the only other chair and set them on the floor. The book on top was an obviously pirated copy of Nietzsche's *Beyond Good and Evil*.

The tiny cabin was crammed with books, most of which, Cooper knew, the XO had picked up in Kaohsiung during a port call there last spring. Taiwan did not observe any of the international copyright conventions, the XO had explained during one of their late-night talks on the bridge, and did not pay union wages and therefore could offer pirated copies of books at a mere fraction of the price of the originals—especially, according to the XO, after you got through bargaining the shopkeepers down, which was a long-standing tradition.

When the *Cook* returned to Kaohsiung later in the year, Cooper was going to buy as many books himself as he had room to accommodate— which wasn't much. They would be the beginning of a library that one day would cover the walls of his study and make him a true member of "the literary elite."

The XO tapped his pipe against the palm of his hand and funneled the ashes that hadn't already fallen onto his lap or the floor into a topless Coors can serving as an ashtray. His own shirt was stained with perspiration around both armpits. He picked up a sheet of yellow paper perforated along both sides and looked at Cooper. "We just received a wire from the Red Cross. I'm afraid I have some bad news for you, Cooper."

Cooper stopped breathing.

"There's been a death in your family."

Flight Risk

EARLY 1950S

Cooper sat at the kitchen table with his brothers, Barry, Stephen, and Benjamin, and his parents, Carl and Esther. He was starving—he had last eaten at school at around 11:15 a.m. and had not dared snack beyond a single oatmeal cookie for fear of being yelled at: "That's enough! You'll spoil your dinner!"

Cooper was sitting at his usual place. Benjamin, a fidgety toddler, was imprisoned in a high chair to Cooper's right. Barry and Stephen were sitting across from Cooper. Cooper's mother was at the end of the table to Cooper's left. Carl was sitting at the end of the table to Cooper's right. Benjamin had to sit next to his father because Esther had just "had it" with him.

Carl usually didn't get away from the store until around 6 p.m. and then had to have time to read the newspaper and have a Corby's and soda, so it was always around 6:30 before they would finally sit down to eat. Dinnertime usually included the *Watertown Daily Times* IQ quiz.

Stephen, who never had fewer than three 100s on his report card in any given marking period, was almost always able to get some of the questions right, but Barry and Cooper almost never were, except by guessing or going along with whatever Stephen said.

Cooper's one moment of glory had come—and gone—when he had blurted out "Backus" to the question "In Greek mythology, who is the god of wine?" He had never forgotten the look on Stephen's face when their father exclaimed—more out of surprise, Cooper could tell, than anything else (like pride, for instance)—"That's right!" At that moment, Stephen had burst into laughter, shaking his head. "It's not *Backus*, stupid. It's Bahk-us: B-A-C-C-H-U-S."

In the moment Cooper swore himself to silence for the remainder and fantasized Stephen choking on a piece of overdone pork chop.

"Wrong Way Corrigan," their father continued, "got his name from going in the wrong direction while (a) flying a plane, (b) playing football, or (c) sailing a yacht?"

Cooper couldn't take his eyes off the flow of melted butter running down the side of a mountain of mashed potatoes on his plate.

Stephen answered "A" and declared himself triumphant, his eyes shining with superiority.

"Anybody else?" Carl asked.

Barry shook his head.

Cooper filled his mouth with a forkful of delicious potatoes.

Esther stared at her plate.

"'A,'" Carl declared.

Stephen shook his head. That was the wrong answer, he insisted, because he absolutely knew for a fact that Wrong Way Carrigan had scored a touchdown for the wrong team.

Carl looked sternly at Stephen. "How much do you want to bet?"

"Five dollars."

Carl turned two pages ahead: "'A,' Flying a plane," he read.

"That's wrong!" Stephen insisted.

Carl folded the newspaper to show Stephen the answer box.

Benjamin's cup of milk hit the floor close to Carl's feet.

Esther jumped up from the table, nearly spilling everybody else's milk, and rushed to the sink, grabbing a dishrag. Kneeling between Benjamin and Carl, she began to soak up the spill, starting with Carl's shoes. After squeezing the dish rag into the sink for a third time, Esther refilled Benjamin's cup and told him to sit still or "your father's going to deal with you."

Cooper filled his mouth with another forkful of potatoes.

As if he hadn't heard a word of the warning just issued, Benjamin began to slither between the tray on his high chair and the slippery metal seat. Grabbing him by the shoulders, Esther replanted him in his seat and tried to push his tray another notch tighter against his stomach but without success.

Esther sat back down.

Benjamin began to squirm again—

Carl slammed a fist on the metal tray of Benjamin's highchair, startling everybody. His fingers were as big as uncooked sausages.

Benjamin began to cry.

"Sit there until we're done. Hear me?" Carl said, pointing a finger.

Benjamin made a face as if tasting something awful.

"I don't care what it says," Stephen said, looking petulant. "Wrong Way Carrigan played football. I read all about it."

Stephen was an authority on just about everything because he had read what seemed like every book there was to read—and remembered all of it.

Carl suddenly pounded his fist on the table, spilling the boys' milk. "I don't want to hear any more about it!" he shouted. "Maybe you're not quite as smart as you think you are there, buster." He glared at Stephen. "If you were, you'd know it was *Corrigan*—not *Carrigan*!"

Cooper flinched as Benjamin's cup hit the floor. He began to tremble.

"You sonuvabitch!"

Cooper bolted out of his chair and ran up the hallway to the front door.

He heard a terrible crashing sound behind him. He heard his mother scream. Flinging the door open, he tumbled down the steps and ran.

Jefferson County Mental Health Clinic

J. COOPER HAYNES

4/27/53 Mrs. H in while Mrs. Ackerman saw Cooper. "Realized after we were here, both needed to get away, so flew to New York for a week. Mr. H is a great baseball fan." Went to a game every day, she visited the shops, went to a game Saturday. They saw some shows. She said she would never fly; flew both ways and "it wasn't bad." Things went very smoothly at home; she telephoned twice.

Cooper was no trouble. "I was afraid there was something really wrong with his head—he had fallen downstairs last year, in the dark, but after we were here last week and you reassured me, I felt I could go away and leave them."

Mrs. H graduated from the U of Minnesota (1937), lived with aunt there. Taught school in Philadelphia, NY, and then Cape Vincent. Used to play the violin, enjoyed conducting the school band.

Belonged to the College Club for several years but gave that up. Has a feeling Mr. H does not like her doing things without him. He says, "Sure, go ahead and do it," but is a little sarcastic and acts hurt when she comes home. They never go out in the evening together, no friends they go around with.

Mr. H has the Red & White Store. After finishing high school, he battered around in NYC, boxed professionally for a while. (Mrs. H passed over this very quickly, seemed a little ashamed of it—she is a college graduate with a cultural emphasis.) Mrs. H is concerned because he keeps the store open at night, especially in the winter. Not enough customers come in to pay for the lights, yet he insists. He's too lenient about credit also. She thinks he should sell the store. They built a new motel last year; if he gave up the store, he would have more time at home.

A Painful Interruption

SEPTEMBER 1982

Dr. Weiss was droning on about how the disease would progress, most likely presenting challenges in the arms and legs, places where he had already experienced weakness. "Have you been noticing any problems with breathing or swallowing?" he asked.

Cooper told himself he did not have to answer. He did not have to do anything. He did not have to continue to sit there.

"If you have not, that's probably a good sign. The rate of progression might not be quite what Dr. Parag anticipates. Over time, though, it will involve every voluntary muscle in your body, including those concerned with swallowing and respiration. Unfortunately, there will be a progressive deterioration in sphincter control as well."

Stop!

"I'm leveling with you here, Mr. Haynes, because I think it's important for you to understand precisely what you are going to be faced with over the coming months. Your wife also, of course—and your children."

Stop! Can't you see what you're doing? You're talking right through me. You're giving me a fucking lecture.

"Longevity can vary from a few months to several years, even a decade or more, as in the case of Stephen Hawking, the famous physicist. Likely you have heard of him."

Cooper had, but until that moment, he had been under the impression Hawking suffered from muscular dystrophy.

"The Hawking kind of longevity, though, I'm sorry to say, is rare. The rate of deterioration can sometimes change, for reasons we do not understand, but the end result is always the same. There is some evidence that sensible exercise can have a positive effect. You're young. I would give that a try if I were you."

Am I supposed to take all this in?

"The good news is that you will experience absolutely no pain, and mentally, you will be as sharp as ever. In other words, there is absolutely no parallel between ALS and something like cancer, which, I'm sure you're aware, can involve a great deal of pain, or Alzheimer's disease, which involves a complete loss of identity and cognitive function—"

Cooper sprang to his feet. The doctor flinched.

"You keep me in the dark for two goddamned weeks—two weeks of me yo-yoing myself between optimism and every nightmare imaginable—and then you sit there and tell me there's no pain? You tell me my life's going to end before it ever really got started—and there's no pain? You tell me I'm condemned to watching myself turn into a goddamn vegetable—I'm not even going to be able to wipe my own ass—and there's no pain?

"Tell me—just when is it you guys lose the ability to feel your patient's pain? After you make your first million? Or are you all just born that way somehow?"

Cooper tossed Dr. Parag's report onto Dr. Weiss's desk.

"Please return that to Dr. Parag with the same regard with which it was sent."

"Mr. Haynes, *please!*"

Cooper started to leave, then turned back. "Have you ever wondered why this is such a sue-happy society, Dr. Weiss? It's not because of all those greedy, opportunistic patients out there, is it? Ever heard of a doctor getting sued for making house calls? Ever heard of a doctor getting sued for driving a 10-year-old Chevy?" Cooper held up two fingers like rabbit ears. "Two weeks, Doctor, you left me in limbo. And don't try to blame it on Ms. World Traveler at Mass General, either. The truth is, the last time I left your office was the last time you gave me a thought. I'm nothing to you but a number on an insurance claim. Actually, I'm not even that, because your office help takes care of all your paperwork for you. Two goddamn weeks. What would you have to say to me right now if I had put *you* through that kind of hell?"

When he reached the parking lot, heart pumping, brain on fire, Cooper found a gleamy, jet-black Trans Am parked adjacent to his dinged, dented, rust-pocked Le Car—so closely adjacent, in fact, it was obvious to Cooper he would have considerable difficulty opening the driver's-side door, much less getting himself through it.

He held the tip of his ignition key against the side of the gleamy Trans Am.

Tessa should be there. He needed to be talked down. He was one tick away from completely losing it. Moving to the front of the Trans Am, Cooper pulled his notebook and a pen from his shirt pocket and wrote,

Thanks to a total lack of consideration on your part, I'm unable to get into my car. Please feel free to leave your seat belt unbuckled.

Cooper ripped his note loose and trapped it under the driver's-side wiper blade. Entering his car through the passenger side, he crawled over to the front seat. He pictured himself kicking the side of the Trans Am several times with a size-16 docksider. Bang! Bang!

When Cooper drove to the intersection where Doctors Park opened onto Central Avenue, the light was red. Driving too fast, Cooper slammed on his brakes and stalled the engine.

Had anybody seen him flame out? He restarted it and glanced at his watch: 7:14.

Tessa would be wild with worry. He should have asked her to meet him at the doctor's office so they could have gotten the bad news together. Now how was he going to tell her? And the boys?

The light changed.

He needed some time to think—to get a handle on all this. He needed a drink—a shot or two of whiskey. He revved the engine and spurted ahead. As he accelerated, Cooper could hear a thumpity-thump coming from the front axle.

Dusk was deepening in earnest when Cooper parked next to a silver Honda showing an antenna poised like the tail on a pedigree pointer. The last time he had been to the Firehouse Restaurant was with Tessa, on the night of her 39th birthday. They had stopped on their way home from dinner in Portsmouth. A work friend had told Tessa that the Firehouse, although not known for its food, had a dance floor and a weekend DJ who played tunes from the '50s and '60s.

Cooper had requested "Unchained Melody," their favorite dance tune, even before they had had a chance to order drinks. Around and around they had twirled, around and around—

Oh my love, my darling...

Cooper cleared his throat. He wiped his cheeks and took a deep breath.

Forty years on Earth, and here he was, sitting in a chronically malfunctioning car, unable to find time or energy enough to write anything more substantial than "little ditties," soon to be rendered completely impotent by a fatal disease, holding nowhere near enough life insurance to see Tessa and the boys through the boys' college years. All this when he should be deep into the midwifery of bringing things of beauty into the world.

America the Beautiful

SEPTEMBER 11, 1967

Cooper and Tessa stood in the same church in which they had been married. Never in his life had Cooper seen so many people crammed into the sanctuary, filling the annex—even at the height of tourist season.

Still groggy from jet lag, Cooper was wearing a brown, double-breasted suit instead of his dress whites, the latter having been lost by the airline between San Francisco and Syracuse.

The choir was singing "America the Beautiful" over audible sobs.

Two of his father's cronies—the same ones who had attended Carl at Cooper and Tessa's wedding—wheeled the casket up to the altar gate. It was draped with an American flag.

Cooper bowed his head. *If only I had finished that piddly little 4-mile run. If only I had hung in just a little longer, toughed it out.*

Happy Hour

SEPTEMBER 1982

The din from the Firehouse lounge area suggested Danville's happy hour had matured well past puberty. Cooper scanned the horseshoe-shaped bar for an empty seat, spotting at least one vacant stool on the other side. The dance floor was still lifeless.

Cooper felt a lump swell in his throat. He could call Tessa and ask her to join him while the floor was empty. They needed plenty of room to move around and around—

But then he would have to explain why he was there when he should be home by now. And given his condition, he might not be able to twirl Tessa the way he used to—he might stumble and take her with him to the floor, the magic gone. Forever.

Cooper laid claim to the stool, which was only recently abandoned judging from an unclaimed tip. Hoisting himself onto the seat, he wondered if the owner of the jet-black Trans Am had discovered the note on his windshield.

A fleshy-jowled man in his 40s sat beside him, holding an old-fashioned and a cigarette in the same hand, preoccupied with a bleach-blonde well past due for a fresh bleaching.

On the other side of him, an animated discussion about the Patriots' prospects in the current season was underway. The man beside him had curly hair, looked a bit disheveled, and seemed the excitable type. He was a bit scrawny, suggesting he burned up a lot of energy just being in neutral. A slightly older, well-groomed man seemed equally invested in the conversation.

Cooper cocked his head to hear their banter while keeping his eyes fixed on the bartender.

Conceivably he could be in a wheelchair by the time the football season ended—and shitting his pants. How could he ask Tessa to deal with *that*? And how could she keep her job and take care of him at the same time? How would she manage to keep the house?

Back when he was working for Bache in Syracuse, he could have purchased a million dollars of life insurance for practically nothing. He declined, figuring it was too early to be concerned about such things.

"Look," the twitchy man interjected, "the problem is *not* Grogan or the Sullivan brothers or this player or that player. You know just as well as I do that that goddamned team, as a team, as a whole, has all the talent it needs to go the distance. What it lacks, the *only* thing it lacks, in my humble opinion, what it has *always* lacked, for Christ's sake, is leadership, pure and simple.

"You can have all the talent in the world, but if the guy calling the shots happens to be an idiot—and even his own mother knows it—you can just forget it. It ain't never gonna happen. Yeah, sure, they'll win a big game now and then, maybe even knock off a contender, catch 'em looking ahead, put just enough Ws together to get our hopes up, like those goddamn Sox do to us every fuckin' year. Hey, if you've got the raw, wet-behind-the-ears talent, right across the board—and I don't care what you say about Grogan; the fact is he's got all the right stuff. All he lacks is the discipline to use it properly, which is what coaching is supposed to be all about, remember? You can't help but win some of the battles—maybe even *all* the battles. Without a real honest-t'-goodness leader, though, a real honest-t'-goodness disciplinarian—a Lombardi, a Paul Brown—you ain't never gonna win the war, the Big One. Truth is, as long as we've got Meyer running the show, we might just as well agree to wait 'til next year and get this season the hell over with—it's DOA. Just like last year, the year before that, and the year before that."

The well-groomed man pulled a slim wallet from his inside jacket pocket and produced a bill from it. "OK, Johnny Boy, I've got a fresh twenty here," he said, then blew on it and waved it, as if to dry the ink. "That says you're as full o' shit today as you were that memorable day you picked Carter in a landslide. You were sitting right about where you are now, as I recall."

"Wow, there's the greatest vote of confidence I've ever had the pleasure of taking advantage of. Are you sure you can afford to lose that much, Counselor? You've got how many kids in school?"

The attorney pulled several more bills from his wallet. "I got a hundred here says *this* is the year they go all the way."

"As my grandfather would say, 'Always bet with your head, never with your heart. Let the other guy do that. You're on, sucker.'"

Cooper tried again to catch the eye of the bartender. He needed a drink before he faced Tessa. Nothing in his life had prepared him for this. The longer he waited, though, the harder it was going to be. He should go home.

Scanning the patrons on the other side of the bar, Cooper rested his eyes on one in particular—a young man in his late 20s or early 30s. He was strikingly athletic—likely a weight lifter, judging from his neck—and was wearing a light-gray, pinstriped suit and a paisley tie knotted with a half Windsor. He was talking to a young woman who seemed close to his age, though her eyes in particular showed early signs of tread wear. She was wearing a lavender blouse.

Cooper was partial to what Tessa referred to as the "blue reds": lavender, lilac, fuchsia, purple, red itself, and, of course, magenta—his favorite color of all. He didn't include indigo in that list because Isaac Newton had effectively made it up, if Cooper remembered correctly, so there would be seven colors in the spectrum instead of only six.

"Half Windsor" squinted and lifted his chin each time he took a drag on his cigarette. *A weight lifter who smokes?* He would then exhale a bluish plume, followed by a few quick puffs—as if signaling to the hinterland in Morse code. An easily triggered giggliness in the woman suggested the long-stemmed drink in front of her was not her first.

"Howdy there, Sport."

The bartender disposed of the empty glass and the unclaimed tip. Cooper caught a glimpse of her nametag: Juli. Her brow was damp with perspiration, her cheeks flushed. She gave the bar surface a cursory swipe with a blue-and-white towel. "What'll it be?"

"Bourbon and *club* soda. One ice cube."

Ever since the time, when he was working for Americana in Illinois, he had ordered a bourbon and soda and had gotten a bourbon and 7 Up, he saw it necessary to add the emphasis.

He shuddered. What was he doing here? *None* of this was real! In a moment he would wake up, and everything would be back to normal.

You've got no fewer than six months but likely no more than two years—three at the most. I'm so very sorry.

Cooper's throat burned. It was all a mistake! Some asshole had mixed up his results. Incompetence was everywhere. It *couldn't* be him!

For one thing, he was too young. For another, he had been doing everything right: taking his vitamins, cutting all the fat off his meat, drinking only one glass of wine a day, being good so he would get his reward in the end.

Justice would prevail.

Juli placed a cocktail napkin over an ugly burn mark on the bar in front of him and set down a sweating glass. It was the kind of glass Cooper especially liked—squat and hefty—substantial feeling.

He started to reach for his wallet, but Juli stopped him with a wink. "First one's on the house."

"Ah, yes, get one free, pay dearly for the rest!" Cooper replied, lifting the cool glass to his lips. He grimaced.

Happy-hour bourbon. Where was the 7 Up when you really needed it?

Cooper was relieved to find the second sip not nearly as substandard as the first.

Cooper studied the way Half Windsor held his drink, the way he held his head, the way he held his hands, the way he smiled. Each gesture or pose seemed calculated for effect—part of a script. Did the lady in lavender not see through it? Or was she just being polite?

Cooper drained his hefty glass and held it up until Juli took notice.

"Thirsty?"

"Something like that."

"Same?"

"Make it Turkey this time, please, and do you have something I could write with?" Cooper made a scribbling gesture.

"Sure thing."

The overweight man to Cooper's left pulled a silver pen from inside his suitcoat, clicked it, and laid it down on the bar in front of Cooper.

"Thank you," Cooper responded.

The man nodded without making eye contact. The flesh on his neck bulged over his collar.

Cooper picked up the pen and watched Half Windsor across the way take a sip of what appeared to be a martini—shaken, not stirred, of course—given the distinctive shape of the glass.

Juli set a fresh drink in front of Cooper, on the same napkin, along with a plastic pen and a small pad of unlined paper. The top sheet showed a few fresh wet marks along with an impression of what appeared to be a phone number written on the previous sheet—probably by a man, judging from the robustness of the impressions.

"There ya go, Sport."

Cooper considered asking Juli for a pencil so he could shade the impression on the pad but decided she was way too busy for that.

A man inadvertently comes across a notepad that appears to carry the impression of a phone number. Starved for excitement, the man uses a pencil to lift the number from the sheet of notepaper, and after a few moments of hesitation, he decides to dial it. An evasive voice on the other end of the line raises further his already raised suspicions, so he tracks down the address corresponding to the phone number by using a reverse-lookup directory. Staking out the address disguised as a homeless man, our hero observes several people, most of them driving expensive European cars, going in and out of a ramshackle house, which itself turns out to be owned by a holding company incorporated in the Cayman Islands. The obvious conclusion is drugs. Sometimes, though, the obvious can be just a little too obvious, and such is the case here. In fact, our hero begins to get the feeling that this whole adventure, starting with his "accidentally" finding the sheet of notepaper, is being staged—that he is being deliberately led down a path, crumb by crumb, into a trap. But why? And by whom?

Cooper lifted his hefty glass to his lips and, taking a measured sip, savored that distinctive velvetiness that is the hallmark of a quality distillate of any stripe. Why hadn't he allowed himself to imbibe a bit of quality stuff more often? From now on, it was going to be nothing but the best! Until, of course, it came time to pay next month's bills.

Cooper took another sip of Turkey, tore the top sheet off the notepad, folded it once, and stuffed it into his shirt pocket. He would attempt to decode the phone number later.

He took up the pen:

Dear Missy,

That jerk trying to get into your panties has herpes. Ask him to say "ah."

Your Guardian Angel

Cooper tore the new top sheet from the pad, folded it twice, and pushed the pen leftward until its owner caught it in his peripheral vision and retrieved it.

Cooper touched the man's arm. "Thank you."

The man nodded.

Cooper waved to Juli, who approached and cocked an ear. The din had grown louder, in proportion likely to the amount of alcohol consumed.

Cooper showed Juli what he was holding. "Would you mind playing post office with this, please?"

He looked toward the farther side of the bar. "The woman talking to the gray suit."

Juli turned. "Lavender blouse?"

"Bingo."

"Your sister?"

"Mother."

Juli grinned and took the twice-folded note into hand.

Cooper took great interest now in the currents and fluctuations in his glass, set in motion, he suspected, by constantly varying gradients of temperature. When he looked up, the giggly lady in the lavender blouse was unfolding his note.

Cooper felt something slither deep in his gut. There was still time. He could slip off his stool and disappear out the door. No one would know.

He watched the lady in lavender cover her mouth with her hand and pull the note onto her lap. He watched paranoia insinuate into Half Windsor's eyes. He watched the lady in lavender hand the note to Half Windsor. He watched Half Windsor scan the bar with ferocious eyes. He watched Half Windsor ask the other bartender to send Juli over. He watched Half Windsor show Juli the note.

There was still time! Just barely!

Cooper watched Juli turn and look straight at him, her eyes semaphores of apprehension.

He winked and raised his glass to Half Windsor. *Cheers—you fucking asshole!*

Half Windsor jabbed his cigarette into an ashtray and pushed himself away from the bar—

Juli's eyes swelled with alarm.

Cooper slid off his stool—

He was an idiot.

7

In Too Deep

Framingham was going on forever! One block of drab, look-alike storefronts after another, after another. There seemed no end—like a line of cell blocks in a prison.

His calf muscles had begun to feel as if they were being twisted into knots, his shoulder blades as if they were being jabbed with an ice pick—jab after jab, unrelenting—the Wizard of Woe had taken over all the levers and dials of destiny.

In fact, wasn't that what life was really all about? Every soul, newly forged, was dropped into a private world with no exit, a lifetime of being subjected to a series of ordeals, to the effect that when you survived one, the next one was a little easier, but when you failed one, the next one was a lot harder, one after another.

Booked

SEPTEMBER 1982

Cooper was sitting in a holding cell at the Danville, New Hampshire, police station on the edge of a cot draped with a wool blanket marked "DPD," waiting for Tessa and the bail bondsman to arrive.

How could it possibly be true he was charged with disorderly conduct and assault?

Cooper probed a gash on his lower lip with his tongue. He touched a tender spot on his temple. He flexed the throbbing knuckles on his right hand. He looked at his watch, but it wasn't where it was supposed to be. He remembered—an officer had taken it along with every other personal effect on his person, including his wallet. He figured it had been about half an hour now since he had called Tessa.

He hung his head. "Just come," he had told her. "I'll explain later."

Cooper lifted his eyes to what sounded like a handful of mashed potatoes striking the wall outside his cell. The fluorescent glare revealed a wet spot on the wall and, on the floor, a brownish lump. It had apparently come from the cell next door—which had taken on a second tenant about fifteen minutes ago. A man had been dragged into it by what sounded like the entire Danville police force. He had shrieked like a coyote caught in a trap until only a few minutes ago, when he had gone silent.

Cooper looked down at his laceless shoes. He took a deep breath and thought back to the time when, seventeen years earlier, he had confided to Tessa his hopes and dreams concerning becoming a writer. Until then, he had not confided them to anyone.

She had listened. She had asked questions. She had offered to read anything he might like to share with her. And *this* was what he was doing in return? Cooper felt a lump at the back of his throat. He heard a metal door rumble open. He wiped his cheeks.

"Goddamn you, Arkie," a voice—that of the officer who had confiscated his personal belongings—growled. "You're gonna clean every goddamned bit of that shit up. Hey! You throw that, and I'll jacket you so goddamn tight, your balls'll turn to prunes. You hear me?"

Cooper startled to the sound of something hard—a nightstick?— striking the metal bars surrounding Arkie's cell. Arkie shrieked and howled.

The same officer appeared at his door. Someone was standing behind him.

"The commissioner's here, Mr. Haynes. And your wife's waiting in the lobby. The commissioner needs your signature on a form, and then you're free to go."

Cooper felt a squeeze in the pit of his stomach. Rising from the cot he had been sitting on, Cooper suddenly felt lightheaded. Hesitating, he imagined himself collapsing—his head cracking open on the concrete floor, blood flowing into the drain.

The man accompanying the officer looked like Santa Claus in street clothes. Cooper followed the officer and Santa Claus into a little room where earlier the officer had fingerprinted him and relieved him of his personal effects, including his watch and shoelaces.

Santa Claus pulled a multicolored form from a worn leather satchel and laid it on a table that was not quite a table, not quite a bench. His nose had the unmistakable tint and texture of a ripe plum. Beneath it, his beard showed a yellowish cast, like the patina of old newspaper. Yesterday's news.

Santa Claus held the form by the upper corners. "OK, see all this fine print down here?" he asked, pointing to the lower part of the form.

Cooper nodded.

"What this says is that if you default on your bond, you lose your house. I get it. Any questions?"

Cooper shook his head. He felt nauseous.

Santa Claus pulled a pen from his pocket protector, his rasps counting the time it took for Cooper to sign the form.

They were going to need a lawyer.

Cooper returned Santa's pen in exchange for the yellow copy of the form he had just signed.

The officer, whose department-issued ID read "J. Gahan," dumped the contents of a small plastic box onto the table—wallet, watch, keys, cameo ring, wedding ring, two quarters and a nickel, worry stone, shoelaces, belt, and, unexpectedly, the business card of "William J. Fraley, Esq."

In Too Deep

Cooper had no idea who William J. Fraley, Esq., was...but he had a vague recollection of the man in the restaurant being called "Counselor." At some point in the commotion, he must have slipped his card into one of Cooper's pockets. Cooper showed the card to Officer Gahan. "Do you know this guy?"

The officer smiled. "Sure do. If I ever needed one o' them guys, he's the one I'd pick."

Cooper studied the card, then stuffed it and his personal effects, including his shoelaces, into empty pockets, and followed Officer Gahan and Santa Claus back into the cell block. As they were passing the cell adjacent to Cooper's, Arkie launched a mucous missile toward Officer Gahan. Officer Gahan deftly ducked and, in almost the same motion, drew his nightstick from his belt and ran it across several metal "strings," generating a staccato of oversized notes.

Arkie reacted by shrieking like a wounded animal.

Officer Gahan sheathed his nightstick and, shaking his head, slid open a metal door with a single pull. As Cooper entered the station foyer, Tessa leaped from an austere chair, took Cooper into her arms, and squeezed him.

Cooper squeezed her back.

"You got the results."

"Yes."

"Your temper kicked in. That's why you're here."

"Yes. I'm so very sorry."

They were the only two people in the room.

"How long?"

"A few months likely, a few years possibly."

Tessa squeezed Cooper again. "I won't let you go."

8

8-Mile Mark

Cooper could see a blue-and-yellow banner spanning the roadway just ahead—another aid station. Water to the left, ERG (electrolyte replacement with glucose) to the right.

Discarded cups littered the roadway, and Cooper felt his spirit deflate. He wasn't a third of the way yet, and already he felt as if he had hit the wall. Or was it more accurate to say *fallen off the wall*?

Whatever the case, the cause had to be, in part, anyway, the fact that he had run eight miles or more only a few times during the entire course of his training, and all those runs had occurred in the early weeks. As far as his body was concerned, the 8-mile mark represented the finish line.

Cooper went with ERG, even though he hated how sweet it was.

The muscles in Cooper's left calf suddenly cramped. The pain was excruciating.

The runner behind him stepped on the heel of Cooper's shoe, sending him crashing into one of the ERG tables.

Dark Distance

SEPTEMBER 1982

Cooper opened his eyes and found himself immersed in inky blackness. Rolling onto his right side, he flinched to the sound of something striking his nightstand. He tried to move his right arm, but it didn't respond! *My disease has accelerated! I'm not going to make it even to six months!*

A reassuring tingling sensation began to spread down Cooper's arm. He took a deep breath. He'd merely been sleeping in the wrong position, cutting off circulation.

Cooper hesitated to put his feet over the side of his bed. Even at 40, he was wary of what might be lurking there, in the dark. He had been well into his teens before he had made a connection between his fear of getting out of bed in the dark and his bed wetting. It had always been a choice between being eaten alive by the monsters lurking under his bed or being punished by his mother for wetting the bed again.

Cooper flexed the fingers of his right hand and marveled anew at his ability to do so.

"Bad dream?" Tessa asked.

Cooper startled. He had assumed she was still asleep.

"Yeah."

"You called out."

"What did I say?"

"I don't know. I was just aware of you saying something." Tessa patted Cooper on the hip. "Do you remember anything?"

"No."

Cooper tried to read the clock on Tessa's nightstand, but its orange face was turned too far askew.

"Can you tell me what time it is, please?" Cooper injected just enough irritation into his voice to make it noticeable.

Tessa rolled toward her nightstand and turned the clock to face Cooper's direction.

Cooper squinted to read the orange dial they had been sharing since Cooper broke his own clock, knocking it onto the floor while trying to grab it in the dark.

It was a little after six o'clock, he thought he saw.

Tessa's voice seemed to carry just enough irritation to match Cooper's. "Two thirty," she announced.

"Are you sure?"

"I am. Please remember, I'm not the one who insisted I keep the clock on my side of the bed. If you'd like to move it to your side, that would be fine."

"I suggested you keep it because you're the one who uses the alarm. That's not the problem. The problem is you keep turning the face so I can't see it."

"I turn it," Tessa said, softening her tone, thereby hardening it, "because the light shines in my eyes. As I believe I have mentioned."

"OK—the light shines in your eyes. But does that mean you have to keep turning it so far that I practically have to get out of bed to read it?"

Silence.

"I'm not out to get you, Cooper."

"I know you aren't."

"But you treat me as if I were. You're treating the kids the same way." Tessa patted Cooper's hip. "I understand why, and that helps—but they don't."

If it were indeed six o'clock, as Cooper had thought it was, the room would not be nearly as dark as it was at that moment. This should have been perfectly obvious to him. He was losing it—even though everything he read and was told about ALS indicated there would be no impact on cognitive function.

"I'm worried about you keeping everything bottled up inside you, Cooper. I'm afraid—"

"Look, it's the middle of the night. This just isn't the time for this."

8-Mile Mark

"You're right, it isn't—but when will it be time, Cooper? When will you talk to me about what's going on and tell me how I can help you?"

"I don't *want* to talk about it. If *you* do, then fine, go ahead and talk about it. Talk to Janice about it, talk to Sheryl, talk to Arden—talk to anybody and everybody you damn well please. As far as I'm concerned, there's nothing to talk about. People live, people die—the sun comes up, the sun goes down. No big deal."

"OK, fine. But please at least consider talking to the boys."

Cooper rolled out of bed and groped his way to the door. He found the clothes he had hung on the back of it.

"Where are you going?"

"I don't know."

Cooper yanked the zipper on his jeans—forgetting he didn't have any underwear on. The pain was swift and excruciating. He made no sound and jerked the zipper back down.

In one of these forced epiphanies, Cooper could see the utter absurdity of the situation—could picture a perennially bumbling Inspector Clouseau in the same situation.

He considered letting Tessa in on the joke but reminded himself he wasn't doing that shit anymore—always smoothing things over, making nice—just to get rid of the knots in his stomach.

Cooper found his shoes under his nightstand and slipped his bare feet into them.

"Stay and talk to me," Tessa pleaded.

"I don't *want* to talk to you. I just want to be left alone. OK?"

Cooper pulled the door shut harder than was necessary. Standing in the dim hallway, he heard one of the boys, probably Noah, the light sleeper, turn in his bed. He sifted the silence for any other signs of wakefulness. Finding none, he felt his way down the stairwell, protecting his head from hitting the low ceiling.

He found his denim jacket in the hallway closet and, after buttoning it halfway, realized it was probably too cold outside for a light jacket over nothing but a T-shirt.

The air was noticeably warmer in the kitchen, which was a direct beneficiary of the air rising from the woodstove in the basement. He wasn't going to miss attending to that goddamn thing! Lugging wood into the basement from the stack at the top of the driveway, bailing creosote-reeking water out of the chimney trap, shoveling ashes from the fire bed—worrying about it all.

Cooper opened the slider door, using both hands, and slipped into the meat cooler in his father's store, or so it felt. The air was colder than he had expected. In the 30s, he'd wager.

He rotated the thermometer in its holder, but the ambient light was too dim for him to be able to read it. He shivered.

When on Judgment Day the clerk read the litany of all the incredibly stupid things he had done in his forty-odd years on Earth, moving to New Hampshire was going to be right up there—just under, likely, allowing himself to believe he could write the Big One.

As a boy he had absolutely loved the snow and the cold—the snow especially—prone to sneaking downstairs at 4 a.m. during a snowstorm to bundle himself up in his snowsuit and overshoes and set about clearing the neighborhood sidewalks with his Radio Flyer snowplow—provided only a few inches had fallen. By first light, he would have rescued the neighborhood from being snowbound.

He swallowed. He would request that someone read *Katy and the Big Snow* at his service, if there was to be one.

He *still* hadn't gotten around to finding out how "Radio Flyer" had come to be a brand name for little red wagons. So many questions, so few answers.

Cooper sat down in one of the deck chairs he had delayed putting away in hopes of at least one last interlude of second summer. As he eased his 206 pounds into it, he heard an ominous ripping sound as more of the

8-Mile Mark

weather-rotted webbing gave way. One more thing he had not gotten around to taking care of—rewebbing the deck chairs.

He shivered, pulling up the collar of his jacket. He propped his feet against the lower runner on the deck and rested his head on the back of his chair. The sky directly overhead was a stargazer's dream—clear, deep, mysterious. Perhaps the ancients had had the right idea after all when they had looked up at night and seen not individual points of light, each separated from all the others, but distinctive clumps—neighborhoods versus individual homes.

For Noah, those clumps were not so much things to be pondered as they were things to be pointed out and identified—Orion, Cassiopeia, Cygnus, Leo, and so on—in conformity with the aims and methods of scientific reductionism.

There was something fundamentally wrong with an education system that valued knowledge of pieces and parts over the experience of awe and wonder.

No, that wasn't quite fair. The system was not the problem. Systems did only what their masters commanded them to do. The real problem was uninvolved, distracted, preoccupied, overwhelmed, exhausted parents.

Parents are teachers first,
braggarts second.

Cooper closed his eyes, bowed his head. Was it possible to squeeze a decade of parenting into a few months? Should one even try?

He felt something bump against his chair. Reaching down, Cooper felt Emily's head emerge from beneath where he was sitting. As he scratched her ears, she pushed her head against his hand. He could hear her purring and wondered if she had heard him come outside or had simply sensed his presence.

Smiling, Cooper recalled Emily's maternal interventions whenever one of the kids got into a snit, how she would suddenly appear and lick the aggrieved party in the face until he was restored to equanimity, how whenever the kids got into an argument, she would jump onto one or the other's lap and reach up to one or the other's face with a paw.

"Hi, girl—aren't you cold out here?"

He shivered. The witching-hour air was sinking ever deeper into him. He should have put his down jacket on. Why was he always in a hurry?

"I think I'm going to have to go in, girl. I'm freezing. I sure wish I had that coat of yours."

Just maybe—in exchange for all the years he was going to be cheated out of—40? 50?—they would let him come back as a Turkish Van—whoever "they" might be.

In 40 years, he would be entirely forgotten. It would be as if he had never existed. Then again, in 4,000 years, it would be as if *nobody* had ever existed!

Cooper shuddered.

He wondered what it would be like to freeze to death—how long it would take for a blessed numbness to set in.

Alas, if he didn't go in pretty soon, he was going to find out!

Rising stiffly from his chair, Cooper scuffed his shoes over the decking, in case Emily decided to beat him to the sliding door. He didn't want to inadvertently step on her.

Cooper smiled toward the small, cat-sized apparition.

"Wanna come in?"

The little ghost did not move.

"OK, see you later. Watch out for the bogeyman."

Cooper pulled the sliding door open, using both hands, and pushed his way through the drapes drawn over the glass. He slid the door closed.

Paying attention to the relative difficulty of opening and closing the sliding door allowed him to gauge roughly how much arm strength he was losing and at what rate. That and opening new jars of strawberry jam.

The air rising from the open stairwell felt warmer against his chilled skin. Cooper hung his jacket on the back of his chair at the table and groped his way into the family room, where he lay down on the couch. He brought his feet up as far as possible and covered himself with the afghans the kids used to make themselves cozy while watching television. The itchy yarn smelled in need of cleaning.

If Tessa weren't so preoccupied with being the best head start director in the entirety of the third quadrant, maybe a few things like that would get done. But wait until he was gone. What would she do then? Cooper felt a tic in the pit of his stomach.

She would do exactly what any other female human, programmed by 4.5 billion years of trial-and-error, survival-of-the-fittest evolution would do when confronted with the loss of her expendable, till-death-do-them-part partner: *She* would get another one.

Suitors would be lined up at the door. She would have her pick.

Cooper took a deep breath. Was this *him* talking?

The world was full of people in *real* pain, and here *he* was wallowing in self-pity instead of concerning himself with how he might be of help to all concerned. He did, indeed, have time left to do exactly that.

If he truly wanted to be deserving of more than a fleeting moment or two of being grieved over, he would march his ass upstairs right this instant and apologize to the only person on Earth who could possibly have put up with his crap for 16 years.

I'm sorry for being such an insufferable asshole.

Cooper cocked an ear to what sounded like the creak of a floorboard. Probably someone upstairs getting up to pee.

The refrigerator was chewing on a cud of kilowatts in the kitchen. Cooper thought he had heard a stair creak.

Another.

"Are you there?"

There were tears in her voice.

"Yup."

Yup? What kind of answer is that? How many ways are there to be a jerk? How come I seem to know them all?

"Are you sleeping down here?"

Cooper wanted to say no. He wanted to say he was just waiting for her to make the first move, to reassure him she would never abandon him, no matter what. He wanted to say he knew he was being a perfect shithead, but he just couldn't seem to help himself. Jerks were like that.

"Yup."

"We've never slept apart in sixteen years."

"I guess you'd better start getting used to it, huh?"

Cooper sensed Tessa leave. He closed his eyes and wept—then startled as Tessa gathered him into her arms and rocked him—

To and fro—

To and fro—

She sang to him,

> *Oh, my love, my darling*
> *I've hungered for your touch*
> *A long lonely time...*

Stay Awake

CIRCA 1950

He was fighting off sleep, his feet drawn up as far from the foot of his bed as he could get them. Sifting the silence for the slightest sound, he heard a solitary cricket chirping outside his south-facing window.

If he went to sleep—if he gave in to fatigue even for a moment—he might not wake up again, as had happened to his great-grandmother Freddie.

"It was a blessing the Good Lord took her in her sleep," Aunt Helena had whispered to him. "She would not have felt a thing."

Smears of rouge on Freddie's ghost-white face had made her look dollish. Cooper remembered her lying stone still in a casket in the place normally occupied by a purplish couch that Cooper had never seen anybody sit on.

"She's with God now," Reverend Bennett had whispered to him. "She was a good woman—pure of heart and soul."

Unlike her next-to-youngest great-grandson, who was looking forward to the day his brother Stephen got run over by a truck, who had once dropped a burning match into a nest of leaves next to the Kirkmans' perky white fence, who had stolen several candy bars from his father's store, who had a hopeless number of dark spots on his soul.

He had to stay awake.

Jefferson County Mental Health Clinic
J. COOPER HAYNES

4/20/53 Cooper thinks the reason he is here is to see why he is gaining so much weight. On the surface this does not seem to bother him, but I suspect that he is somewhat self-conscious of it. He cannot remember when he started to gain weight, but he thinks it was shortly after he was in the hospital after his fall last year; he fractured his skull and was in the hospital several days. When I asked him how this happened, he said he had a playroom on the third floor of their home and was running too fast downstairs one evening after playing with his electric train, afraid the bogeyman might get him.

He is a friendly child and very likable. He talked easily about school, friends, and activities and spontaneously mentioned interest in fishing and gardening. He said he would like to own a greenhouse when he grows up. He apparently does have some outside activities such as baseball, basketball, and swimming, but these seem minimal when compared to the amount of time he claimed to spend watching television.

Of his siblings, he likes Barry (10) and Stephen (12) better than Benjamin. Significantly, he said, "They use me for a punching bag, but I'm getting used to it." He showed no hostility toward any of his family and, except for this remark, did not make any remarks that could be interpreted as such.

The Blacky was administered, and he enjoyed this very much. He asked for more cards to see and did not seem to want to leave the interview situation.

Blacky: On this test, Cooper expresses strong needs for love and attention and mixed feelings toward his sibs. He is consciously jealous but extremely guilty about any hostility he expresses, which is very easily aroused and expressed.

The guilt arouses some hostility toward parents (especially father), and he reacts by alternating conformity and seeking punishment.

Another difficulty in adjustment is suggested by Cooper's record. He appears to be somewhat confused by masculine and feminine roles. He seems to be trying to repress a desire to identify with his mother and, in his efforts to do so, may be criticizing her and at the same time any traits within himself that he perceives as feminine. He is trying now to identify with his father but, so far, is having only partial success. (His present aggressive behavior with other children, his desire to wrestle, pounding his pillow, etc. are all obviously attempts to work

out the hostility aroused by feelings of insufficient affection;
however, they are also attempts to be more masculine and to
identify with his father, who was once a boxer.) His relationship
with his father is apparently not very close. When he grows up,
he wants to "better" him.

BPP:bl

Nightcap

EARLY OCTOBER 1982

It was 2:42 a.m. when Cooper decided he needed stronger medicine to knock himself out. The over-the-counter sleep aid had not worked.

Since his diagnosis, Cooper had been having more trouble than usual getting his brain to shut itself down, as if it were trying to think every thought possible before it was too late.

He made his way downstairs, got his winter jacket out of the hall closet, and reached for a bottle of Jim Beam from the shelf above the coatrack. He zipped his down jacket up to the very top.

The bottle of Beam was more than half full.

He would try to remember to put a load of logs in the woodstove before he went back to bed. Doing that always made it easier to revive the stove in the morning.

Stepping out to the back deck, Cooper eased himself into the deck chair, fully prepared to escape from it at the first hint of rotting webbing ripping. He shifted his weight back and forth to test whether it was safe for him to settle in. Removing the cap from the Jim Beam, Cooper elevated the bottle in a gesture of salutation: "Here's to an eternity of good night's sleep."

He took a hit, then shuddered—as if to a spoonful of cod liver oil. Waiting for the burning sensation in his throat to subside, Cooper savored a lightness of being no more substantial than a lone snowflake or a feathery fluff of chickadee down.

No physical mass! No psychic pain! He understood how people could get hooked on drugs. Life was entirely too difficult to cope with in the absence of at least one discretionary means of escape.

He wondered what his very last moment would be like and took another hit. He bowed his head.

All those years he had spent denying himself, disciplining himself, sacrificing all the little todays for the sake of the Big Tomorrows, doing his push-ups all the way down, all the way up, smug in an abiding certitude his day would come, because it was the meek, after all—Ferdinand the Bulls, chickadees, the SEAL training washouts—who would inherit the earth. All for naught.

He had to pee.

Setting his bottle of bourbon down on the deck, Cooper eased himself from his chair, cozied up to the deck railing, unzipped his fly, and began to sway, as if in rhythm to a heavy sea. He could hear his stream begin to puddle on the ground below.

What was it about peeing off one's deck that males found so irresistible? Cooper suspected it had something to do with the male impulse to own stuff. For males, ownership was both vital and absolute. If you wanted to put piles of junk on your front lawn, if you wanted to play loud music 24-7, if you wanted to run your leaf blower Sunday mornings, there wasn't a goddamn thing anybody could do about it! Cooper recalled the photo Les Kosinski's wife, Kathy, had taken of Les and Cooper peeing off the back porch on the farmhouse in Oswego, New York, that Cooper and Tessa had lived in for three poverty-stricken years.

"Dueling Bozos," Kathy had labeled the photo. Cooper grinned.

Les and Kathy had visited Cooper and Tessa over a weekend to help Cooper celebrate finishing *Chocolate Charlie*—his second novel. He had mailed the manuscript off to the Simon Manning Agency in New York three days earlier, at the agency's invitation, accompanied by a $75 money order.

The euphoria of that weekend had lingered until three months and two follow-up letters later, when Cooper finally received a form letter from the Simon Manning Agency telling him his "finely crafted novel, *Naughty at Night*, although not marketable in its present form, showed great promise."

Naughty at Night?

He had written no such thing! But for an additional $750, Mr. Manning would be happy to work with Cooper "on a one-on-one basis" to fashion a salable property.

How could he have been so stupid?

The $75 "reading fee" should have been red flag enough, for God's sake! Time and again, Cooper would expect people to do the right thing, only to have his trust betrayed. And so what would he do then? He would do the same thing all over again! He was an idiot!

With his dwindling stream beginning to splatter off the lower deck rail—likely doing a number on his shoes—Cooper stepped backward and finished on the floor of the deck.

Screw it. What did it matter?

Despite being in an advanced state of unsteadiness, Cooper managed to get himself zipped up without incident. Easing himself back into his chair, he took another hit and, looking roughly northward, in the general direction of Bangor, Maine, imagined Stephen King at his desk pounding out his next bestseller—in the middle of the night, of course—completely certain of it being published once he had finished writing it.

Cooper smiled. A few years earlier, when he was trying to find a way out of technical writing, Cooper had been interviewed by an ex-English teacher for a marketing communications job at Digitronics. No sooner had he disclosed a long-standing aspiration to be a writer—by implication, then, *not* a marketing writer—than the former teacher had mentioned that, in "a previous life," he had taught English at the University of Maine and had given Stephen King a C in his class. The ex-teacher had thought King a "terrible writer" and not overly bright and had seemed as eager to share this grave—

so to speak—assessment with Cooper as Cooper had been eager to share his literary aspirations with the ex-teacher.

Given the choice, Cooper hoped he would opt to be a "terrible," "not overly bright" writer over being a dead-ended middle manager desperately trying to make meaning out of little more than envy and jealousy. He couldn't be sure, though. Everyone had their price.

Truth be told, King's former English teacher had probably contributed more to American letters than he ever realized. He might just have taught a fledgling horror writer that one of the most important lessons most wannabe writers, including present company, refused to learn was to provide the reader with what the reader wanted to read, not necessarily what the wannabe author wanted to write.

Cooper took a deep breath, a long line of rejections queuing up to prove the point:

"Thank you for sending us *Chocolate Charlie*. While we found your project engaging and evocative, we do not think we could be successful in placing it in today's market."

Cooper swallowed.

"While we very much enjoyed *Gabriel: King of Hearts*, we find very little call for this kind of thing."

"We are only interested in the realistic fiction of today's market—

"...does not fit in...

"...is not appropriate...

"...is not right...

"We're sorry..."

Cooper wiped his cheeks. He took another hit.

The inescapable truth was that people read *not* to be enlightened, *not* to be rescued, *not* to be challenged, but to be enthralled, to be transported, to be relieved of the relentless burdens of reality for some immeasurable span of time. Why had that simple truth been so difficult for him to accept?

He took another hit.

8-Mile Mark

His bird feeders were just barely discernible in the ambient glow, hanging against a dark background. He should have filled them when he had gotten home from work. He would fill them in the morning, he had told himself.

Actually, this would probably be a good time to stop feeding his feathery friends altogether—before winter set in—so they would have plenty of time to find alternative sources of food.

If only he had taken out more life insurance—if only he had pursued a *real* career from the get-go—he wouldn't be having this conversation with himself.

He took another hit.

Their financial situation would likely start deteriorating just as soon as he was no longer able to work—which, Cooper sensed, could be relatively soon. They had no savings. They had no wealthy relatives.

Easing himself up from his chair, Cooper climbed onto the top runner of the deck railing and, swinging his legs over to the other side, clutching his bottle of whiskey by the neck, thrust himself forward with enough force to carry him over the ferns he had planted along the deck front.

Landing hard, Cooper stumbled awkwardly forward and ended up on his back, miraculously holding his bottle of whiskey upright. It quickly became apparent, however, that although Cooper had managed not to lose a single drop of his "sleep aid," he had lost one of his shoes from his sockless feet.

Rolling onto his hands and knees, Cooper swept the clammy grass with his free hand until he found the errant shoe. He slipped it on.

Getting to his feet, Cooper took a couple more hits of whiskey, spilling as much of it down the front of himself as he managed to swallow. He shook his head. He staggered to where the empty bird feeders were hanging from a board nailed horizontally to a small pine. He set his whiskey bottle next to the galvanized trash can in which he kept birdseed and, reaching above the empty feeder, grasped the brass clip he used to attach the feeder to an eye screw protruding from the bottom edge of the horizontal board. Using his thumb, Cooper tried to pull the spring-loaded latch open, but it wouldn't budge.

His arm having weakened, Cooper shook it loosely at his side, flexed it a few times, and tried again to pull the latch down with his thumb. He lifted himself onto his toes in an effort to gain better leverage, but still the latch would not yield.

God-damn-it!

Cooper shook his arm at his side, flexed it a few times, and holding the clip with his left hand this time, pulled on the latch with his right thumb—

Goddamn sonuvabitch!

Retrieving his bottle from beside the seed can, Cooper raised the neck to his mouth, staggered backward a few steps, and chugged.

He leaned forward, wiped his mouth on his sleeve, and straightened. He could make out his car parked at the top of the driveway.

Piece o' shit!

He gripped the empty bottle at about the middle.

He placed a foot on the pitcher's rubber—it was the seventh game of the World Series, ninth inning with two outs. Three to two.

He took a signal for a fastball, straight down the pipe. This was it, now or never. He pumped—*Piece o' shit!*

He stumbled, now sprawled onto his back—his head bounced off the ground. A flash of white heat, a flood of light, a rumble.

"Cooper? Are you there?"

Cooper tried to get up—tried to make a sound. His fingers found the bottle—he grasped the bottle by the neck and heard the empty bottle hit the deck.

"Cooper? Oh my God!"

A Chilling Effect

FEBRUARY 1974

Emerging from Dr. Ashmore's office at Iowa State University, Cooper approached a set of glass doors that opened onto Duff Avenue.

Tessa had dropped him off on campus earlier—hours ago, it seemed—on her way to her Friday afternoon guitar lesson. She had wanted to go with him to his appointment, but Cooper had insisted she keep her own appointment, knowing how much she looked forward to her only real respite from two babies in diapers and a 4-year-old who had not yet outgrown his terrible twos.

Cooper had missed both of his morning classes—Chaucer at 9 a.m., linguistics at 11 a.m.—because he had not been able to get his elderly Plymouth wagon started. He knew the moment he scraped enough frost from the kitchen window to be able to read the thermometer—23 degrees below zero—he didn't have a chance, but he had to make the attempt anyway.

As of fifteen minutes ago, he was missing the 3 p.m. section of freshman comp he was teaching.

Missing a session of a course he was taking at Iowa State University—which was more a means to an end—didn't bother him all that much. Missing a session of a course he was teaching, however—in which he was helping twenty-one tender souls think critically and express their thoughts effectively—bothered him a whole bunch.

Teaching was the first job he had ever held, other than writing, of course, that fit him like a suit tailored to his measurements. How many times had he caught himself looking forward to his next class as he had once looked forward to the next episode of *Davy Crockett* on ABC?

Reaching the doors, Cooper paused just out of the range of the needle-sharp claws of arctic cold he knew awaited him.

Although their apartment was only a few blocks away, Cooper felt so fatigued, so utterly devoid of strength and energy, that he thought about calling the sitter and asking her to tell Tessa to pick him up when she got home. He would be waiting in the lobby until she arrived.

But it was Friday. Tessa would be going directly to the store from her guitar lesson to do her weekly grocery shopping. She wouldn't be getting home for probably two hours. He would walk.

He wasn't about to sit in the lobby for two hours, no matter how shitty he felt. The red splotches that had broken out all over his body, head to foot, two days earlier, following a three-day bout with a 104° fever, were as ugly as ever. Dr. Ashmore had given him a free sample of a drug he said would diminish the redness, but it hadn't had time to take effect yet. Keeping his gloves on, Cooper wiped clammy perspiration from his upper lip and forehead and pulled his coat sleeve over the unsightly splotches on his wrists.

He took a deep breath. Just three more months and he'd be done. He was in sight of the finish line. All he had to do was just hang in there.

But then, of course, he would need to find a job—at a time, unfortunately, when all the postings for creative-writing positions were calling for people who had published several books to rave reviews in *The New York Times* and at least three articles of scholarly criticism...and they might also prefer you be Black and female.

Cooper waited for an elderly woman to shuffle through the glass doors. He was torn between staying well back, to prevent the woman from seeing his leprous face, and rushing forward to hold the door for her.

But then it was too late. The woman smiled mostly toothlessly as she hobbled past him.

It seemed to take all of Cooper's strength to open the same door the old woman had just opened without assistance. For a moment, the outside air seemed warmer than it could possibly be, but once Cooper stepped past the closing doors, an implosion of arctic air took his breath away.

He needed to get himself a heavier jacket—a *winter* jacket—as soon as he got a job.

Walking north on Duff Avenue, Cooper found himself headed almost directly into the wind. He pressed his collar against his throat, where logic would place a button or a snap but the manufacturer had placed neither. A steady flow of tears, it seemed, was all that was keeping Cooper's eyeballs from freezing. He hated February—even more than he hated November.

8-Mile Mark

He startled to a sharp blast of horn and, falling backward, struck his head on the curb. Dazed, he got to his feet, wobbled, and continued to cross the street.

A man appeared. "Sir! Are you all right?"

He was. He continued to cross the street. Picking up his pace, limping, Cooper could hear only the groans and plaits of tree limbs being tortured by the wind. Reaching the next cross street, Cooper bore left, walked out of sight of Duff Avenue, and stepped behind an ancient oak. Collapsing onto the frozen ground, he squeezed himself into a fetal ball.

He could feel blood leaking from his scalp. He closed his eyes.

9

Second Fall

Cooper's left calf spasmed into a knot before he had a chance to order it not to. He staggered and tried to break his fall. Pain exploded in his right wrist.

Faces were looking down at him, judging him, not seeing who he *really* was.

"You're done!"

No!

Called Out

EARLY TO MID-1950S

Stephen had just invited Cooper to play Simon Says in the backyard of their home on Point Street. The last time Stephen had included Cooper in an official Brainian activity was when he invited him to go swimming with them in one of their secret spots. This mystery spot turned out to be an area of flat rock on the south shore of Wilson's Bay, near the terminus of the Dablon Point Road. No sooner had Cooper taken his clothes off than Troy Tessier had grabbed Cooper's clothes and initiated a game of Keep Away. The teasing had been merciless: *Tee-ny wee-ny, teeny-teeny weeny—tee-ny wee-ny, teeny-teeny weeny.* When Cooper started to cry, the Brainians jumped on their bikes and left Cooper behind in his underpants.

"I've gotta go to the bathroom," Cooper announced. "I'll be right back."

Cooper ran to the back porch, bounded up the steps, and blasted through the kitchen door to a residual odor of pork and broccoli.

Esther glared at him from the sink, her lips pressed into a thin red line.

"Don't do that! You're going to break something! How many times do I have to tell you?"

In a flash, Cooper extracted two molasses cookies from the cookie jar his mother kept beside the refrigerator. He stuffed them in his jacket pockets.

"That's it! No more! You just had your supper!"

Entering the living room, Cooper turned on the TV and, leaving the sound low, listened for reassuring sounds from the backyard. He listened until he was sure Stephen and his fellow Brainians were still in the backyard, then turned up the volume on the TV, careful not to turn it up loud enough for his mother to think it might wake up Benjamin. He tiptoed into the front hall and eased himself out the front door. Standing at the top of the steps, he cocked an ear in the general direction of the backyard.

He could hear voices.

A long, deep-throated blast from the direction of the river was answered by a single, higher-pitched whistle. Two lakers—one big, one smaller—were passing port side to port side saying hello.

Cooper often imagined himself aboard a laker, snug in a warm bed in a water-tight cabin, reading Holling C. Holling's *Paddle-to-the-Sea* beneath the covers with a flashlight, surrounded by one thousand cans of Planters Peanuts. Enough to last forever.

Cooper listened a moment longer, then skulked down the steps and slipped through the open gate. He slinked up the sidewalk toward the street corner. Keeping his head below the top of the picket fence, Cooper ran to where a thicket of shrubs stood just inside the fence, between him and a clear view of the backyard, then ran diagonally across the intersection and up the far side of Lake Street to a grove of chestnut trees that lined a vacant field between Lake Street and the cemetery behind St. John's.

The sun had already disappeared behind the tree line, so there wasn't much daylight. Cooper didn't need much, though, to find the handmade ladder he kept hidden behind a clump of milkweeds. Placing the ladder against the field side of one of the chestnut trees, Cooper climbed to the platform he had nailed across two not-quite-horizontal tree branches. He then hoisted the ladder up and hung it by the top rung on a nail driven into one of the upper limbs. Standing on the platform, clutching a branch to steady himself, Cooper pulled his Wham-O slingshot out of his ammo box, followed by a couple of recently shucked chestnuts.

Cooper rested his back against the muscular trunk of the tree and drew in a deep breath. A few crickets seemed to be celebrating the evening. Listening to their mysteriously synchronized bleats, Cooper felt a sense of kinship with them so deep, it brought tears to the brink.

Cooper could still hear voices coming. By now, Stephen and his fellow Brainians had realized Cooper wasn't coming back.

Idiots!

Closing his eyes, Cooper breathed deeply of the dew-laden air, then, remembering the treasure in his jacket pockets, pulled a cookie from one of them and took a generous bite. Breaking off one of the residual corners, he crumbed it and spilled the crumbs onto the ground below for his little friends.

He stiffened suddenly to a familiar beck and call: "Coo-per! It's time to come in!"

Stuffing the rest of his cookie into his mouth, Cooper zipped his jacket up and then, folding his legs, wrapped his arms around his knees and squeezed them against his chest. Closing his eyes, he imagined running away to Canada, where he could lie beside a stream and bask in the sound of rushing water, where all the Bambis and Thumpers in the forest would be his friends, where he could read his favorite books anytime he wanted— over and over.

"Cooper? Don't make me call your father!"

Second Fall

Cooper dropped his chestnuts back in his ammo box, followed by his slingshot, and unhooked his ladder. Squatting near the edge of his platform, he wondered what it would be like to fall out of his tree fort and land on his head.

Jefferson County Mental Health Clinic

J. COOPER HAYNES

4/27/53 Cooper was eager to "do some more tests today," and so the Stanford-Binet was administered. Previously, some of his behavior had suggested that doing well in school was important to him, and it seemed worthwhile to find out if he was pushing himself. The test was not completed today, as Cooper showed signs of fatigue, but it will be completed in next interview.

He apparently enjoyed those tests that he was able to do well, but he became rather worried whenever he found a test beyond him. He frequently asked for reassurance on his answers but gradually accepted the fact that it was up to him to do the tests and on the whole was reasonably self-reliant. His attention was very good until near the end of the tests when he complained of being tired.

One interesting answer to a comprehensive question reflects Cooper's defensiveness in relationships with his peers. He apparently shows hostility very easily and finds it important to assert himself in minor situations. He probably interprets many harmless situations as threatening to his ego. His overall behavior on the test indicates that it is important for him to do well in school but that there is not too much anxiety associated with this. *BPP:bl*

10

Overheating

Between Framingham and Natick, Cooper expected to see the 10-mile mark now for what seemed like an hour and a half. Everything ached, burned, or throbbed: He had already fallen two times, his calf muscles seemed on the verge of spasming, both hands were bruised and chafed, his right wrist throbbed, his forehead burned, his eyes smarted. The latter problem, Cooper surmised, was largely a function of wearing a helmet and sweatband, which was serving to trap the heat and excessive moisture. The only solution seemed to be to stop whenever he needed to, like right now.

Moving out of the flow of traffic, Cooper pulled off his helmet and used his left hand to squeeze as much liquid out of his sweatband as he could.

What in God's name am I doing? This is stupid!

A man in uniform was staring at him. He was going to make him stop!

No!

Cooper shuffled back into motion. He tried not to limp, to make himself shuffle faster, to show them what he was made of. He had to show them that J. Cooper Haynes was no quitter.

Cooper grabbed a cup of ERG.

Road Rage

OCTOBER 1982

Cooper pulled a pint of Jim Beam from his glove compartment and, holding the bottle between his knees, unscrewed the cap. He simply could not face his 53.7-mile commute home on the Everett Turnpike without a little "pick-me-up," as his Aunt Helena called cocktails.

"Snakebite," his Uncle Doc called them.

He deserved whatever little pleasures he could allow himself now.

He had been putting life's little pleasures off for his entire life, and now there was only today—this moment—and he was going to use this moment, dammit, to allow himself a little blessed numbness.

Cooper lifted the pint in a gesture of salutation. "Looks like you had the right idea after all, Pops. Numb out and be happy."

Cooper took a quick look in the rearview mirror, then took a swig and relished the burn.

He recalled the twenty-seven bottles of Corby's he and Benjamin had found after their father's death, when Cooper was home on bereavement leave. The largest stash was found in the basement of the Shaffer house. And still more in the marina office, the motel office, and a farmhouse Carl owned on Tibbetts Point Road.

Benjamin, only 16 at the time, had been shocked. He had no idea his father was an alcoholic. Then again, nobody seemed to have any idea—except Cooper.

Cooper recalled the time he had brought Bill Snyder, his best buddy at Clarkson, home for a weekend. Cooper was a junior, on his way to flunking German for the first time, and Bill was a pro baseball–aspiring sophomore. They were both math majors. They were out cruising in Cooper's '56 Buick Special, the Blue Goose, when Cooper spotted his father's burgundy Buick headed in the direction of Tibbetts Point Road. Cooper had known instantly where his father was headed and why.

Staying well back, Cooper followed his father up a winding road that traced the alternating convexes and concaves of the St. Lawrence shoreline. Turning into an unpaved driveway about a quarter of a mile long, Cooper drove toward a forlorn-looking house on the right, a saggy-roofed barn on the left. As he progressed, he could see sunlight glint off a car parked behind the tall weeds between the barn and the house.

When he had driven about two-thirds up the driveway, his father suddenly appeared from the direction of the house, hurrying as if he had forgotten something.

Cooper had never forgotten his father's face as they passed each other at the top of the driveway—how his father had looked like a scared little boy. Cooper did not wait for the owner of a second car to emerge from the house. He didn't need to. He knew who it was.

Was he the only one who knew?

Cooper took another hit of Jim Beam.

I really wanted to embarrass you that day, Pop. Did you know that? Did you have any sense of that at all? You thought I was just taking my college buddy on a tour of my home turf, am I right?

Cooper took another drink and, sensing encroachment, checked his rearview mirror. A mass of chrome was bearing down on him. He searched ahead for an opening in the slow-speed lane to his right, but there wasn't one. His only option was to move into the high-speed lane. As a general practice, Cooper avoided high-speed lanes because his Le Car offered little protection against being crushed in a collision of any magnitude. About to merge left, with trepidation, Cooper was visited by a wildly voluptuous thought—

He could stay right where he was!

Bless me, Father, for I have sinned.

The truck behind him crept closer.

Get the hell out of my way, bucko! Time is money!

Overheating

He was already going the speed limit. If he went faster to accommodate this asshole's pathological addiction to speed, he would risk getting a ticket, which was the last thing he needed. Besides, he had a perfect right to be where he was. He didn't have to make any more of an effort to let this asshole past him, and he didn't have to allow himself to be intimidated either.

Looking again in his rearview mirror, Cooper watched the truck surge dangerously close to his rear bumper but forbade his foot from pressing down on the accelerator the slightest bit more. To ensure compliance, he commanded his foot to ease off a bit. Maybe even a little more than just a bit.

The truck eased back about two car lengths, then surged closer.

Cooper checked his speed. He was doing a little over 60 miles per hour—admittedly, a bit slow.

What if that all-important "reasonable man" of his Cornell Law days were sitting on his shoulder right now? What would *he* say? Cooper watched the speedometer needle creep up until it pointed to 64.

The truck maintained the same separation—as if towed by the Le Car. It was one of those custom jobs—chrome everywhere and lots of hand-painted decals. The truck's headlights flashed.

Cooper searched ahead. There was still no place for him to merge into the right lane.

The truck's headlights flashed again. Cooper watched the needle on his speedometer drop to 56, 55, 54—and heard the deep blare of a truck horn.

He touched the brake pedal—just enough to trigger his brake lights—and grinned at the happy sound of 18 locked tires skid-marking the highway.

Cooper turned on his blinker and, merging into the left lane, sped up to 65, 70, 72. He looked in the rearview mirror. There was no sign of the truck.

Taking another hit of Jim Beam, he screwed the cap back on the bottle and tossed the bottle onto the passenger seat. His whole problem was he had spent almost his entire life being too nice. As in too sympathetic, too accommodating, too deferential, too empathetic—in a world that interpreted *all* those things as weaknesses. Character flaws.

Cooper felt as if he had just emerged from spending ten years shivering in a dark cave only to find himself 200 yards from a double-decker motel on a superhighway. The truth of the matter was *niceness was weakness.*

Traffic had thinned a bit. Seeing an opportunity, Cooper moved into the middle lane and then into the slow-speed lane. He glanced in the rearview mirror. The same truck was approaching from the middle lane. It was going to pass him.

Once it was beside him, instead of passing, it started to merge right into him!

This cannot be happening!

Cooper swerved into the breakdown lane and immediately straightened to avoid hitting a guardrail, but the truck kept coming at him, now moving into the breakdown lane!

Moving a little more to the right, as much as he dared, Cooper waited for a long expanse of guardrail to end, then turned a little to the right and straddled the crest of an embankment. As the truck passed by, horn blaring, Cooper steered back onto the breakdown lane and slammed on his brakes.

He looked at the disappearing truck. He bowed his head.

Several minutes passed before Cooper could calm himself enough to pull back onto the highway. When he got onto Route 101, he stopped at a mailbox beside the road and stuffed his bottle of Beam into it. *Merry Christmas.*

When he arrived home, he managed to slam the driver's-side door hard enough, on the first try, for the latch to catch.

It was a faulty parking brake that started the problem with the driver's-side door. Cooper hadn't thought to warn Tessa about it.

Union ware; buyer beware!

A few months back, she had parked the Le Car at the top of the driveway, only to have it roll down and across the street, taking out the quaint wishing well in front of the neighbor's house. Cooper wished he had simply made a joke out of the whole thing—especially the wishing-well part—instead of allowing himself to get caught up in what the damage meant in terms of budget impact and hassle. But, of course, that's not what he had done.

Too late now.

Regret hath the greatest of company.

With Halloween just around the corner, Cooper considered locking his car but couldn't face trying to get the lock to work. Latching the door was one thing, locking it quite another. One had to turn the key at the right moment while pressing against the door as hard as possible.

The TV was on in the family room when Cooper transitioned from the mudroom. It was uncomfortably loud. It wasn't garbage that was going to pollute the world; it was noise.

He had forgotten his tote. Screw it. What did it matter anyway?

Cooper wiped his feet on the mudroom mat even though there was nothing to wipe and, entering the family room, tried not to notice the usual detritus of three boys—the school packs, the shoes and jackets, the hockey paraphernalia, the couch pillows and afghans, and the inserts from recently arrived magazines.

Noah, sitting on the near end of the couch, looked up from a *Discover* magazine.

"Hi, Pop!"

Luke, sitting on the other end of the couch, was reading what appeared to be *Sports Illustrated*. Zak, not present, was likely down in the basement playroom.

Noah jumped up from the couch and greeted Cooper with a kiss on each cheek. "How was your day?"

"Good," Cooper lied. "How was yours?"

"I kicked butt on a grammar test."

"Ah, good man. I thought they stopped teaching grammar in school."

"Miss Kapels still does."

"Good for her." Cooper started to step through the minefield of their belongings.

He paused. "Guys—the shoes belong in the mudroom. The jackets belong in the closet. The afghans belong on the couch. And none of this is news, am I right?"

"Hi, Pop," Luke said without looking up.

"Hi, Luke. What's the score?"

"Score?"

"In general."

Luke smiled. "We're winning."

"Good. It's about time."

Cooper continued into the kitchen, and Tessa approached from the stove. She kissed him, held him—tight—then turned back to the stove.

Cooper hung his jacket in the hall closet, went upstairs, and changed into his "grungies."

He debated whether or not to lie down. He needed a little distance right now anyway; he just didn't want to be too obvious about it. She might ask questions. He couldn't handle any questions right now. He lay down and closed his eyes.

The woodstove might need tending if someone hadn't thought to stoke it in the last couple of hours. The coals might already be too low to start a fresh log. Tessa sometimes remembered to check it, but she always had plenty of other things to do when she got home from work.

T'hell with it. If it goes out, it goes out. He didn't have to worry about things like that anymore. It was all their problem now.

Cooper sighed and then rolled out of bed and made his way down to the basement, where he found Zak well along in building a block castle around Queen Emily, who, eyes half closed, seemed well pleased with the attention she was getting.

"Hi, Zak."

"Hi, Pop."

"Got a friend there?"

"Yep."

"Would you build a castle like that for me someday?"

"Sure, Pop."

"Great. I'll take you up on it. I'd like mine made of gold and silver, though, OK?"

"OK, Pop."

Cooper stoked the stove, adjusted the vent, and checked the water level in the cleanout. Then he climbed the stairs to the kitchen and slowly poured himself a modest measure of Rossi Rhine.

Tessa had recently replenished his supply with a smaller jug. He had dropped the full-gallon size. Twice.

It wouldn't be long before Tessa would have to start zipping and unzipping his fly every time he needed to pee.

"How was your day?" Tessa invited—to get a read on him, Cooper knew.

Cooper stood a moment near his place at the table to gauge the level of heat rising from the basement, then moved to his usual debriefing spot, near the entrance to the dining room.

"Other than some jerk trying to run me off the road—great."

Tessa stared.

"How about you?"

"No, *you*," Tessa insisted. "What happened?"

Cooper took a sip of wine, then summarized his encounter with the 18-wheeler.

Tessa was aghast. "That's horrible! You could have been killed!"

Cooper wondered if the kids were listening. He took another sip of wine. His thumb was twitching.

Was that a hint of disapproval he saw in Tessa's eyes?

She turned off the front burners on the stove and pushed the hot frying pans onto the back burners. He could tell that she wanted to say more, ask questions, challenge his anger. Undoubtedly, she wanted to know whether he had provoked the driver of the 18-wheeler.

"I hate having you on those roads."

"Yeah."

Cooper set his wineglass down on the counter next to the stove and leaned against the counter behind him. "Something bothering you?" he asked.

Tessa opened the oven door and, pulling out a cookie tray loaded with asparagus stalks, set it on an array of hot pads. She shut the door and turned the oven off. "I spoke with a therapist today. He used to be the rector at St. Paul's. Lynn told me about him. He retired from the priesthood to become a family therapist. He got his degree at UNH. His name is George Quigley. He's very nice." Tessa looked to Cooper. "This would be for me, Cooper. You could involve yourself or not, as you saw fit. That would be entirely up to you. I know how you feel about therapists. Whatever you choose to do, though, I would support it any way I could. Twice over."

Cooper threw his arms up. "Oh Jesus, *that's* what we need! Another goddamn pickpocket in our lives. Here, I'll just tell you what he'll say: 'Mrs. Haynes, it's perfectly all right to bury a dead man before he's officially dead. People do it all the time. It's all perfectly natural. It's even legal. Life goes on. There's absolutely no reason to feel guilty. Go in peace.' How's that? No charge."

Tessa's eyes showed disappointment and a bit of hurt but no anger. "That is *not* what I need at all. What I need is to talk to somebody about what you refuse to talk about. He's very good, Cooper." Tessa paused. "I'd like you to come with me sometime."

Cooper felt Emily bump up against his legs. She had a low tolerance for any kind of strife in her family.

"If you want to talk to somebody, then go talk to somebody."

Noah and Luke were staring wide-eyed from the family room. Zak was peering from the basement stairwell—half looking, half hiding. There was terror in Zak's 10-year-old eyes.

Overheating

They shouldn't be seeing this. What am I doing? I'm a goddamn idiot!

Fleeing from the kitchen, Cooper stormed upstairs and slammed the bedroom door. One of Aunt Estelle's lithographs fell from the wall and struck the bowl to his grandmother's antique chamber set, leaving a jagged cavity on the lip toward the wall.

It was ruined. Fuck it!

Cooper smashed a fist through the hollow door. A pulse of excruciating pain shot through his knuckles. He pulled his hand through the jagged rupture—too quickly, too incautiously—and lacerated it.

Sinking to his knees then, Cooper drew himself into a ball and, holding his bloody hand against his chest, whimpered. *Take me now. No more pain.*

Tessa was beside him, kneeling, holding a wet washcloth on his hand and forearm.

"I love you to pieces, Cooper. You can't chase me away, no matter how hard you try. I will pass every test you come up with. Let me take care of you. Grant me that privilege."

Hot Coffee

OCTOBER 1982

Cooper was racing a set of footsteps approaching from behind. He was not winning! He tried to walk faster, desperate for every little victory he could get.

Reaching the glass entry doors, Cooper pulled the handle on one of them with greater than normal force. The previous morning, he had not been so deliberate and had not been able to pull the door open on the first attempt—or on the second.

Using his 212 pounds as a counterweight, Cooper held the door open for a plumpish, plain-faced woman wearing too-tight jeans and lavender running shoes. He cringed at a nonzero prospect of being called out for being a sexist pig.

Having received a simple thank-you, Cooper followed the woman into the foyer, where he switched his tote to his left hand and, slipping his badge out of his jacket pocket, held it up as he walked past the guard station. The guard, preoccupied with a group of two men and a woman, did not so much as glance in Cooper's direction.

About halfway up the corridor, Cooper was surprised to pass the freckle-faced, strawberry-blond man who had chastised him in front of his colleagues for having left the coffeepot empty.

Freckles was just about to enter the Faraday Conference Room toting a slim, burgundy briefcase with brass corner plates and combination locks.

Straight-arming his way into the men's room, Cooper dropped his tote to the floor and claimed an unoccupied urinal.

Would you rather be told you weren't going to die of an incurable disease after all or make it to the toilet just in the nick of time? Tough one.

Standing at one of the sinks for a quick rinse, Cooper found himself stealing glances at a balding Black man standing at a sink to Cooper's left. He had just emerged from one of the stalls.

The man was wearing a set of baggy, dark-green work clothes and had a ring of keys dangling from his belt. Something about him—*everything* about him—triggered in Cooper that nagging disquietude he would experience whenever he sensed he was in the presence of someone who felt looked down upon.

He looked the man in the eye and nodded.

Our greatest need,
Our greatest gift,
Me seeing thee,
Thee seeing me.

En route to his cubicle, Cooper stopped off to check his mail slot and was surprised to find something in it—a sign-up sheet for Digitronics' annual United Way drive.

Overheating

Cooper crunched the sign-up sheet with his free hand and dropped it in the first wastebasket he came to. He moved on, then stopped, turned around, and retrieved the crunched-up sheet.

He passed his cubicle and looked in Dana's, expecting to find it dark.

Her desk lamp was on. Was she *really* in this early, or had she left her light on overnight, playing the old *leave-your-light-on-to-make-them-think-you're-still-at-it* trick?

A WGBH tote was lying on her visitor chair. Her coffee mug was missing.

He remembered she had a doc review at 8 a.m. She should be done by 10.

Cooper pulled a soggy tuna sandwich from his tote and, placing it beside his terminal, logged in to his account. He had four new messages.

There was going to be a full disk backup tomorrow night. *Great way to spend an evening.*

Discount certificates for snow tires were available at Personnel. *How about instituting a true merit pay system instead?*

The site for the farewell luncheon for Roy Jacobs had been changed. *How many of the attendees would remember Roy's name five years from now?*

A big shot from Carnegie Mellon would be lecturing on the "Fifth Generation Computer" in the auditorium next Thursday. *Bring your own popcorn.*

He hit D, pressed Return, and stared at the blank screen.

Tomorrow Houghton-Mifflin would summon him to Boston to discuss a six-figure contract. Dr. Weiss would leave a message about a new miracle cure for ALS.

Cooper grabbed his mug. Several people were standing around the coffee alcove watching a pot fill. If someone had commanded them to stand there wasting precious moments of their lives, they would have taken up arms!

He found himself listening in on a conversation between two young men standing to his left, one of whom was showing a beard as black as Lucifer's tongue. The other was wearing a shirt that looked suspiciously like a pajama top.

Judging from the volume and content of their conversation, it seemed to be one that was intended to be overheard. It didn't take long to get the gist of the subject at hand: Chinese restaurants in San Francisco. Or, better, *authentic* Chinese restaurants in San Francisco. Apparently Lucifer's Tongue had recently visited San Francisco and was describing, with celebratory verve, the "authentic" fare he had experienced at a particular restaurant. It had been the first "real thing" he had experienced since he had last visited Chinatown in New York. The "real thing," everyone watching the excruciatingly slow-filling pot was soon to learn, was, number one, where they didn't serve any alcoholic beverages, not even Tsingtao; number two, no one spoke anything but Chinese; and number three, there was no English translation on the menu.

You did *get that I can both speak and read Mandarin, right?*

Cooper pictured himself turning to Lucifer's Tongue with a big smile and launching into a high-pitched monologue of singsong gibberish. He could only wish he had the balls to actually do stuff like that.

He hung back until everyone waiting had filled their mug and left the alcove. When he had finished filling his own mug, there was only enough coffee left in the pot for perhaps half a mugful.

Cooper scanned the posted instructions, willed himself into motion, and in a minute or two was watching a grudgingly slow trickle begin to darken an empty pot, bottom to top.

As Cooper waited for the pot to fill, the alcove began to accumulate a fresh crop of pot watchers. He felt an obligation to explain to these people why he was still standing at the head of the queue holding a full mug but, of course, said nothing.

Fuck 'em!

When the last dribble had yielded to the relentless tyranny of gravity, Cooper picked the pot up by the handle and turned to leave. "Boss's waiting," he announced. "Back in a jiffy."

A burgundy briefcase with brass corner plates and combination locks was lying open on a table the size and general shape of a stretch limo.

Overheating

"Coffee's ready," Cooper announced.

A dozen or more faces showed consternation.

"It's the real thing."

Cooper approached the freckle-faced man with strawberry-blond hair. "Warm that up for you, sir?"

The man directed a look of confusion from Cooper to the man's half-empty—or was it half-full?—mug. When the mug overflowed, Cooper continued pouring, thereby soaking several sheets of numbery numbers neatly arranged into columny columns.

"Hey!" The man rolled his chair backward and, jumping to his feet, pushed Cooper with considerable violence, sending him crashing against an adjacent chair and sprawling onto the floor.

Soaked in scalding-hot coffee, Cooper got to his feet and, trying to hold the saturated fabric of his shirt away from the scalded flesh of his chest, walked as casually to the door as he could manage.

He turned back to see Freckles frantically blotting his columny columns of numbery numbers, using a handkerchief.

Cooper bowed. "Sorry."

He closed the door behind him. It was over.

You're done!

11

Uncharted Territory

Somewhere between the 10 and 11 mile markers, Cooper realized he had run farther than he had at any point in his six-month training regimen. All he could do now, though, was put as good a face on defeat as he possibly could. For the kids' sake.

Humility is the last lesson learned, the first forgot.

Cooper searched ahead for a water station and caught a glimpse of a well-attended lawn behind a wrought-iron fence. It was the kind of lawn that, despite being taken care of, allowed, even encouraged, a little wildness. The buds on the shrubs were swollen with promise. Another week and they would begin to pop. A new cycle would have begun.

Cooper had forgotten to include in his to-do list for Tessa and the boys how to care for the shrubs he had planted along the front of the house last April. If they didn't get watered at least twice a week in the summer, they would never make it. They hadn't had enough time yet to establish themselves. They would need a little help.

All because Ed Ojai, the builder, had stolen their topsoil to sell elsewhere, leaving them with nothing but silty subsoil, hidden with just enough trucked-in topsoil, stolen from someone else, to keep the deception intact until he had gotten his money and left town in the dark of night.

Then there was the "kiln-dried" lumber that had bled sap for nearly a year; and the insulation that had been so poorly installed, Cooper had had to take it all out and reinstall it himself; and the cracks that had mysteriously crept into the concrete foundation, leaking snowmelt in the spring; and the bathroom window that had been installed at about the same angle as the Tower of Pisa's lean; and the kitchen floor that was so warped, you could rock your chair on it; and the gritty, sloppy paint job; and the linoleum that had worn out in less than a year; and the stairwell that had been built with such a low ceiling at the bottom that they had not been able to get their queen-size box springs up the stairs; and the water that had come gushing out of the light fixture over the kitchen table one morning, to the sound of a flushing toilet; and the driveway that was less than half the width specified in the contract.

He really, really should have been a Victorian. He really, really should have lived in a time when pride in workmanship was the rule rather than the exception and the measure of a man was expressed in terms of his contributions to his community rather than in terms of his material wealth.

The purpose of your life
And mine—
is to be useful;
You in your way
Me in mine;
More of philosophy
Dear Horatio
is a waste of time.

He was thirsty beyond measure, and his core temperature was well into the danger zone. He could feel it. *Danger! Danger!*

He needed to stop. He would try to just make it to the next water station—it had to be close by.

Mount Jackson

OCTOBER 1982

Cooper needed to rest, even though it had only been about a half hour since his last break. The boys had gone on ahead, as boys cannot help but do when there's an adult to be beaten to the top of a mountain.

Cooper propped his walking stick—an old hockey stick minus the business end—against the trunk of a gnarly fir tree and, slipping off his backpack, sat down on a hunk of ancient granite. He drank hardily from his water bottle, then dug out a bag of gorp from his pack and funneled a handful, which was heavy on the peanuts, into his mouth.

No longer hearing snippets of voices from above, Cooper suspected the boys had already reached the summit and were looking for a viewing spot, as he had asked them to do. He massaged his calves, took another handful of gorp and drink of water—and shivered. He was cooling down rapidly.

He licked chocolate residue from the palm of his hand, then pulled a fisherman's sweater from his pack and attempted to pull it over his head. He winced from a cramp in his right arm. When he had suffered a similar cramp at the trailhead trying to pull his pack on, Luke had had to come to his aid.

For an anxious moment, Cooper found himself trapped—unable to get the sweater all the way on or all the way off. He pictured himself hiking the rest of the way to the summit in his present state—as if wearing a straitjacket.

Finally able to get the sweater all the way on, Cooper resumed climbing. He wasn't dead yet! He could still climb a 4,000-foot mountain, if only in fits and starts.

Surveying his immediate environment, Cooper noticed there were two distinct tiers—an upper tier, consisting of stunted and disfigured firs standing no more than twelve feet tall, and a lower tier, consisting of lushly plumed seedlings, standing no more than a foot tall. There was no in-between growth. Apparently, the mature firs had to die out sufficiently for enough sunlight to reach the ground to trigger the germination of the next generation. Once they became elderly and moribund, it would trigger the germination of the next generation, and so on and so on—life to death, death to life. But for some kind of modulating mechanism to limit the number of generations, there would be too many trees to support at any given time in so harsh an environment.

Nature was a marvel of resourcefulness. Of a kind of intelligence, actually.

Reaching an outcropping no more than a few hundred yards from the summit, Cooper paused to peer through a gap in the low growth toward the northeast, in the direction of the Franconia Range. He could easily identify Mount Lafayette, the tallest of a group of peaks that included both Mount Liberty and Mount Flume.

Before getting his diagnosis, Cooper had intended to climb these peaks with the kids—when time availed. Now it was likely too late. In theory, they could still do it, but with winter coming on, it was unlikely they would have a chance to climb any one of the three peaks until spring—late spring—when odds were he would be bound to a wheelchair or interred in a bronze urn.

The autumn foliage was past prime, with the fiery reds and bold oranges of the maples having given way to the duller cranberries and rusts of the oaks. Soon all would be dead, another cycle having run its course in an eternal series.

Cooper found himself wondering anew if there were sentient creatures anywhere else in the universe. He used to believe it highly likely—back in the days when driving across the continent to hear Carl Sagan deliver a 50-minute talk on that subject seemed like a perfectly reasonable thing to do—but now he wasn't so sure. Too many coincidences seemed to be required in precisely the right order. The unlikeliness of it all truly boggled the mind.

Ranking high among Cooper's disappointments was not getting a reply from Lewis Thomas, the famous biologist and essayist. Cooper had written Thomas asking for his thoughts on whether all life on Earth had derived from the same anomalous event—a particular collection of proteins managing to replicate itself—or whether there had been multiple instances of such.

The question seemed key. If all life had evolved from an event that had occurred only once in the entire 4.5-billion-year history of the Earth, then it seemed highly unlikely there could be life elsewhere in the universe—*or at least within our galaxy.* In fact, it would appear that life had been reserved for this one little orb, just as the authors of Genesis had it.

Even though Cooper understood that people like Lewis Thomas did not have the time or the will to answer the hundreds if not thousands of requests they were typically deluged with—they had to draw the line somewhere—still.

Still there was an outside chance that the Truth Fairy would visit him at the moment of his death and whisper in his ear the answers to all his questions.

Paradise aplenty!

Maybe *that* was the deal. If you had been naughty, you are sentenced to an eternity of asking questions and getting no answers—or getting the answers in a foreign language, like Swahili. But if you had been good, really good, you get to hear—and comprehend—all the answers.

Cooper followed a trail of yellow blazes on trees and rocks until he came upon Noah, Luke, and Zak sitting in a row, gazing upon what seemed like half of creation.

A lump formed in Cooper's throat. Tears welled. This was going to be hard.

He wished Tessa were there. She would know exactly what to say and how to say it. She wouldn't need to find the courage. It would already be there.

The eastern horizon, perhaps ten miles away, maybe more, was dominated by three pyramid-shaped peaks. All three were tree covered, indicating they were no taller than the present peak. In the foreground, a valley extended roughly north to south. There was no sign of human encroachment.

Cooper had rehearsed the words in his head at least a hundred times, even in the middle of the night, but now, with the curtain about to rise, he found himself all but paralyzed with fright and misgivings.

"Beautiful, eh?"

Noah: "Sure is."

Luke: "What took you so long, Pop?" Luke was always ready with a good-natured barb.

"Well, interestingly enough, that brings me to the reason I asked you up here today."

Interestingly enough? Good grief. You're a writer, Cooper. So, what? You can't come up with a more memorable opening line, in league with—

It was the best of times, it was the worst of times.

Call me Ishmael.

Last night I dreamt I went to Manderley again.

Mother died today. Or, maybe, yesterday; I can't be sure.

It was a bright cold day in April, and the clocks were striking thirteen.

"So we could carry you down?" Zak was unable to resist a barb of his own.

"Well, actually that just might be the case," Cooper rejoined. "See those three peaks in a row over there?" Cooper pointed toward the eastern horizon. "I'd like you to look at those a minute while I tell you something. This is something I should have already told you so you could understand what's been going on with me—why I've been such an asshole.

"There's a peak over there for each of you. It doesn't matter who chooses which one. You can all choose the same one if you want. It doesn't matter. OK?"

Zak: "Is this a game?"

Cooper: "I wish it were, Zak. Right over those three peaks is where the sun would have come up this morning."

Slipping his pack off, Cooper lowered himself onto one knee, and then the other, directly behind the boys. All three were sitting cross-legged.

Cooper leaned back on his haunches to minimize the weight on his knees. He swallowed.

"The other day, I ended up in jail because I attacked a perfectly innocent man in a bar. I was upset, and I lost control. I've had trouble with anger my whole life.

"The reason I was so upset." Cooper paused. "This is hard." He looked up. A turkey vulture, wings fully extended on either side, was circling and soaring overhead. "Remember those tests I had in Boston a couple weeks ago?" Noah and Luke nodded. Zak started to turn to Cooper.

Cooper patted Zak on the shoulder. "I just got the results from my doctor." Cooper paused. "He told me I had tested positive for an incurable disease called ALS. Lou Gehrig's disease. Stephen Hawking has it. There is no cure. Most people who get it only live a couple of years after diagnosis. You guys and your mom are going to have to take extra special care of each other."

In an instant, all three boys were in Cooper's arms.

"I am so very sorry," Cooper managed.

They wept.

Uncharted Territory

12

Out of Reach

The halfway point was only two miles away, but it might as well have been two million. A bridge too far is a bridge too far.

It was time to allow reality its due.

He was done.

Hearing a strained wheezing sound, Cooper glanced left and recognized a man he had seen earlier. His licorice-black beard and garish Hawaiian shirt made him hard to miss, but it was his labored wheezing that Cooper took most notice of. One runner handicapped by too much weight, the other, himself, by too little. Poles apart yet the same.

Cooper stopped for water. He wobbled as he drank. He poured a cupful of water over his head. Another. And another.

When Cooper started up again, the Wheezer was no longer in sight. He apparently had not stopped. Cooper would try to catch up with him.

Why not?

There was no tomorrow.

No Way Out

OCTOBER 1982

A bank of boiling clouds—purplish green—was approaching from the west. The atmosphere was sodden—stifling.

A breeze now—fraught with portent. It was too late to make it to safe ground. He was too slow; if only he hadn't ventured out so far. A rumble not thunder— something else—continuous, growing louder.

He dared a glimpse over his shoulder and felt his stomach jump against his spine. A massive vortex was undulating directly toward him! He dropped to the ground and lay flat. The stiff stubble of harvested grain lacerated his flesh.

He tried to dig his fingers into the ground but it was like baked clay, impenetrable. He summoned all his strength.

He felt himself begin to ascend—as if by the sucking power of a giant vacuum! He felt himself begin to rotate—around and around, faster and faster, like on a carnival ride.

He was going to be flung into oblivion. It was just a matter of time!

Cooper woke with a start. Tessa was patting him on the hip. He lay still to give Tessa time to go back to sleep.

After moments that felt like hours, Cooper lifted the clock from his nightstand and held the orangey face close. He squinted to make out 2:40. He listened to Tessa breathe.

He closed his eyes, swallowed, and felt just enough constriction in his throat not to be able to pretend he didn't notice. He had been feeling this same sensation, or thought he had, over the past week or so. Maybe not every time he swallowed, but ever more frequently, it seemed.

Staring into the gloom, Cooper focused on a raft of formless speckles as it floated across his field of vision, right to left. He wondered, as he had on so many previous occasions—in particular when he had lain awake deep into the night for fear of dying and being cast into hell—what those little speckles were. And why they moved as they did—always from one side to the other.

And why he could jerk them back into view simply by blinking his eyes.

So many things, big and small, he had wanted to know—to understand or stand under—but now could not. The music had stopped, and there was no chair left for him to claim.

Not that there would ever have been enough time for such a project, but it sure would have been nice nonetheless to have been able to cling to a child's illusion of timelessness a little longer.

Cooper slid his arm toward Tessa until his hand made contact.

Another lump. He tried to swallow it. He sensed his lungs laboring a bit harder than only recently had been normal. He dabbed his eyes with the top sheet and, easing himself out of bed, felt his way into the bathroom. Making sure the seat was down, he eased himself onto it.

He grinned. How many adult males were there in the world who sat on the seat to pee at night?

How might such a statistic be collected?

Rising too quickly, Cooper leaned forward, hands on knees, to a rush of dizziness. He took a few deep breaths. Feeling his way to his chest of drawers on the other side of the room, he slowly cracked open the second drawer from the top.

He wished there was a way he could be sure one of the boys would cherish his beautiful old chest as much as he had—then pass it on to someone else who would love it and keep it, just as his grandmother had done and her mother before that. There seemed to be a diminishing appreciation in the world for beautiful artifacts—for beauty in general. If it was ugly, loud, or garish, it was "in." If it was beautiful, restrained, or subtle, it was "out."

Maybe Zak would keep it. Of the three boys, he seemed to be the one naturally inclined toward developing an abiding affection for inanimate things. All three boys were tender at their core, though, and because of this, they were going to have a rough time of it in the world.

How different his own life might have been had he had someone to ease *him* into the world.

Out of Reach

157

Lifting a pair of briefs from the drawer, Cooper stepped into them—one foot safely through a leg hole, the other foot safely through the other leg hole. No sooner had he pulled them up, however, than he could sense he had put them on backward. The story of his life.

He debated whether to ignore this little violation of the "proper order of things" or to take the time to make it right. Sliding his Jockeys to the floor, he stepped out of them, turned them 180 degrees, and pulled them up again.

He decided to leave the drawer cracked open. If it bound, even slightly, the whole chest would rattle, and the jig would be up, as they say.

Moving cautiously toward the door, Cooper lifted his clothes from the hook on the back and put them on, working not to lose his balance. He pulled his shoes from under his nightstand, slipped them on—leaving his socks behind—and faced the bed.

He swallowed, touched his lips with his fingers, and blew a kiss toward Tessa. The night-light in the boys' bathroom was casting a dim glow into the hallway. Pulling the door just short of triggering the latch, Cooper stole slowly up the hallway. Near the end, he bore left and navigated around the wicker hamper that stood between Luke's room and Zak's. The door being open, Cooper entered Luke's room and, reaching Luke's bed, found a leg, an arm, a shoulder, and, finally, a downy head.

Luke's position seemed awkward, and Cooper was pretty sure he knew why. Probing farther, he located the edge of Luke's pillow, and soon thereafter encountered Emily's silky fur. She began to rev up her motor, not that she ever needed much of an excuse.

Easing himself onto the edge of Luke's bed, Cooper laid a hand on Luke's arm and soon found himself remembering when Luke was in the fifth grade, peddling his first volume of poems, titled *Sorry About the Title*, door-to-door in the neighborhood.

Cooper shook Luke gently, to no obvious effect, and then shook a little harder. Luke shot upright.

"It's Pop," Cooper whispered. "Everything's OK. I just needed to tell you how much I love you and that I'm very proud to have you as a son. I *know* you're going to write a lot of good stuff."

Luke leaned forward and wrapped his arms around Cooper. They squeezed each other.

Cooper swallowed.

"Careful when you lie back down," he whispered. "Emily's on your pillow."

Luke uttered a few grunts and settled into his previous contortion. Cooper tucked the covers around Luke's shoulders and stroked his head. Emily's "beasty sounds," as Tessa called them, lulled him back to sleep.

Lifting himself from the edge of Luke's bed, Cooper made his way to the door, eased himself around the hamper between the two rooms, and entered Zak's room. Zak's was wide open, likely left that way to invite visitors. It was not unusual for Emily to visit all three members of her brood in succession any night she wasn't outdoors.

Finding the edge of Zak's bed, Cooper quietly sat down and tried, with several shakes, to awaken the same hibernating "bear cub" he and Tessa, a few years earlier, had struggled to wake to a sufficient level of consciousness for him to realize he had wet his bed and needed to turn off the raucous device (Wee Alert) a pediatrician had told them would solve Zak's bed-wetting problem once and for all.

It was behavior modification at its worst. Everybody else in the house would be fully awake, including Noah, who would compound the uproar by banging on a drum while marching up and down the hallway.

Nothing would work. They would turn on every light. They would wash Zak's face with cold water. They would hold the alarm up close to Zak's ear. Tessa would hold Zak's face in both hands and talk to him. Through it all— although Zak's eyes would be as open as everybody else's—Zak would be fast asleep. It wasn't until a few years later that Tessa discovered (with no help from the we-know-best medical establishment) that Zak's coma-like slumber and daytime driftiness were caused by an allergic reaction to cow's milk. Once Tessa switched Zak to goat's milk, all that went away. Not after a few days or weeks, but instantly. Gone.

Zak was lying on his stomach.

"You awake, Zak?"

Grunt.

"It's Pop. You awake?"

Grunt.

"I just wanted to tell you how much I love you and that I'm very proud to have you as a son."

"I love you too, Pop."

"So you *are* awake," he whispered. "Now you can go back to sleep."

Cooper stroked Zak's back for a few moments, as if in grateful acknowledgment of all those unsolicited backrubs Zak had given him. They had been far and away the best backrubs Cooper had ever received, owing largely to the fact that Zak would not stop until you deliberately released him from duty. It was like eating shrimp from a bottomless bowl.

Zak the caregiver, Zak the empathizer, Zak the romantic. And maybe Zak the keeper of a beautiful old chest of drawers.

How long would it be, though, before the caregiver, the empathizer, the romantic—the keeper of beautiful things—would start building walls and moats around himself as essential protection against the world?

Cooper took a quick breath, patted Zak on the back, and eased up from Zak's bed. "Goodnight, my friend."

"G'night, Pop."

Creeping back into the hallway, Cooper bore left and, moving straight on, passed through Noah's open doorway. He scuffed his feet from this point on lest he trip over one of Noah's three-ring computer manuals; or a tome of similar size and weight, such as *Gray's Anatomy*; or a volume or two of *Encyclopedia Britannica*.

Of the three boys, Noah had always shown the least inclination toward surrounding himself with anything resembling order. It had likely been inevitable that Noah and his control-freak, everything-in-its-place father had spent a large part of their early years together butting heads.

Cooper reached for the edge of the same bed he had slept in at Noah's age and, finding Noah's hand, gently gripped it. Noah stirred but did not awaken.

Bowing his head, Cooper forced himself to remember the moment, almost five years earlier, when he fractured Noah's wrist. Cooper was to begin a new job he knew he would eventually hate. Noah had reflexively put his hands behind his back following a kick from his father to fend off a second blow. It was the second blow that did the damage.

A kick. From his father. Tears welled.

Resting his hand on Noah's shoulder, Cooper shook him once gently, knowing nothing more would be needed. Noah was as light a sleeper as Zak was deep.

All things tended to sum to zero.

Noah sat upright.

"It's Pop," Cooper whispered. "I was just thinking about you, what a fine young man you've turned out to be. I just wanted to tell you how very proud I am of you, how very much I love you, and how sorry I am that I wasn't a better father to you when you most needed me to be."

Noah hugged Cooper, and they squeezed each other.

Tears spilled down Cooper's cheeks. "You can go back to sleep now," he whispered.

"Why are you up so late, Pop? What time is it?"

"I couldn't sleep. I'll be OK now, though. Good night, my friend."

"'Night, Pop."

Cooper stood up and asked, "Will you remember this in the morning?"

"Yep."

"Good."

Cooper negotiated his way through the clutter and stood in the hallway for a few moments, bathed in the soft light still emanating into the hallway. A flood of memories now: The 20-hour labor at Bay General in Chula Vista. The intoxicating moment of birth five hours past the time he was supposed to be back aboard his ship. His mother's response when he called home with the news of Noah's birth: "You aren't going to name him *that*, are you?"

The XO of his ship, the father of five, convincing the CO to go easy on Cooper for going AWOL, after explaining to the CO what a Lamaze birth was and why it required the participation of the father.

The police escort up I-81—lights flashing, siren wailing—when Tessa was in labor with Luke. Overhead, flocks of Canadian geese in formation, heralding the moment when Luke would be born in the hallway between the labor and delivery rooms.

Tessa threatened to give birth to Zak in the lobby at the Oswego hospital—reporters present—if they wouldn't allow her husband in the delivery room so he could coach her through another Lamaze birth.

Cooper wiped his cheeks. Thanks to Tessa, their sons would be able to say to themselves, in those inevitable moments when it mattered more than anything else, "My dad was there, in the room. He helped catch me when I slid down the chute. My dad really loved me."

At the top of the stairs, Cooper cocked an ear toward the master bedroom and listened. The only sound was a low hum coming up the stairway from below. Tears ran down his cheeks. He could just slip back into the bedroom, crawl back into bed, and bask in Tessa's warm presence for the rest of the night, for the rest of his life.

He swallowed. He wiped his cheeks.

Grasping the handrail with his left hand, Cooper descended the stairs holding his right hand up to protect his head from bumping against the ceiling on the lower part of the stairwell. If Tessa had to sell the house and move, she would have to contend with getting their queen-size box springs down the stairs, which would require removing part of the stairwell ceiling, as had been the case in getting the same box springs up.

She could handle it. He had shielded her a little too much from having to deal with such things, but she would learn. As would the boys. They would do whatever had to be done. Necessity was the mother of invention, to be sure, but also of cooperation.

Cooper felt his way into the kitchen and, standing at the top of the stairwell to the basement, basked in a current of warm air rising from the woodstove below.

Shit! He was pretty sure he had forgotten to include bailing out the chimney trap in his list of chores and reminders. If the trap wasn't bailed out every two or three days, creosote-polluted water would leak from the trap and foul the basement floor, as had already happened once. The carpeting would have to be replaced in its entirety. Worse, though, the acrid odor would never go away. It would stink up the whole house forever! He imagined the boys could take turns doing it each week. Whoever's turn it was to empty the dishwasher that day could be responsible for bailing out the chimney trap.

Cooper entered the garage through the side door, climbed the steps to the loft, unlocked the door with a key only barely hidden, then pulled the chain on the green-and-brass banker's lamp Tessa had given him a few Christmases ago. He left the door unlocked.

Cooper's desk consisted of two fire-engine-red file cabinets serving as pedestals and a hollow door, varnished, serving as the desktop. A good portion of the desktop surface was taken up by the modem and terminal that Digitronics had loaned him so he could work at home a day or two a week to cut down on his commuting. Someone from the company was supposed to have picked it up by now.

Cooper pulled a small silver key from his pocket, unlocked the two file cabinets, lifted a bottle of Wild Turkey and a glass from the bottom drawer of the one, and removed his Grandmother Spafford's old lockbox from the bottom drawer of the other.

Cooper had kept only two things back from the auction his mother had held to "get rid of" five generations of family heirlooms: that lockbox—for which Cooper did not have a key, only an emotional attachment—and the old walnut chest of drawers that was now his. "The Spafford chest," Grandmother Spafford called it.

Lifting the lid on the lockbox, Cooper removed two fat envelopes bound with colored rubber bands and an amber vial containing the unused portion of the painkiller his mother had been prescribed following her hip surgery. She had only used one tablet. She was a tough old bird.

Having become aware of how chilly it was, Cooper turned the electric heater up higher, then sat down in his roller chair and closed his eyes. This *was* the right thing to do, he assured himself, for all concerned.

Cooper broke the seal on the bottle of Wild Turkey, filled his glass to about half full—half empty?—and took a robust sip. He shuddered.

Slipping the rubber bands from the two fat envelopes, Cooper read the first one:

For Tessa, in the event of my death

He took another gulp of whiskey but did not shudder this time. Cooper slipped several sheets from the envelope and unfolded them.

Dearest Tessa,

I once told you I would gladly sacrifice my life to save yours.
I wouldn't even have to think about it. Of course, such noble
declarations must, of their very nature, be treated as highly suspect,
especially from someone who loses control at the very sight of your
underwear, whether or not you're in it. But I truly meant it when
I first said it, and I truly mean it now. Of course, at the time I first
said it, I had visions of standing, sword in hand, between you and
a horde of fire-breathing dragons. I've always tended to be a bit of
a romantic, as you well know. However, as you also well know, we

don't live in that kind of world. There simply aren't any (literal) fire–breathing dragons for me to protect you against.

I cannot tell you how cheated I feel that the only dragons I can slay for you now are those inside me, killing me softly. But slay them I must, and slay them I shall. To do otherwise would be to put you and the boys through the worst kind of hell—far worse than anything I have put you through over the past 16 years.

If you are reading this, you are in pain. I'm sorry. You will find this pain, though, I firmly believe, far more like that of a hypodermic needle—clean and quick, ultimately healing—than that of a long, slow, horrific goodbye. Time will be your friend now rather than your constant tormentor.

Please allow yourself to feel as loved as I am desperately trying to make you feel. No woman has ever been more deserving of this kind of love. And in time (not too soon, though, goddamnit), please find someone else to share your life with, with my blessing. Life does indeed go on—is indeed only for the living. (Just make sure, whoever he is, he doesn't harbor any dreams about becoming the Poet Laureate of the Universe. You certainly don't need any more of that kind of shit!)

Please, please accept this last act for the gift it is meant to be. 'Tis, truly, "a far, far better thing I do than I have ever done."

Cooper pulled a pen from his college beer mug and realized he had neglected to include all the pens and pencils he had "borrowed" from Dig-itronics on the list of things to be returned.

What *else* had he forgotten?

Ah, yes. The yellow legal pads he used to write first drafts of his own stuff.

Cooper unfolded the to-do list he had drawn up over the past several days and added two entries, making his print as legible as was in his power in the moment to make it:

37. Zak, Luke, and Noah: Please make sure you bail all the water out the chimney trap, located at the bottom of the chimney, at least twice a week. Please use the pail next to the stove to collect the water. Whoever has dishwasher duty for the week might also be assigned clean-out duty. Please work it out among yourselves. I know I can count on you.

38. Tessa: Please return to Digitronics all the pens and pencils you will find in my college mug and all the yellow pads in the bottom drawer of the left-hand file cabinet. Someone is supposed to pick up the computer equipment. You can just include these other items when they show up. Thank you much. (Yes, I am a hopeless control freak!)

Cooper took another sip of whiskey and smiled. The one good thing about knowing when you were going to die was being able to leave everything in good order.

He refilled his glass to about halfway, took a sip, and another, then sealed the first envelope and took up the second.

To Luke, Noah, and Zak, in the event of my death

Cooper removed several sheets from the envelope, unfolded them, and took another sip of whiskey. What a wonderful buzz he was getting!

Dear Noah, Luke, and Zak,

Because fate has intervened and I can no longer "be there" for you in person, I'm leaving you with a few fatherly pontifications in my stead. My hope is that you will find them of some help toward living a life worth all the considerable bother—

no easy task, even under the best of circumstances. Please feel free to take what you think is worth taking and leave the rest.

If you would be happy, my friends—

Recognize the difference between craving and yearning, gratification and fulfillment. A dog barks, we reach for a bone. A cat rubs against our leg, do we reach also for a bone?

Strive to love, accept, and sacrifice without expectation or condition. In committing ourselves to a life of spontaneous generosity and compassion, we assure ourselves of everything we will ever really need.

Discover early in your uncertain tenure on this Earth the gifts with which you were uniquely graced. Tarry not till the hour of regret.

Judge every opportunity, every possibility, every choice on the basis of whether it will add to or diminish the cordwood of your self-regard. Go with what will always feel warm and cozy, even on the coldest of deep-winter nights.

Keep your expectations in line with the reality in which you live—especially in regard to love, security, success, and happiness itself. The less you expect, the more surprised by happiness you can be.

Plan for the future but live in the present. Avoid postponing happiness for that mythical day when one's ship finally comes in. Choose it for now.

What am I doing? What right do I have to pontificate to anybody? What are my credentials?

Jumping to his feet, Cooper began ripping the sheets into the smallest shreds he was able to achieve with compromised hands, tossing these into the air.

Leaving nothing behind is a helluva lot better than leaving a pile of shit, is it not?

As the last of his confetti settled, Cooper took another chug of bourbon and, dumping the contents of his mother's pill vial onto his desktop, popped a tablet into his mouth. He washed it down with another chug of bourbon. When they found him, he would look as if he were asleep. Tears scudded down his cheeks.

> *As the right to vote implies the right not to,*
> *so the right to live implies the right not to.*

Cooper popped another pill into his mouth and followed it with another sip of whiskey. He bowed his head. The world was a grotesque, irredeemable, fucked-up place. He would be so very glad to be rid of it!

He took another sip of whiskey. He felt tired. More than tired. More than more-than-tired. It was as if he had been tag-teaming with Holden Caulfield, taking turns patrolling the edge of a field of tall grass, unable to sleep for fear innocents would emerge and plunge into an abyss before he could catch them.

He popped another pill and took another chug of whiskey. As he inhaled the dryness of the electrically heated air, his nostrils tingled. The room had begun to move—sort of float. He closed his eyes.

Noah again: "Papa? Are you up there?"

O Jesus! Oh God! Cooper locked the door.

"Papa—are you there?"

It was all going to shit!

Silence.

The doorknob rattled. There was a tap on the door.

"I'm scared, Papa! Please open the door."

Cooper took a gulp of whiskey—and shuddered.

He had to be strong.

He startled to a sharp rap on the door.

Tessa: "Are you in there, Cooper?"

Oh, Jesus!

"Are you all right?" Tessa rattled the doorknob, urgently begging, "Please let us know, Cooper. Say something—make a sound, anything. Please."

"Papa, please."

All three boys had begun to cry. Cooper took another chug of whiskey. They would understand—this was best.

"We love you, Cooper. We love you to pieces. Please let us take care of you." Tessa's voice trailed off. The boys continued begging.

Cooper took a deep breath. He closed his eyes as still more tears streamed down his cheeks.

He startled to his phone ringing.

"Somebody wants to talk to you, Cooper. On the phone. Please answer," Tessa pressed.

Another ring. Cooper took the receiver off the hook and placed it on the desk. The phone stopped ringing, but the pleading continued.

A voice on the phone, low and in the distance, said, "This is George Quigley."

"Please talk to him, Cooper. Please. We'll leave if you pick up."

Cooper wiped his cheeks and picked up the receiver.

"Are you there, Cooper?"

This cannot be happening!

"Can you hear me?"

Cooper shook his head as the voice on the line persisted.

"I will assume you can hear me. I'm terribly sorry about intruding like this, Mr. Haynes, especially at such an ungodly hour. I realize I'm violating your privacy, and I'm very sorry about that, but the situation does seem to call for something a little out of the ordinary. May I call you Cooper?"

Cooper shook his head.

"You can call me George. If you'll allow me to, Cooper, I'd like to talk to you for a few minutes. Would that be OK? After I'm done, you can go ahead with whatever it was you were doing, or maybe call it a night and go back to bed. You're in charge. May I ask you a question, Cooper? Do you have a gun? Your wife mentioned she thought you might still have a pistol your father brought back from Europe at the end of World War II. Do you have a gun, Cooper?"

No answer.

"All I'm going to do here, Cooper, with your permission, is I'm just going to tell you a little story. I know: It's almost four o'clock in the morning, hardly an appropriate time to be telling stories, and you're probably going to think I'm just stalling for time until the cavalry arrives. But that isn't going to happen, Cooper. That would be overstepping my bounds, and I won't do that."

Cooper widened his eyes as if to keep two leaden curtains from dropping shut.

He was tired. Very, very tired. Getting incredibly drunk was hard work.

"If you need a recommendation concerning the quality of my storytelling, Cooper, I can refer you to my granddaughter, Peaches, who lives with my wife and me. She's just upstairs. I can get her here in a jiffy. She wouldn't mind a bit."

He should *not* have gone into the boys' bedrooms. He should have wrapped his piece-o'-shit car around a telephone pole—except he probably would have missed the goddamn thing and ended up in the shallow end of somebody's swimming pool.

George was persistent. "In a previous life, Cooper, I was an Episcopal priest. I left the ministry several years ago—six to be exact—to become a full-time therapist. I took two things with me when I left the ministry: a compassion for people in more pain than any human being should be made to bear and a penchant for telling stories that either make a point or stir the pot. All I'm asking of you, Cooper, is that you just bear with me for a bit. OK? Are you game?"

Cooper remained silent.

"I'll take that as a yes."

George went on to tell a story about a man who was immigrating to America to pursue a lifelong dream. He was making the passage across the Atlantic aboard an old freighter because this was the only passage he could afford. He was alone because he didn't have enough money to bring his family along. He intended to send for them later, after he had made enough money in America to pay for their passage.

One night, after he had been drinking rather heavily, trying to numb the pain of loneliness and allay the anxiety he felt over what lay ahead, he was standing at the railing thinking about his wife and children, when he was set upon by several members of the ship's crew who robbed him of everything he had been saving for the past several years. His assailants then threw their dazed and drunken victim into the cold, dark waters of the Atlantic Ocean.

George's pillowy voice reminded Cooper of the woman who had served as his mother's after-school, and sometimes live-in, helper, back when Cooper was a child. Helen would read bedtime stories to him, her soft voice delivering all of his favorite stories about determination and hard work. Cooper had always dreaded the moment she would announce it was time to go to sleep.

George continued, "Fortunately, this young man was stronger than he knew. A good swimmer in his youth, he was unfazed by cold water, and he was able to keep himself afloat until the eastern horizon began to glow. Sober now and painfully aware of his plight, our victim hoped dawn would bring salvation—that he would see land in the distance, or a ship on the horizon, or even a piece of driftwood he could cling to. But all he saw, in whatever direction he looked, was emptiness—a vast expanse of undulating mounds of water. At one point, after the sun had fully risen, our victim thought he caught a glimpse of sunlight reflecting off something shiny—the windshield on a pilothouse, perhaps—but then realized it was just the crest of a wave playing tricks on him. Now dangerously chilled, our victim continued to search the horizon, clinging to nothing more substantial than a leaky raft of hope for several hours more, but the result was always the same—nothing."

Out of Reach

Cooper scolded himself for having not written to Helen years ago to tell her how much he cherished those warm memories she had given him.

"Our victim's arms and legs started to grow heavier and weaker. He began to gag on the saltwater he was inhaling, and the chill was creeping ever deeper into the very marrow of his being. His leaky raft of hope had all but deflated into the deadweight of despair when something caught his eye—a sleek, glistening triangle, protruding from the surface about 50 feet from where he was treading water. It was a shark. A second fin appeared—smaller than the first, diametrically opposed."

A mantle clock chimed the hour, the distinctive sound somehow reassuring Cooper.

"First, our victim could think only of fighting these ancient killing machines to the death. He would take them on with his bare hands, as David faced Goliath. But feeling the inevitability of his fate, he allowed himself to see, and accept, that this was the stuff of childhood fantasies. Resisting would merely set himself up for one last defeat. He was a dead man—why prolong the inevitable?"

Cooper picked up a painkiller from his desk. *One or two more tablets should do it!*

"The most he could do was to deny the sharks the pleasure of inflicting on him what had to be the ultimate horror for any human being."

Cooper held the tablet with two fingers.

"And so he pulled a penknife from his pocket and slashed his wrists, vertically, releasing the knife to the abyss. So numb from the cold was he at this point that he felt nothing."

The tablet was pressed between his lips.

"Right as he was about to slip into eternal slumber, off in the distance, where he had looked so many times before, he thought he saw something.

"Toward the west, just above the horizon, something dark against a bank of puffy white clouds—a ship!"

Cooper bowed his head. He unlocked the door and collapsed.

13

Halfway There

It had been a long time—seemingly days—since Cooper had been able to host a positive thought. Of course, it no longer mattered. The most he could do now was shuffle his way to the next milestone. Which was where? He had no idea.

Wait a minute—what was he hearing? Were those voices?

He lifted his eyes—yes, female voices. It was the girls of Wellesley College, which meant he had made it to the halfway mark!

Could it be? Holy shit! He had actually made 13 miles—plus change. Not bad for a guy losing muscle mass by the minute, even by the second.

Cooper followed the runners ahead of him into a corridor of exuberant young women.

"Good work, Danny D, you're gonna make it!"

"Hang in there, Jim. You can do it!"

"Halfway, Adidas—you've got it made!"

Most of the runners were going out of their way for a high-five. Cooper decided not to follow suit. He couldn't afford to expend the energy. It was all he could do just to make eye contact.

He saw the joyous expression on one girl's face change the moment she noticed him—the blood.

She held up a thumb. Cooper nodded.

Another girl extended a hand toward him. "C'mon," her eyes seemed to say.

Cooper slapped the girl's hand.

Looking him in the eye, she said, "Hang in there, Little Engine! You can do it! Keep going! You're halfway there!"

Cooper slapped more hands. He broke into a jog. His calves didn't spasm. The burning between his shoulders seemed to abate. His vision seemed to clear despite the tears now flowing down his cheeks.

He would go a little farther. He would try to make it to the next marker. That would be it...period!

Medicine Man

OCTOBER 1982

It felt strange to be alive. It felt even stranger to be sitting in George Quigley's office glancing now and then through a set of French doors into a well-kept backyard, where Elizabeth, George's wife of 49 years, appeared to be winterizing her gardens. George was sitting in a comfy upholstered chair.

Earlier, upon entering the room, Cooper had taken notice of a school-teacher's desk arranged at an angle in a corner. George had bought it at an auction, he explained, when the grade school he had attended "500 years ago" was scheduled to be demolished. "I got it for five bucks," George boasted. "Of course, then I had to pay someone to truck it across three states. Suddenly a fantastic deal had become a not-so-great deal—as my dear wife felt it her moral duty to point out to me, more than once. So I refinished it myself, to save paying someone. Not a bad job for an amateur, wouldn't you say?"

"It's gorgeous."

"What am I offered?"

"You wouldn't sell it."

"You're right. My granddaughter, Peaches—I mentioned her to you— has already laid claim to it. She wants to be a teacher someday. She's only six, and already she has her life all mapped out. She's one of those. All business."

About half the wall space in the room was taken up with bookshelves, while most of the rest of the wall space was taken up with framed items, including a not-quite-plumb array of professional certificates and diplomas.

A trio of framed photographs stood on a shelf behind George's desk, a little to the right. The middle photo, smaller than the other two, showed a young girl in a coquettish pose. She appeared to be the mistress of her own fate. To the left, a young man, early 30s, grinning, presumably over the unlikely presence of a squirrel on one shoulder. He looked an even blend of George and Elizabeth. The photo on the right showed a young woman, also early 30s, in the company of a large, shaggy dog. The photo of the girl was matted in ivory. The photos of the young man and that of the young woman were matted in black.

George obviously had a story to tell. He had been engaging in small talk as a way, Cooper knew, of setting him at ease. So far, it hadn't had the desired effect. In fact, Cooper felt even more anxious now—claustrophobic, actually—than he had on the drive over.

He did *not* want to be there. Sitting in George's cozy office, painfully alive, was not only anticlimactic; it was humiliating—like sitting in a room full of blank-faced swabbies waiting to be banished to the fleet.

"Would you like to talk about last night, Cooper? We don't have to, of course. We can talk about anything you might want to talk about." George glanced at his watch. "I don't have another appointment until 4:30."

Cooper noticed Elizabeth studying a clump of birch trees. She was shading her eyes with one hand and assessing the progression of autumn perhaps, as revealed by the gradual alchemization of emerald into gold.

Why did birch trees tend to grow in clumps? Was it for the same reason birds tended to clump? Or fish? Or cars on the interstate?

Halfway There

Elizabeth seemed completely absorbed in her work, wholly at ease. Cooper envied her. He had never been at peace in his entire life. The sword of Damocles always seemed to be hanging over his head.

He looked at the two photographs framed in black. How could a parent survive the loss of a child?

Cooper looked to George. "I have a question."

"Shoot."

"That story you told me last night. It seemed eerily apt—like you made it up on the spot to fit the situation."

George settled back in his chair.

"You did, didn't you? You knew certain things about me—from your sessions with Tessa—and you used those to create a story for effect. Am I right?"

George smiled.

"May I tell you another story, as a roundabout way of answering your question?"

"Shoot."

"When I was in the third grade, my teacher, Miss Kapels, whose desk is sitting over there, invited a medicine man to talk to the class about the tradition of oral storytelling. How long do you think it takes someone to become a medicine man?"

Cooper shrugged.

"Sixty-four years. And it takes—what? Four or five years to go through medical school? To be fair, though, we're talking two different kinds of medicine—spiritual on the one hand and physical or mechanical on the other.

"So this medicine man picked a student and spent a good half hour interviewing her. Patti Rockwell. At the end of the interview, the medicine man proceeded to tell us a story based on what he knew about Patti. It seemed like he was reading from a book. It was amazing!"

Cooper relaxed a bit more into his seat.

George continued, smiling, "I was so taken by what seemed to me an act of pure magic that I started making up stories myself—and praying to the Good Lord to help me with the effort. I needed all the help I could get because I wasn't very good." He chuckled. "In my case, it took quite a while for the Good Lord to get to me on his to-do list, but once he did, things really began to click. My stories got better, and I got more and more confident. Confidence, as I'm sure you're aware, is key to this kind of thing working."

Cooper realized he did not want this session to end. *Why is this always happening?* he wondered. *You find a sweet spot in your day, but you can't really take advantage of it.*

George got up from his chair and closed the French doors. He lingered a moment, his eyes fixed on Elizabeth, who was working near a border fence.

"There's not always all the hope we would like there to be, but there is, I believe, always at least a glimmer or two, no matter how desperate or dire a particular situation might seem. Hope by itself, though, can't do the job. Hope needs help. It needs time and space, a field of dreams. Hope needs for you to stay alive as long as you can possibly stand it—"

He was surrounded by daffodils—King Alfreds—their golden trumpets uplifted toward the sun, the source of all life; the revealer of all mystery. Amid them, a headstone.

Cooper shivered.

"Cold?"

"I'm fine."

"Be sure to tell me if you aren't."

"I will."

"Let me put all my cards on the table, Cooper. All I would like to accomplish today, if I may, is to see if I can convince you to hang in there a little while longer. This is not so much for the obvious reasons—for the sake of your family or to give the medical establishment more time to find a cure, though these are certainly worthy enough goals. When that one-of-a-kind impossibility that is you comes to an end, I just want you to be at peace with yourself. You're not at peace with yourself right now, are you?"

Halfway There

Cooper kept his eyes fixed on the rectangular carpet on which a glass-topped table in front of him was resting. He liked looking for designs in the warp and weave of things.

"I'm not going to try to accomplish this by preaching to you, so if you're concerned about that, please don't be. What I do here—in this room—is all I do. I'm a psychotherapist."

Cooper could feel his right thumb twitching. "I have a friend at work—Dana Hill—who started the same day I did. She's been seeing a shrink for over fourteen years, and as far as I can tell, she hasn't gotten one thing to show for it. She's a poet, but she hasn't been able to write a single word in all that time. She's gay, but despite all of the therapy, she hasn't been able to come to terms with what that means for her. She has relationships with other women, but they never work out. In fact, they're highly destructive because—*I* think, anyway—she chooses partners who have even more problems than she does. And even though she wants desperately to come out to her parents—to finally get that monkey off her back—she just can't get herself to do it. She can't even get herself to come out to her two older brothers, who are probably more approachable than her rigid, domineering, Methodist minister father and dutiful doormat mother, who's embittered after living a lifetime with a man and religion who have controlled her every thought and move. Every time Dana goes home to visit, she comes back unglued. It takes her days to calm down. She spends Christmas with us every year instead of being with her own family. This woman comes from a family where nobody ever listened to her—nobody ever treated her like a real person, and they still don't. Going home is like stepping back into the same old nightmare, even after all of that 'therapy.'"

"No problem. Your concerns are perfectly legitimate. Most people lack the courage to voice them. You obviously do not have that problem. Good for you." George smiled. "You might want to work on the tone of your delivery. People tend to hear better when they're not being scolded."

Cooper nodded.

George slipped on a pair of amber-rimmed glasses and opened a file folder on his lap. "As I'm sure you at least suspect, I already know a little about you, from your wife, who appears to know you very well. Would you agree?"

Cooper nodded.

"On the basis of this information, I put together something to share with you here, to see what you think of it." George smiled. "Just sit back and relax for a few moments, and I'll read it to you."

Cooper gazed beyond the French doors. Elizabeth had disappeared. He closed his eyes.

Daffodils—King Alfred's—everywhere, as far as the eye could see. Tessa was running ahead of him, looking over her shoulder, motioning. "This way!" she seemed to be saying. "Follow me!"

"The hero child," George began, "is the adult in the family. By assuming more responsibility than anyone their age should ever be allowed or expected to assume, they miss out on a spontaneous and carefree childhood. Heroes distract outsiders from the family's problems, or dysfunction, by being model students, sports stars, prom queens, goody two-shoes. As adults, heroes tend to be rigid, controlling, and highly judgmental—of themselves as well as others. They achieve outward success and receive much positive attention but tend not to be in touch with or develop their true self. Heroes tend to be compulsive and driven because deep inside, they feel inadequate and insecure. The hero child is often the family member who has the hardest time coming to terms with the damage done to them in their most vulnerable years. They would rather deny and suffer than seek help and thrive.

"The hero tends to be responsible, dependable, hardworking, high achieving, focused, generous, persevering, loyal, powerful, and organized. They readily volunteer for leadership roles.

"The hero also tends to be judgmental, inflexible, wary of intimacy, driven, unable to play, unreasonable in their expectations, fearful of failing, easily made to feel guilty, negligent toward their own needs, constantly seeking approval—especially from those who can least give it—and constantly feeling inadequate because nothing they do is ever quite good enough."

"That's me, alright," Cooper said emphatically.

George smiled. "I had a feeling you might say that."

He slipped off his glasses. "This is just one of the roles that people who grow up in alcoholic families tend to assume within the family. Besides the hero, there is a scapegoat, a caretaker, and a lost child. You clearly fit the hero profile, but any one family member can assume more than one role, which is usually the case whenever there are fewer than four siblings or when any particular sibling just isn't up to the task for whatever reason."

Cooper was beginning to feel trapped.

"Let me tell you about the scapegoat's profile," George said, slipping his glasses back on: "The scapegoat is the child the family feels ashamed of. Scapegoats are nothing but trouble. Everything is their fault. These children are usually the most sensitive and caring, which is why they feel such tremendous hurt. They are romantics who become very cynical and distrustful. They have a lot of self-hatred."

George looked to Cooper.

He was beginning to feel coerced.

George continued, "Mistreat good people long enough, and those good people are going to suffer real damage. How could it be otherwise? Take as an analogy our lakes and streams. How much can we mistreat them before incremental damage becomes so great, they can no longer sustain life?"

George returned his folder to the end table next to his chair and continued, "What may surprise you even more, Cooper, is that one or more of those four profiles applies to some 60 million people in this country." George grimaced. "Including me—a classic caretaker if there ever was one.

"When someone is alcoholic, a parent, for example—my mother, your father—they are not alcoholic in a vacuum. They're alcoholic in a particular context. The primary context in which they are alcoholic is, of course, their family, and every family member, including the children—*especially* the children—cannot help but be affected by it. It's like when your boss at work is in a bad mood. No one goes untouched by it. Is he mad at me? What did I do? Is he going to call me into his office and fire me for being a fraud? How can I protect myself?'"

Cooper bowed his head and took a deep breath.

George continued, "Alcoholism is not like diabetes or COPD, affecting only the individual. It's a systemic disease, and if you think about it, how could it be otherwise? If someone's world revolves around maintaining unencumbered access to booze, as if their very life depended on it—and in a way, it does, because that is precisely the nature of the alcoholic's need—they will start doing some pretty desperate things if their sustenance is cut off or threatened in some way, just as one would respond to their air supply being cut off. Picture a diver, deep under the sea, whose air hose has been severed on a sharp coral. He's flailing and grasping and not thinking a whole helluva lot about you and your needs or anything else about you."

George paused.

Cooper felt a hundred years older than he was an hour ago.

"There are layers here. Alcoholism is a disease, a physical addiction, but it's also a culture—a set of behaviors and expectations that get passed down from one generation to the next. We see this in adult children of alcoholics who tend to do unto their own children what the alcoholics in their childhood did unto them. It's sort of an eye for an eye without the intentionality. For example, an adult child might manifest anger-fueled violence in counterpart to the alcohol-fueled violence he experienced as a child. The behavior is very much the same in both cases—bruises and broken bones—and so, unfortunately, are the results."

Tessa had been doing more than giving George a little background on him; she had been ratting him out. How else would George know about all the "bruises and broken bones"? Wasn't that an ethical breach? A betrayal?

"Are you an adult child of an alcoholic, Cooper?"

Halfway There

Silence.

"Was your father an alcoholic? Did he or anyone else in your family mistreat you?"

Cooper leaned forward.

"Please stay if you can possibly stand it, Cooper. What's to be gained at this point by running out of here full of righteous indignation?"

Daffodils—King Alfred's—everywhere, as far as the eye could see. Tessa was still running ahead of him.

Cooper remained seated.

George resumed, "One of the ways we can at least begin to deal with things we don't really want to deal with is to give them voice—to say them out loud."

"OK, my father was an alcoholic son of a bitch. Is that what you want to hear?"

"Is that what you want to say?" George asked. "Was he abusive toward you? Was he abusive toward other members of your family you might have thought it your duty to protect?"

"Yes!"

"And are you mad as hell at that alcoholic son of a bitch, Cooper?"

Fuck you.

"How could you not be—right? How could all that anger, all that rage, Cooper, not affect you in some very profound ways? How could it not be the filter through which you viewed an ever-disappointing world filled with all manner of jerks and assholes? How could you not be profoundly hopeless and despairing? There were no acknowledgments of serious injury. There were no apologies. There were no resolutions or reconciliations."

Cooper pulled a fresh tissue from a box on the table in front of him and wiped his eyes. He cleared his throat. He fantasized about bolting from George's torture chamber.

"There's a sticky wicket here, Cooper. We call it *denial*. Unfortunately, the typical adult child of an alcoholic, as in the case of the typical alcoholic, tends to deny having any problems that might warrant having to make any fundamental changes. He isn't the one who has a problem; therefore, he isn't the one who has to make changes. It's everybody else who needs to make changes. It's an obtrusive spouse. It's a recalcitrant eldest son. It's an unappreciative boss. It's the other drivers on the highway. It's *them* who need to be sitting where you are—and hopefully will remain sitting for a few minutes longer.

"Unfortunately, no adult can move beyond anger and despair until he or she can somehow break out of his or her denial. And even though denial is one of the most powerful forces, if not the most powerful force in the human psyche—ask any drunk, ask any addict—anyone who really wants to break free can do it.

"And there's the rub. You have to really want to. You have to want to break out a lot more than you want to stay in. If you're addicted to the status quo, however—the sadness, the self-pity, the rage, the victimization—you're pretty much doomed to a life of hell on earth."

Cooper was very aware of his perspiration.

"Before healing can begin, the adult child usually has to reach some kind of crisis point—utter exhaustion, for example, from trying to make his parents love him. His pain becomes so intense that the status quo is no longer bearable. Something has to give."

Cooper wiped his upper lip with a hand and then with a tissue.

"You're dying, Cooper, and I can't save you." George cleared his throat. "But I can offer you a choice. Check out of this world more or less in the state you're in now, consumed with rage and self-pity and all manner of other toxins to the soul—in other words, essentially already dead—or go out of this world at peace with yourself and your world."

Daffodils—King Alfred's—everywhere, as far as the eye could see. Tessa was running ahead of him, looking over her shoulder, motioning. "This way!" she seemed to be saying. "Follow me!"

"I'm curious, Cooper, as to how many pills you swallowed the other night."

Halfway There   183

"I don't remember. Four or five, I would have to guess."

"Out of how many?"

"Ten."

"Did you swallow those four or five pills all at once?"

"One at a time. They were horse pills."

"And you washed each one down with whiskey?"

"Yes."

"A just-large-enough-swallow of whiskey to do the job, or a bit more?"

"I don't recall exactly, but likely a bit more."

"So which is more likely to have occurred first—unconsciousness or death?"

"Apparently, I passed out."

"From the combination of the four or five 'horse pills' and half a fifth of 100-proof whiskey?"

"Yes."

"But if you really wanted to die, Cooper, why not dissolve all 10 pills in a single glass of whiskey and ingest them all at once?"

Cooper bowed his head.

"You don't want to die, Cooper. You just want the pain to stop."

14

Inner Turmoil

The surge of hopefulness he had allowed himself to feel earlier had dissipated, like raindrops on hot pavement. He needed water, but if he stopped here, just west of Wellesley Village, he might never get started again. Everything might freeze up.

This was a really stupid idea, Cooper! Why has Tessa stuck with you all these years? How much could even the most loyal and loving of spouses take in the face of one harebrained scheme after another being foisted upon her? Case in point: Buying that run-down farmhouse in New York.

Had he *really* done that?

Cooper noticed a man passing him on the left. It was the Wheezer! He felt a spark of adrenaline. He would try to keep up.

Cooper consumed as much ERG as he could keep down, then poured a cupful of water over his head. And a second.

He staggered, steadied himself, began again to put one foot in front of the other.

The Wheezer was no longer in sight.

On his right, Cooper noticed two young boys. A woman, presumably their mother, standing just behind them, was scanning the runners as they ran up the hill.

Noah, Luke, and Zak would be searching for a glimpse of his bright-red "The Little Engine That Could" T-shirt. He wondered if Tessa, Dana, and the boys had managed to rendezvous.

He pictured them waiting to catch sight of him turning onto Boylston Street. The boys would never forget it.

By the time he was just west of Wellesley Village, the proverbial needle had crept back into the red zone. He was on fire—and he tumbled to the pavement. His brain felt like mush. There was a taste of blood in his mouth. He spit out a piece of tooth.

Pulling himself to his feet once more, he staggered into motion.

Fighting Fire

CIRCA 1953

Cooper was deep into choreographing a ten-alarm fire. All hell was breaking loose on Cape Vincent's Point Street, with hoses and fire trucks everywhere. He was forced to roll more globs of modeling clay into hoses to fight the worst fire ever.

He paused to slurp some diluted Pepsi Cola from a glass and crunched the remnants of an ice cube with his teeth. He liked the cold sensation. He would rather freeze to death than burn to death.

His mother had told him several times to pick up his mess before Cub Scouts or she would call his father home from the store to give him "the business." She was "sick and tired" of him not minding her.

Cooper hated Cub Scouts. Even more, he hated playing with other kids. He especially hated it when older kids, like his brother Stephen, took stuff away from him. Why couldn't he just play by himself?

He was in the middle of a major fire. The entire city block was in flames. If he put all his hoses down now, hundreds of people would burn to death— many of them women and children. They needed to be rescued, and only he could do it!

Stephen wouldn't let Cooper participate in any Brainian make-believes, so he was constantly having to make up his own. He didn't mind all that much, though, because it was much safer to be by himself. No one could betray him, or make fun of him, or beat him up for no reason.

He sensed his mother's presence. Without looking up, he sounded another alarm. Now the whole city was burning!

"I told you to pick everything up!"

Cooper made siren sounds, louder and louder.

He sensed his mother leave the room. He paused, straining to hear his mother give the operator the telephone number for the store: 3-4-2. He heard her tell his father, in the high-pitched voice she used when she was "beside herself," to come home and give Cooper "the business" because she "just could not take it anymore." He heard her hang up and return to the scene of what was now a 12-alarm fire.

She told him his father was on the way from the store and that he needed to wait in his room—"or else."

Cooper moved a hose to contend with a fresh outbreak of flames. It wasn't looking good.

His mother grabbed him by the arm and pulled him to his feet. Cooper tried to shake himself free, but he wasn't strong enough. His mother whacked his bottom, then pulled him to the stairs and waited at the bottom until he disappeared from the landing. "You *stay* up there until your father gets here."

Closing the door to his bedroom, Cooper raised the sash on his east-facing window and lowered himself onto a vine-covered arbor. He crawled atop the arbor to the side farthest from the kitchen, then climbed down to the ground, using the vines as ropes.

He made a beeline for a gap between the picket fence and a large elm and slid through it. From there, Cooper scurried to his tree fort on the south-west corner of Lake Street. He had only just pulled the ladder up when his father arrived home in the Jeep he used for delivering groceries.

Cooper watched his father enter the house. His parents soon emerged onto the front stoop. He saw his mother point in his direction. She knew about his fort.

He was *not* going to come down from the only safe place he knew.

Cooper's father marched across the intersection and stood at the bottom of Cooper's tree.

"Get down from there right now! I can't have this! I can't be called away from the store every five minutes like this to deal with your bad behavior."

Cooper was holding his slingshot and a chestnut. He had several more chestnuts stuffed in his pockets.

"Get your ass down here—right now!"

"Why? What do you care?" Cooper couldn't believe the words coming out of his mouth.

"OK, that's it! That's all the sass I'm going to take. You'd better be out of that tree and in the house in three minutes or you're going to spend a week in your room."

Returning to his Jeep, Cooper's father made a U-turn and drove back the way he had come.

Cooper considered making a run for it, but where would he go? Where would he hide?

When Cooper's father returned, he pulled a fire extinguisher from the back of his Jeep and lugged it to Cooper's tree.

Cooper recognized it from the back room of the store. He assured himself his father would never spray him with a fire extinguisher, any more than Cooper would shoot his father with a slingshot. It was just a scare tactic.

"Get down from there—right now! This is your last chance."

Cooper pretended not to hear.

The spray from the extinguisher was shockingly cold. It stung Cooper's eyes. It burned his skin.

Cooper fell from the platform and landed on his back. He was momentarily breathless, but immediately sprung to his feet and began to sprint. As he ran, he could hear his father calling from behind, "Get back here!"

Cooper could run fast when he had to.

Jefferson County Mental Health Clinic

J. COOPER HAYNES

5/11/53 The Binet was completed. Cooper has a chronological age of 9 yrs. 8 months and an MA of 13 years, 5 months. This gives him an IQ of 139.

BLP:bl

Fact-Checking

OCTOBER 1982

Cooper wondered if having French doors in a temperate climate was an extravagance due to heat loss. The daylight pouring into George Quigley's office kept him from casting further judgment.

A gust of wind sent a vortex of leaves scurrying across the patio just outside the doors. Cooper had been disappointed that Elizabeth was not on duty. There was something reassuring about people tending gardens. What if a majority of the Earth's 4.5 billion residents regarded the planet as one big garden?

"Just for the fun of it," George said, looking up from a yellow tablet lying on his lap, "let's string all this information together and see what we've got. Tell me if I get anything wrong or if I miss anything."

Cooper muttered something that sounded like compliance.

"All through your high school years," George began, "you would typically stay up every night until two or three o'clock in the morning doing academic work of one sort or other—not just homework but well beyond

Inner Turmoil

189

that—and as a result, you graduated valedictorian of your class"—George looked at his notes—"with a 96.4 average. Have I got that right?"

"Yes, but there were only twenty-nine kids in my class."

"You took the New York State regents exam in trigonometry a semester early and got a perfect score on it. Am I right?"

Cooper nodded. He began to shake one of his feet.

"You were president of your class in your freshman through junior years and student body president in your senior year. You played two varsity sports. You were awarded a General Motors Scholarship to study physics and math at Clarkson College, where you were president of your class in your junior and senior years. You played a leadership role in several other organizations and even founded a few, including the Clarkson Rocket Society. Your goal, you confessed, was to be tapped into Phalanx, which was the highest honor any student could receive at Clarkson. Because of a faltering academic record, however, highlighted by your flunking German, twice, you went untapped. You had invited your parents to attend the tapping ceremony, but you were passed over." George looked at Cooper.

Cooper nodded.

"In the summer before you went off to law school, you attempted to swim across Lake Ontario from Kingston to Cape Vincent—a distance of about 21 miles. Less than a mile short of your goal, you had to be pulled from the water suffering from acute hypothermia and what turned out to be a ruptured lung."

Cooper stared straight ahead, saying nothing.

"You're probably not going to believe this, Cooper, but you could have made it all the way across Lake Ontario instead of coming up a mile short. You could have slogged your way up the corporate ladder and become CEO of Corning Glass. You could have made it all the way through SEAL training—and kicked some ass in the jungles of Vietnam. You could have written the Great American Novel—ten times over. You could have become a courtroom virtuoso. You could have become Emperor of the Universe—and *still* it would not have been enough. Even if your father had lived, Cooper, and were alive today, he *still* wouldn't love you, at least not in the way you needed him to love you—that is, just as you are."

Cooper again pulled a tissue from the box in front of him.

"Your father was not capable of it. He was too distracted, too self-preoccupied, to care about anything other than all those bottles that you and your brother found after he died. That was it for him. That was his whole life. Not being able to love you had absolutely nothing to do with *you* and everything to do with *him*—with *his* self-loathing, *his* failures.

"I know how attached you are to the notion you are essentially an unworthy, unlovable 'piece o' shit,' whose only recourse to salvation is to accomplish some superhuman feat, some outward indication of inward worthiness—like writing the Great American Novel, like completing the 'toughest military training program in the world'—anything that might *finally* cause your father to take notice and say, 'This is my beloved son, with whom I am well pleased.'"

Cooper held silent. After dabbing his eyes again, he took a deep breath and looked at the photos behind George's desk.

"Those photos behind your desk," Cooper said. "May I ask about those?"

"Are you trying to change the subject?"

"Yes."

George turned and looked behind him. "These two are my son and daughter-in-law; this one, Peaches, my granddaughter. Her name is Stephanie, but she'll always be Peaches to me. She lives with us, as I believe I mentioned."

Cooper nodded. "You did. Her parents are deceased?"

"Yes."

"I should not have asked."

"Everything in this room is fair game, Cooper, or it wouldn't be here."

"You want people to ask about them?"

Inner Turmoil

"I allow the possibility. Every human being on this planet has heartbreak in their lives. What if we were all to shut ourselves up in separate rooms with nothing in them but our individual suffering?"

"What happened?"

"They were living in Providence. It was a Saturday night. They were on their way home from seeing a play at Trinity Rep. A driver ran a red light and hit them broadside. Edward died at the scene. Elizabeth died an hour later."

"I'm sorry."

"As I said, we all have heartbreak in our lives."

"What happened to the driver of the other car?"

"She was given a breathalyzer test at the scene and was arrested for DUI. It turned out she was a state senator who had three priors. Her license was revoked for thirty days, and she had to pay a fine."

Cooper shook his head.

"I know—I wished for her the same kind of suffering. I wanted to burn down the houses of all those who had enabled her, with them inside. Justice being the illusive angel she is, however, I had to settle for what my mother had done to cope starting at 4:30 every afternoon—drink myself into oblivion.

"One morning I woke up on that couch you're sitting on reeking of vomit. There was a fresh bottle of Carstairs on the table and a note. 'Clean up your mess,' it read. 'No one else is going to do it.'"

George smiled. "Let me show you something." He got up from his chair and disappeared for a moment, then reappeared holding a full bottle of Carstairs. He placed it on the table in front of Cooper.

"I keep it beneath the photos of Edward and Elizabeth. There's a little credenza there, below the shelves. Even though I can't see it, I know it's there."

He returned to his chair, his eyes locking on Cooper. "Those three young gentlemen of yours don't need a hero. They certainly don't need a martyr. All they need is you—to be with you for as long as they can have you. You know this."

Cooper was sitting in a cozy room on a cold winter's night in the company of a sizzling woodstove, surrounded by shelves filled with books.

Tessa was sitting next to him. Noah was sitting next to Tessa. Luke was sitting next to Noah. Zak was sitting next to Luke.

"Are there any more pills, Cooper?"

"No."

"If there were, would you tell me?"

"No."

"If your sons asked you to turn them over—to them—would you?"

15

Challenge Accepted

Fifteen miles behind him, 11 to go: 10 plus 1, 5 plus 5 plus 1, plus 385 yards—

How much farther could he go? A hundred yards? Two hundred? Ten? Zero?

How close was he to collapsing? His legs were all but nonfunctional. He was just going through the motions.

He needed water. He needed to cool down. He needed to stop. *You're done!*

A man a few steps ahead caught Cooper's eye. He looked familiar—the Wheezer was still ambulatory!

Cooper moved a little ahead of him and held out a hand. The Wheezer slapped it. "See you at the finish," he said between gasps.

Cooper held up a thumb.

Sins of the Father

OCTOBER 1982

A gust of wind sprayed rain like hail against the French doors. "Apparently the phone had rung," Cooper continued. "I didn't hear it because my bedroom was sort of off by itself."

"Sort of?"

"It wasn't part of the second-floor bedroom area."

"As was the case regarding your Point Street bedroom, if I recall correctly."

Cooper nodded.

"You were Cinderella, and the rest of your family—your mother and brother Stephen, in particular—were sort of the stepmother and stepsister?"

Cooper smiled. "Good analogy. Anyway, I woke up to my mother shaking me. She was in a panic. Somebody was trying to break down the door to one of the cabins at our motel, which was located just across Esselstyne Street, a block from the river. I got dressed assuming I was backup. My father would already be on scene taking care of things. He would handle it; I was just a kid."

"How old?"

"I was 17 or 18—just home from college for the summer."

George nodded.

"When I got to the scene of the crime, it didn't take me long to figure out I wasn't backup. I was it."

George smiled. "From scapegoat to hero in an instant?"

"Yeah, I guess so, except I had no idea what to do because this kind of thing had never happened before in my little hometown, as far as I knew.

"Joe Harmon, a regular customer from Syracuse, a large tub of a man, was trying to kick in the door to the cabin adjacent to his. He had already kicked in the screen."

"Would it be fair to say, Cooper, that you had an antipathy toward people who are overweight?"

"They made my skin crawl."

"As was the case when you were yourself overweight?"

Cooper stared at George, offering no explanation.

"Please continue."

"Joe's wife, Jane, was there, as was Tom Grimshaw, the village's constable. Joe's wife was trying to talk her husband down: 'Now, Joey, I'm sure that man didn't mean to park in your spot'—which, as it turned out, wasn't the real issue.

"Jane tended to speak in a soft, cloying voice that was so saccharine, you almost had to put your nose up against hers in order to hear her. She was almost as tall as her husband, who had to be six four, and was always dressed to the nines. A real pair. They were husband and wife but also mother and son, it felt like. And probably brother and sister. They had been staying at our motel on a regular basis for at least ten years.

"Grimshaw was just standing there, as if in shock. The guy behind the door had to be feeling his life was in mortal danger. Joe was effectively a 300-plus-pound battering ram and was not only drunk as a skunk but obviously out of his fucking mind. Sooner or later, he was going to break through the cabin door—and then what? Grimshaw didn't even have a nightstick.

"I had seen Joe and Jane a few hours earlier. They were sitting on the veranda at the Carleton Hotel, sipping cocktails. They were with another couple.

"The Carleton was one of those old wooden hotels that used to be common along the St. Lawrence, back when the Thousand Islands area was a playground for the rich and famous—before they could jet off to Europe or to the Caribbean for the weekend. There had been three or four such structures in Cape Vincent alone. They're all gone now. Anyway, Joe and Jane were practically fixtures at the Carleton, probably because it was the only place in town you could show off your jewelry and not look totally out of place. In retrospect, I think the Harmons were acting out some kind of fantasy. Back in Syracuse, they were just a salesman and his wife—but then they would drive up to Cape Vincent for the weekend and pretend they were really something.

"I would have avoided them at the hotel—this is all coming back to me. Usually I can't remember shit to save my life. I was dating a girl who was waitressing at that hotel, and I was stopping by to pick her up. I would have avoided them except there was no way I could have gotten into the hotel without them seeing me.

Challenge Accepted
197

"When the Harmons saw me, they called me over and made a big fuss over me in front of their friends. They were always doing that kind of thing, to my eternal embarrassment, especially Jane. Jane would mention that I was quite the swimmer.

"Tell them how far your big swim was, Cooper.

"Twenty-one miles, but I didn't quite finish.

"Jane didn't mention the 'I didn't quite finish' part.

"Isn't that something!

"It would get worse: She would tell people I was going to be president one day because I was even better looking than JFK.

"I suspect she did this as a way of putting her husband down for being so fat, but he never seemed to catch on. He would just sit there, chewing on a cigar. He was always chewing on a cigar.

"Jane made eye contact with me in an attempt, I suspect, to read my intentions. What was I going to do? What did she need to do or say to keep her husband out of jail?

"'Now, Joey,' she said, or similar, 'if you'll just calm down, I'm sure that nice man will come out and move his car.' She's embarrassed half to death, of course, and wants this unpleasantness to end so everybody can start pretending it never happened. But her Joey is not listening. Instead, he's screaming bloody murder at that 'Jew bastard' for taking his parking spot.

"The irony was there weren't any officially designated parking spots. This was not the Sheraton Tara. This was a little twelve-cabin motel in Upper Slabovia, and all there was for parking was a narrow strip of lawn between the sidewalk and the street. Guests parked their cars on this strip on a first-come, first-served basis, headed either inward or outward. There was always plenty of room, even when the motel was full, which I don't think it was on that particular night. But, of course, that wasn't the real issue. The real issue was the guy who stole Joe's parking space was a 'Jew bastard.'

"When I heard 'Jew bastard' for maybe the third time, I lost it. I put a hammerlock around Fatso's throat and dragged him to his car, him back-pedaling, Jane screaming. In trying to get him into the back seat, I tore his shirt.

"The village constable pulled me off him.

"Once the Harmons had left, never to be seen again, the 'Jew bastard' came out of his room. He was white as a sheet, as they say. He thanked me for saving his life and offered me a $20 bill.

"I don't know why I hadn't noticed it on the way over to the motel. I hadn't looked, I guess. I was distracted. Anyway, there it was—parked behind my brother Stephen's Chevy—my father's maroon Buick. It had obviously been there the whole time."

Cooper bowed his head. He swallowed and wiped his cheeks.

"What would you say to him, Cooper, right now—at this moment—if he were sitting here instead of me? In fact, let's pretend I'm him. I'm your father, and I'm sitting here right now. What are you going to say to me?"

Cooper shook his head.

"I know. You hate this kind of thing. But let's just see what you've got to say. You've just noticed your father's car parked behind your brother's. You've just been put in a situation you should never have been put in—a trigger situation in which all that anger in you, all that rage, has just exploded out of proportion to what the situation called for. You're very upset. You're scared to death over what those demons inside you might do in the future. And there's your father's car, right where it's been the whole time."

Cooper jumped to his feet and, glaring at George, kicked the desk.

"Coward!" he yelled.

"Count to 10!" George implored.

Cooper's temper was still gaining speed—he felt the blare of a horn, the urgency of oncoming traffic.

He slammed the brakes.

Challenge Accepted 199

Gasping for a breath, he began to count.

"All that rage, Cooper, is like a wild, rampaging river. You have a choice. You can let it have its way, to no good end, or you can channel it toward some truly noble end. Which is it going to be?"

Cooper sat in silence.

"You were blessed with many gifts, Cooper. Let me help you make the best use of them in the time you have left. Don't quit."

16

New Resolve

Cooper's right eye was so badly swollen, he could barely see out of it. His hockey helmet had not provided much protection, the problem being there had not been any way to test it without risking injury.

The Wheezer was no longer in sight, having obviously surged ahead. There were enough runners on the roadway for him to be obscured by the crowd.

He would try to marshal enough resolve to jog the rest of the way to the firehouse. He would stop there—and would finish on a high note!

A short, shirtless man passed Cooper and, accepting a bottle of beer from a spectator, chugged the contents to a roar of approval. Once the bottle was emptied—mostly, it would seem, to spillage—the imbiber returned it to the supplier.

Cheers!

The man pulled a red bandanna from around his head, wiped off his face and brow, and put it back on.

Cooper moved closer to the imbiber and held out a hand. The man slapped it.

Cooper slapped the man's hand in return and broke into a jog.

Man in the Mirror

MAY 1964

Even though Cooper was facing away from the only window in his bedroom of the Shaffer house in Cape Vincent, he could tell from the brightness of the ambient light that another day was already half shot.

His mouth tasted of stale beer and a 2 a.m. hot sausage sandwich from Nick's Diner. He was covered by a single bedsheet, damp with perspiration.

Rolling onto his back, Cooper probed for the stretched-out body of Tex, his beagle buddy. A lump formed at the back of his throat. He had not gotten to say goodbye to her. He would have come home had he known his parents were going to put her down. They hadn't wanted to upset him, they said.

For 12 years, Tex had been his best buddy and constant companion—best fishing buddy, in particular.

She was supposed to have been Benjamin's dog, but she had latched on to Cooper, and he onto her, from the first day. Cooper was Huckleberry; Tex was Jim.

They would go fishing almost every day, all summer long, just the two of them—Huckleberry and Jim. Tex would ride on the bow of Cooper's outboard to Cooper's favorite fishing spot, near Remington's Dock, her ears flowing in the airstream, and would jump into the river the moment Cooper dropped the anchor. She would swim the fifty yards or so to shore and hunt rabbits all the time Cooper was fishing. He would hear her yelping in the distance. When it was time to go home, Cooper would call her—he only needed to call her once—and she would swim out to him. He would lift her into his boat by the scruff of her neck, whereupon she would transfer her wetness to Cooper. *Magical days.*

Cooper wiped his cheeks and, swinging his legs out of bed, felt the flesh around his middle shift into flaccid folds. He shivered.

On entering the bathroom across a short hallway, Cooper unloaded the remnants of the seven or eight bottles of Red Cap Ale he had drunk the night before.

He forced himself to look at the reflection in the mirror, noting the faint purplish stretch marks around his trunk.

The bathroom scale was located at the far end of the room, behind an old-fashioned tub—interestingly, where it was not within easy sight. Cooper couldn't remember the last time he had weighed himself with it—probably prior to the family moving from their Point Street home to their Esselstyne Street home, which would have been five or six years ago.

The dial on the scales bounced back and forth, then settled on 232.

Cooper felt a sickening tightening in the pit of his stomach.

He stepped off the scale—back on, back off, back on. *Two hundred and thirty-two pounds! Jesus H. Christ!*

Returning to his bedroom, Cooper switched on the overhead light and rummaged around in his closet until he found an old pair of high-top sneakers, black and white. He pulled on the only bathing suit he could find, which was too small even with the tie-string fully loosened, and the biggest sweatshirt he could find. Sitting on the edge of his bed, Cooper put on his sneakers.

He would run around the perimeter of the fish ponds. He would skip breakfast.

Upon reaching the ponds, Cooper followed a little-used dirt road to the upper ponds, which bordered the sprawling school grounds. No one would see him, other than a few frogs and a killdeer or two.

Surveying the outer perimeter of the honeycomb of ponds, Cooper figured it was probably just about a mile all the way around. He would start with that and build up from there.

The sun felt hot on his face—as if he were sitting too close to a bonfire. There was a slight breeze. He took a deep breath—and launched into a lumbering gait. After maybe 100 yards, he was already breathing hard.

About a quarter of the way around, he knew he wasn't going to make it all the way. His face was at the kindling point, his blood at the boiling point.

Halfway around, Cooper began to fantasize plunging into one of the ponds, despite the slime floating on the surface. He slowed his pace—what had been a mere pinch in his right side began now to feel like the jab of an ice pick.

About three-quarters of the way around, a voice began to whisper in his ear that it was really *two* miles all the way.

About a pond length away from where he had started—an hour and a half ago, it seemed—his side stitch had grown into what felt like a scalpel carving out his kidney. His breathing had devolved into wheezy gasps. His face now felt like it was burning. His legs felt like they had begun to turn into cooked spaghetti.

When finally he stopped—after making sure he hadn't fallen short of his precise starting point, even an inch—he leaned forward and braced himself with his hands on his knees.

Sweat stung his eyes. He had nothing dry to wipe his brow with. He had never been so grotesquely out of shape in his life—but he had made it all the way around!

And tomorrow he would do it again. And the day after that. Every day he would run a little farther and/or a little faster.

A Moonlit Epiphany

OCTOBER 1982

Cooper had been refusing to read his nightstand clock for what seemed like hours now. He simply *had* to get up. His brain was chasing its own tail. He had to break the cycle.

Rolling toward Tessa, Cooper noticed an unusually strong light around the perimeter of the shade over Tessa's desk. The moon was either full or very close to it. He would go for a walk.

He loved it when it felt as if he were the only person in the world out and about. He loved the tranquility that was part and parcel of it. Cooper found his shirt and jeans on the backside of the door and pulled them on. He would go without socks, he decided, rather than risk waking Tessa.

Shoes in hand, Cooper made his way down the stairs and into the kitchen. He sat in the chair and put on his shoes, wishing to Christ he had risked getting a pair of socks out of his chest of drawers. It was damned cold out! He could tell by the feel of the house.

Snapping on the deck light, Cooper read the thermometer: 34 degrees. Way too cold for just a denim jacket!

He fetched a down jacket and gloves from the hall closet and, pulling these on, eased himself out the sliding door—and immediately stepped back into the kitchen.

He had promised Tessa he would leave a note whenever he left the house, telling her where he was going and when he expected to be back. There were to be no unexplained absences.

Cooper wrote "Walking" on a sticky pad. He didn't know when he would be back. He left the sticky pad on the kitchen table and slipped back outside.

The world at large bore a silvery patina. His bird feeders were clearly visible, as was the seed level in each one. There appeared to be plenty of seed for his feathered friends to eat at first light.

Cooper had no idea what time it was—so it could be whatever time he wanted it to be or no time at all, as, in the latter case, whenever he became totally immersed in a project.

Descending the driveway, Cooper breathed deeply of the 34-degree air, grateful for having bothered to check the outside temperature before leaving the house. His reward was being warm and snug in a down jacket—except, of course, for his feet.

To the south, the moon was about two-thirds across its arc and was just shy of being full.

At the bottom of the driveway, Cooper bore right, toward the end of the Garrison Lane cul-de-sac—away, that is, from a stronger likelihood of the magic of the moment being interrupted by an intrusion of headlights.

He started out on the right-hand side of the road, but then, as was his habit, he soon drifted into the center. Just past the Mercers' house, he paused and, lifting his eyes, drew in a deep breath through his nose. He closed his eyes.

Which is it going to be, Cooper?

Truth be told, there was not enough time for him to do anything meaningful—certainly not enough time to read all those great books he had been intending to get at one day, or to ponder all those great ideas he had been intending to get to one day, or to travel to all those great locations he had been intending to visit—one day.

So *what* then? Realistically speaking?

If only there was a way to assure himself of a certain amount of time—just enough for him to give the Big One a shot! The truth of the matter was, of course, the Big One just wasn't in him.

He had to come to terms with the fact that J. Cooper Haynes was not "special." He had no "special" talents or aptitudes. He had no "special" raison d'être.

Cooper looked up at the few stars that were visible—the brightest of the bright.

Unfortunately, he was not one of them. Instead, he was one of those countless billions of stars in the background whose light was just strong enough to be visible but no greater.

It came to him in a flash. He knew what he needed to do. Cooper resumed walking. He walked a little faster—he broke into a jog.

By the time he reached the farther end of the cul-de-sac, instead of feeling on the verge of collapse, he felt as if he could go a bit farther—not to the moon and back, but, well, at least a bit and a half more.

The return leg was slightly uphill, but Cooper did not slow. Even where the road was steepest, from about the Andersons' house on up to the Desmonds', he did not slow down. At the top of the incline, Cooper felt so exhilarated, he did five jumping jacks on the spot—in the middle of the road—then dropped onto all fours and pumped out five push-ups, keeping his back perfectly straight, touching his nose to the cold pavement on each downstroke.

"Down—one. Down—two. Down—three."

"Hooyah, Lieutenant. You son of a bitch!"

Rising a little too quickly, Cooper slumped to a rush of lightheadedness. He drew in a deep breath through his nose and looked eastward. The sky above the tree line was just beginning to glow.

If something was not theoretically impossible, it had to be theoretically possible. Right?

There was enough time! He just might pull it off!

He wasn't dead yet!

A Plan to Finish

OCTOBER 1982

It was raining. The French doors were closed.

George smiled. "You look like the cat that swallowed the canary."

Cooper was all but beaming. "I'm running again."

"For president?"

Cooper grinned. "Maybe next year."

"I'll look forward to that. How does it feel—running again?"

"Exhilarating—except for having to walk partway."

"I suspect a lot of people entering middle age have to do that. What's this about, Cooper? You're up to something. I can smell it. You're not taking up running again just for the sake of taking up running again, are you?"

"I need to finish that run, George—one way or another."

"Handicapped by ALS instead of cellulitis?"

"Something like that. I couldn't find a 4-mile race nearby, but there's a 5-mile Turkey Trot every November right here in Danville. I might run that one and call it good enough. It's held every year on the day before

Thanksgiving, so I'd have two months to get into shape enough to pull it off. Getting my time down would be the hardest part."

George looked hard at Cooper. "I understand your needing to do something like that, Cooper, but I have to ask whether you might be setting yourself up for another disappointment. Don't those races usually include at least one shorter distance?"

"Yeah, 5K for kids. I'm afraid sitting at the children's table just wouldn't cut it."

George held silent a moment. "What does Tessa think about this?"

Cooper offered up a sheepish grin.

17

Not Alone

Cooper sagged to a sitting position, then collapsed onto his back.

You're done!

He had hoped to get to the 16-mile mark.

My papa made it all the way to the 16-mile mark in the Boston Marathon even though he had ALS.

A woman in an orange vest helped Cooper sit up and drink. He drank and drank.

He retched.

The woman removed Cooper's helmet and poured cold water on his head—cup after cup.

She then wrapped an Ace bandage around Cooper's wrist, bandaged the abrasions on his forehead, and helped him to his feet.

He wobbled.

An orange-and-white ambulance was parked offroad to Cooper's right, in the shade of a tree. Several runners were huddled near the ambulance, some with blankets draped over their shoulders. One person was lying on the ground being attended to. He could feel a pull in that direction.

The woman asked him if he wanted to stop here—it was a good place, she said.

Cooper shook his head.

"OK, keep hydrating. Load up before you get to the Newton firehouse. OK?"

Cooper nodded.

"Good luck."

Cooper nodded.

As if on cue, a girl offered a cup, which he grabbed—then dropped.

The girl was profusely apologetic. Cooper tried to smile as he trudged onward.

Another woman offered a cup. This time, he grasped it with both hands. He tried to smile in thanks.

Lifting it to his swollen lips, he drank—and gagged. Stomach acid burned the back of his nose.

He wobbled. The woman poured water over his head—she put a wet towel to his lips.

"Suck," she said.

The woman wrapped the towel around Cooper's neck. She did not ask him to stop. She did not threaten to get help. She must know—there is no tomorrow.

"Take it with you," she said.

Cooper nodded.

A Thing of Beauty

OCTOBER 1982

Cooper awoke to cramps in both calves.

Tessa stirred—then was still.

What he wouldn't give to be able to sleep like she could! He eased himself out of bed, dressed soundlessly, and eased himself out the door. He didn't know what time it was. He had all but stopped looking at clocks.

He made his way to his office. It was only the second time he had been there since that terrible night. It felt strange—like standing on an empty stage long after the curtain had dropped.

He turned on the heat, put his headphones on, and slipped Beethoven's Ninth into his cassette player. *I need to finish that run, George—one way or another.*

Cooper pictured himself passing the 1-mile mark totally in control, feeling like he could run forever; passing the 2-mile mark, pumping his arms; passing the 3-mile mark, feeling undiminished. He turned up the sound.

He pictured a humongous polar bear charging a pack of hideous, gargoyle-like demons, the bear sinking its fangs deep into the soft underbelly of another demon, the bear ripping the head off another demon. *Sonsabitches!*

Cooper looked at the print of Monet's *The Poppy Field near Argenteuil* Tessa had given him. He closed his eyes. If only he could create one thing of such beauty—just one.

Resting his head against the back of his chair, Cooper peered up at a tail of insulation foil hanging from the ceiling. *One ringy-dingy, two ringy-dingys. Hello? Anybody there? Anybody listening?*

How many times—how many *hours*—had he spent kneeling in front of the statue of Mary at St. Vincent's waiting for a sign that someone in the celestial realm was watching over him? How many times had he said the rosary, over and over, until his knees ached?

It had to hurt. That's the way it worked. It was all about pain. Tears ran down his cheeks as Beethoven's masterpiece soared.

Training Partners

OCTOBER 1982

Cooper was trudging up an incline of about eight degrees. It was the only incline of consequence on the shorter of his two training courses.

Noah was riding shotgun beside him, on his bike, in likeness to a picket ship attending to a larger, less lethal vessel. Tessa had insisted someone be with Cooper whenever he expected to be out of sight of the house. He hadn't resisted. There was no need.

The hill extended from a pond on Cooper's left to the intersection of Evans Road with Pudding Hill Road. As usual, the top of Evans Road seemed to retreat two steps for every step Cooper took toward it.

He had tried to discipline himself not to sneak glances ahead, but he hadn't done very well in that regard. As a loose tooth had to be wriggled, so a receding horizon had to be measured.

At this point in the struggle, Cooper would try to keep in mind that he had less than a mile to go and that once he got to the top of Evans Road, it would be more or less downhill from there.

A pebble shot out like a bullet from under Noah's front tire, causing Noah to almost lose control of his bike. Noah was struggling to keep his balance, Cooper knew, because he was having to go so slowly.

"You want some water, Pop?"

"At the top."

Pause.

"How can the universe be infinite, Pop, if it had a beginning?"

"Later."

"Does Stephen Hawking have the same disease as you?"

"Yes."

"Hasn't he had it a long time, though?"

"Yes."

"He's done a lot of science work all the time he's had the disease, right?"

"Yes."

"Maybe you'll have it a long time, too."

Cooper stopped and braced himself with his hands on his knees. His legs began to prickle.

Noah stopped beside him.

"Noah, would you *please* stop talking to me while I'm running? I can't talk to you and get up this goddamn hill at the same time. I just don't have the strength. Can't you see that?"

Noah looked wounded.

Cooper resumed trudging up the incline. At the top, he wrapped his arms around Noah and hugged him.

"I'm sorry," Cooper rasped. "I am not angry at *you*. I am angry at what's happening to me." Cooper squeezed Noah tighter. "I'm glad you're here. But please don't ask me any more questions. I just don't have the strength to answer you. OK?"

Cooper wiped his cheeks.

Noah wiped his. "Would you like me to run with you instead of riding my bike?"

"Yes!" Cooper grinned. "That should shut you up!"

18

This Is a Test

Where the hell is it? Cooper had been expecting the Newton Fire Station to come into view for what seemed like hours. It was the perfect place for him to call it quits. It was a marathon landmark in itself. It was located past the halfway mark but before Heartbreak Hill, for which he had zero appetite. Cooper would be admired for what he had been able to accomplish—17.3 miles with a gorilla on his back the whole way. Good enough!

The *Danville Daily Record* might do a story on him.

Cooper lifted his eyes again—and there it was! Two stories, red brick, four bays. He had made it. Seventeen miles!

Cooper stopped in front of the station and, feeling suddenly lightheaded, propped himself, hands on his knees. Two men in uniform helped him to a chair at the back of one of the engine bays. Several other runners were huddled there. Some prone.

Cooper accepted a cup of ERG and forced himself to drink—slowly, though, so as not to upset his stomach.

He took off his helmet and poured several cupfuls of water over his head. He felt something aggressively cold on the back of his neck—an ice pack.

He drank a few sips of water and shivered.

A light was shining in his eyes. "You need to be evaluated for a concussion," a woman said.

"Someone's waiting for me at the top of Heartbreak Hill," Cooper lied.

"That's three and a half more miles," a woman stated. "Uphill."

He would be OK, he insisted.

Another woman held an ice pack against Cooper's temple. Cooper recoiled from a sharp sting. The woman warned him not to push it.

"You belong in a hospital," she warned.

She told him there were plenty of places over the next few miles where he could drop out and be taken care of. She wound gauze around his head and taped it. Wishing him luck, she left.

Three and a half miles to the top of Heartbreak Hill. That would be an amazing achievement! He had to try!

Cooper limped to where runners were turning onto Commonwealth Avenue. Breaking into a gimpy jog, Cooper fixed his eyes on the pavement. Almost immediately he detected a steepening grade underfoot, even though the infamous Hills of Newton were still over 3 miles away.

A man wearing a tuxedo and carrying an uncorked bottle of wine, balanced on a silver tray, passed him on his left, to cheers from the curbsides.

Cooper envied the man's energy. What he wouldn't give for just a fraction of it.

Race "Red-dee"

NOVEMBER 25, 1982

Cooper knew almost nothing about wine, but he could tell by how this one felt in his mouth—smooth and silky—that George had spared no expense.

"A few more carbs?" George asked, eyeing Cooper's tomato-stained plate.

Cooper patted his belly—what was left of it. That morning, Cooper had weighed in at 172 pounds. He had lost 40 pounds over the past four months, at the cost, inevitably, of weakening himself.

"I'm only running five miles," he reminded George.

Cooper noticed the kids exchanging whispers. Shortly thereafter, he noticed Noah steal out of the room and return momentarily holding a package that was hastily wrapped in bright-red crepe paper. Noah smiled with self-conscious pleasure as he handed it to Cooper. "It's from the three of us."

"No, it isn't," Zak corrected. "It's from *me* until *you* guys pay your share."

Zak the accountant. As a matter of general practice, the other two boys generally spent whatever money they were gifted as soon as opportunity allowed, or they managed somehow to lose it. *Who stole my money?* Apparently, the same gremlin who stole socks from the wash also stole loose change from wherever.

The package had that distinctive shirt-for-dad shape.

"Well, now," Cooper said. "What can this be?"

Cooper opened the package with excruciating slowness.

"C'mon, Pop," Luke ordered, "open it!"

Cooper held up a bright-red "The Little Engine That Could" T-shirt. A bright-red sweatband and a pair of bright-red shorts were also folded in the box. He tucked the neck of the T-shirt under his chin.

"You sure look *red-dee*, Pop," Zak quipped.

Cooper raised his wineglass.

"I am. Thank you."

Turkey Trot

NOVEMBER 26, 1982

It seemed half a century since Cooper had passed the plaque marking the entry to "Danville's Tuttle Farms / 1832." All shapes and sizes of people were passing him—tall people, short people. Young people, old people, fat people, skinny people. Even a woman who looked old enough to be Cooper's grandmother.

He should have waited! He had not given himself enough time to get into respectable shape.

Looking ahead, Cooper could see a stream of runners ascending a hill he had taken note of on his reconnaissance mission. Hills were his potential undoing. He simply did not have the stamina to defeat all comers.

On reaching a crossroad at the foot of the hill, Cooper bore right, started up the incline, and soon realized he was not going to be able to make it to the top of the hill without pausing to take a breather.

Slowing his pace, Cooper looked ahead again, just long enough to assess the distance to the top of the hill. He guessed the length of about three football fields.

A whiff of cow manure seemed to take on the role of smelling salts.

Keeping his focus on the pavement, Cooper crossed over a red stripe and the numeral 4.

The 4-mile mark—finally! Only 1 mile to go—and it was all downhill.

Cooper picked up his pace a little bit more.

Reaching the crest of the hill, Cooper could hear labored breathing close behind.

A man roughly his own age, thinner and a bit taller, appeared briefly on his left, then passed him. The wet area on the back of the man's shirt formed the capital letter V.

Cooper forced himself to keep pace with V-Man, about five yards back.

As he mounted a brief incline, Cooper caught sight of the redbrick buildings that stood close to the finish line, where he hoped Tessa and the boys would be waiting.

Again picking up his pace, Cooper pulled even with V-Man—and sensed the moment their egos locked.

V-Man surged ahead.

Cooper pulled even.

V-Man surged ahead.

Cooper pulled even, then raised V-Man one and surged ahead.

V-Man matched Cooper's move in kind and raised him one.

Straining to counter, Cooper felt a sharp pain in his right calf. Howling, he lost his balance and suddenly found himself sprawled out on the pavement. He was saved from serious injury by a hockey helmet and several joint protectors.

Struggling to get to his feet, Cooper was assisted by a man wearing a gray sweatshirt.

19

Collision Course

Eighteen miles?

Had he covered only one mile since making it to the Newton firehouse? *One lousy mile?*

By his reckoning, he should be only a mile and a half from the top of Heartbreak Hill, not two and a half miles. One and a half he might have been able to handle, but two and a half?

It *couldn't* be two and a half! It *had* to be one and a half! Tears welled.

The woman at the firehouse had tried to warn him. *Everybody* had tried to warn him!

A face in the crowd, to his right, startled him. For just a fraction of a moment, it looked like her—Tessa!

She had the same raven hair, the same exotic cheekbones, the same regal bearing—

Without warning, Cooper collapsed—striking his head on the pavement. Instantly, he realized he no longer had a helmet on. He must have left it back at the fire station.

First Date

NOVEMBER 12, 1966

Cooper and Jeb had the best intentions when they invited Tessa and her housemate Lisa on a double date at a restaurant in Troy, New York. They had been wearing their Officer Candidate School (OCS) uniforms, and a couple men at a table near their own had kept lobbing antimilitary insults their way—"murderers," "baby killers," and the like—until a fed-up Jeb had stood and invited the two ununiformed males out to the parking lot. At the time, Cooper, at 6 feet, 2 inches, weighed over 200 pounds, and Jeb looked every bit the muscled farm boy from Montana he was.

What these two men didn't know—about Cooper, at least—was that he had volunteered for military service in lieu of accepting a "critical skills" deferment from Corning Glass, which status would, in effect, have condemned some hapless kid into being drafted in Cooper's stead and likely billeted to the infantry to serve as cannon fodder for the Viet Cong. In effect, Cooper had conceivably saved the life of someone he did not know and would never cross paths with.

A similar arrangement during the Civil War had allowed the male elite of Boston and New York to avoid military service by paying a surrogate to serve in their stead. Cooper had never understood how Mister Lincoln could have allowed such a practice to go on. Political expediency? To keep the moneyed elites from opposing the war?

In any event, it was not an evening for a brawl, even though Jeb was obviously spoiling for one. To Cooper's disappointment, Jeb turned out to be one of those sweet-tempered, soft-spoken Jekyll types who turned into a belligerent asshole upon consuming more alcohol than he could handle. The swiftness and extent of Jeb's Hyde-like metamorphosis was nothing short of startling, not to mention embarrassing, not to mention alarming.

Cooper had not seen it coming. How could he have? This occasion was the first opportunity for such an anomaly to manifest since Cooper and Jeb entered OCS three weeks earlier.

It had scared the hell out of him. Not only did it jeopardize the rest of the weekend; it also cast doubt on the possibility of there ever being another such weekend.

And what if Jeb got hauled off to jail for disorderly conduct? What then?

The evening air was unusually warm for mid-November—a perfect complement outside to what Cooper was feeling inside.

As he and Tessa followed Jeb and Lisa across the parking lot, Cooper slowed his pace to increase the time it would take to reach Jeb's car.

Cooper wished he could make time stop altogether. In just 36 hours, he and Jeb would be on their way back to Newport and 14 more weeks of OCS, to be followed by, for Cooper, 16 weeks of Basic Underwater Demolition/ SEAL (BUD/S) training—although it was far from certain he would be able to qualify for the program. Despite all the weight he had lost in his first three weeks at OCS, Cooper knew full well he wasn't even close to being in good enough shape to pass the BUD/S qualifying tests. Especially the pull-up part. Not to mention the running part.

He had never been a very good runner—and he hadn't been on a pull-up bar since the third grade—when he turned out to be the only boy in gym class who couldn't do a single palms-out pull-up. Not one.

Cooper took a few more steps before finally summoning the courage to bump Tessa's left hand with his right hand as if by accident.

A few steps later, Cooper felt Tessa's hand bump his. He had to take the risk! *There is no tomorrow!*

Cooper grasped Tessa's hand and held his breath. He firmed his grip. Tessa firmed hers. He realized that if he didn't take a breath pretty soon, he was going to pass out. They continued to walk in silence, and Cooper wondered what Tessa was thinking:

That he was going to try to put the make on her just as soon as they got into the back seat of Jeb's car?

That he was too fat to take seriously, despite all the weight he had lost since she first met him, at his brother Stephen's wedding?

That he looked ridiculous with all his hair shaved off?

That he had talked too much?

That he had been a typical asshole male interested only in himself?

How might he let her know he had never talked to anyone like that before in his entire life? How might he let her know he had talked so much only because Tessa had drawn him out without his being aware of it? In truth, he hated to talk about himself. He was a born listener. Or, more precisely, a born interviewer.

Like Tessa herself—she had asked questions and follow-up questions. She had made comments. She had looked him in the eye.

As Lisa's head disappeared below the roof of Jeb's car, Cooper's stomach felt as if he had swallowed a shot of whiskey and an ice cube both at the same time. It was now or never!

Cooper stopped walking; he stopped breathing. He turned to Tessa. He stared into her eyes.

He leaned tentatively toward her—ready to retreat at the slightest hint of rejection. He leaned closer, not breathing...the moment the cotton of his lips touched the silk of hers, he knew.

Did she?

20

Heartbreak Hill

He wasn't sure where he was. Someone gave him ERG in a cup. He drank—someone poured water over his head. Wobbling dangerously, he resumed putting one foot in front of the other.

After 100 yards or so, he was able to increase his pace from little more than a chain-gang shuffle to an uneven jog. Searching ahead, he discerned what looked suspiciously like the top of a hill.

Heartbreak! Just a couple of hundred yards ahead! From there it was just 5 miles—*downhill*—to the finish line.

One mile five times over. One mile, then another. One step, then another.

He sensed a tap at the door to hope. He cracked it open. It was a dangerous thing to do. *I think I can, I think I can—*

He opened the door a little farther. *I think I can, I think I can—*

He crested the hill! *It was all downhill now!*

He picked up his pace a little more. He could endure *anything* for 5 miles. He fixed his eyes on the pavement immediately ahead. He vowed not to lift them again until he was certain of being at or beyond the 21-mile mark.

But then, strangely, he felt as if he were climbing again. *Something was wrong!*

He lifted his eyes. He winced. He shook his head. He had reached the *bottom* of Heartbreak Hill—*not* the top.

He sank to his knees and bowed his head. He would have to take comfort in likely being the only ALS patient in the world to have run 21 miles. The kids would be proud.

There had to be a Heartbreak Hill in hell, where the damned were told paradise was just past the top. All they needed to do to earn their way out of eternal misery was to get to the top of that hill.

Of course, the hill would never end. It would just keep going and going—

Cooper wobbled, lurched—and struck his head on the pavement.

When he opened his eyes—he wasn't sure how long he had been unconscious. He struggled to get to his feet. He took a cup of water from "Boston College." It hurt to hold the cup. It hurt to drink from it.

He poured the remaining water over his head, then glanced at his watch. He had trouble focusing on the digits. He thought he could make out a "5" and maybe a "3" and maybe another "3"—5:33?

If he had it right, the winners had crossed the finish line over three hours ago. To keep going at this point was to continue to embarrass himself—a helicopter passed overhead, rotors throbbing. A second copter passed overhead.

Cooper's ears were ringing, brain buzzing. He sank to his knees.

He sensed someone close by—

A rotund man with a black beard and a garish Hawaiian shirt helped Cooper to his feet, held a hand toward him, palm up. Cooper slapped at it, missed, tried again, connected.

Brainian Initiation

EARLY 1950S

They were sitting cross-legged around a flickering flame from a single candle. Stephen had earlier invited Cooper into Stephen's playroom on the third floor of their house on Point Street. Troy Tessier was sitting on one side of Stephen, Barry on the other. Richard Favre and Morrie Dunfey completed the circle. Cooper could smell Morrie from across the circle.

Troy was almost as smart as Stephen. Barry was the next smartest, then Richard, and finally Morrie. Among the four of them, they knew just about everything there was to know.

Stephen, solemn as a nun, pulled a ribbon off a scroll of yellow paper and unrolled it. He was wearing his Boy Scout kerchief and his merit badge sash. Stephen had more merit badges than anybody ever.

"Candidate J. Cooper Haynes," Stephen read, "it is hereby decreed that before you can be officially inducted into the exultant and esteemed citizenry of the Royal Republic of Brainia, you must successfully pass the official Trials of Suitability."

Stephen's face looked spectral in the flickering candlelight—like in a horror movie. Stephen looked at Cooper. "Does the candidate here present solemnly accede to this requirement?"

"He does." Cooper's voice sounded as if he were on the verge of tears. He cleared his throat. "He does," Cooper repeated, a little more forthrightly. His voice was always doing that—like when he knew he was about to be called on to read out loud in class.

Stephen looked again at his scroll. "In order to pass the official Trials of Suitability, the candidate must do everything he is told. If the candidate should refuse or otherwise fail to comply, he shall be forbidden from becoming a citizen of the Royal Republic of Brainia for all time." Stephen stared at Cooper. "Does the candidate here present solemnly accede to this mandate?"

Stephen knew a lot of big words. Cooper cleared his throat as quietly as he could. "He does."

"So let it be written," Stephen intoned, "so let it be done."

Stephen nodded toward Troy, who rose and tied a blindfold in need of washing over Cooper's eyes.

Heartbreak Hill

Cooper thought of the time last spring when he had walked into Stephen and Barry's room to borrow a couple of comic books from their closet and found Troy and Stephen standing in the dark in women's underwear. He would never forget the look on their faces. Cooper was supposed to be at his violin lesson at Mrs. Halloran's, but she had greeted him at the door looking all watery eyed and stuffed up and told him she had a bad cold and couldn't give him his lesson. She could barely talk over her coughing.

"If at any time the candidate should remove this blindfold," Stephen admonished, "he will be automatically expelled from these proceedings. All rise."

Cooper rose. Someone grasped his arm and began to lead him as if he were a blind billy goat.

He couldn't imagine anything worse than actually being blind. He was keenly thankful he wasn't.

He could tell that whoever was leading him had a flashlight, because at one point he shined it directly at Cooper's blindfold, apparently to test whether this person might be able to see through the folds of the dirty cloth. He could tell it was only one person, too, because he could only hear one set of steps besides his own on the creaky floorboards. At one point, Cooper thought he heard giggles followed by an authoritative shush. But he couldn't be sure. Sometimes sounds play tricks on you when you are listening too hard.

Cooper remembered the time Stephen had him pinned to the floor and was bouncing on his chest. In desperation, Cooper had wrapped his legs around Stephen's shoulders, from behind, and thrust him backward—bam! Stephen's head had bounced off the floor.

Stephen had long since gotten even, so all Stephen was likely going to do now, Cooper assured himself, was what he had done to Richard and Morrie when they had been initiated.

Even if Stephen was out to get him again, what was the worst thing he could do? Scare him a little? Big deal. So let him have his fun. What did he care? He could take anything they could dish out.

The hand gripping his arm signaled him to stop, then a hand on each shoulder turned him, as if positioning him. "Sit," a muffled voice instructed. The voice sounded as if someone were talking through cloth.

OK, *now* he knew what they were up to. When he tried to sit down, there would be no chair there, like in musical chairs. All right, let them have a little laugh. Big deal.

Cooper landed on the seat of a chair.

"You will sit until instructed otherwise," a muffled voice commanded. "If you get up for any reason, you will automatically be disqualified."

Not to worry. As long as he was sitting, he was safe.

Listening for the slightest sound, Cooper could now and then make out a squeaking floorboard, seemingly from farther and farther away. Then he thought he heard the door to Stephen's door click shut.

He felt a chill in the pit of his stomach. They were locking him in the attic...in the dark!

No. They were just making it seem that way. They would be waiting nearby to see if he would panic. They were testing him.

He would pass. He would outlast them. He caught the scent of melting wax. He was back where he had started!

Tilting his head backward a bit, Cooper tried to look through any gap there might be between the blindfold and his face, hoping to detect a flicker of light, but he couldn't detect any.

The only sound now was a sort of high-pitched hiss in his ears. Maybe they *had* abandoned him—to see how long he would sit in the dark.

Now a different sound, from behind! The sound of someone or some-*thing* putting weight on a floorboard.

He held his breath and heard the same sound—this time in front of him.

Then from one side. Then the other. Then in front again.

Silence.

Now a different sound! Regular, like breathing from behind, in front, everywhere!

He felt that if he reached out, something would bite his hand off and then devour him piece by piece.

Something light as a raindrop touched the top of his head, again, and again! Something was drooling on him!

Screams now! Seemingly from every direction!

Cooper pulled off his blindfold and, jumping up from his chair, tried to orient himself with outstretched arms. It was too dark for him to gauge where the stairwell was.

Jefferson County Mental Health Clinic

J. COOPER HAYNES

5/18/53 Mrs. McKenzie insisted that there was no point in coming to the clinic unless Cooper was along, and so Cooper was in briefly. After a few moments, he asked what I wanted to see him for. When I said "To see how you are getting along," he answered "The appointment was really for my mother, wasn't it?" with a large grin. His insight may surpass his mother's.

He talked today of his brother Stephen, toward whom he admitted "very bad feelings." Stephen apparently teases him a great deal about being fat. We talked about the time mothers have to spend with their different children, and Cooper decided that a mother should try to keep it even. He apparently likes Barry much better, at the moment anyway.

Cooper discussed his "fatness" and decided he was not too fat and that exercise would be a good thing. He is very disappointed that there are not more facilities for organized boys' play in Cape Vincent and spontaneously mentioned that he was going to ask his father to get together with the truant officer in an effort to

build up something of this sort. This was encouraged, and it is to be hoped that Mr. H will do as Cooper suggests.
BLP:bl

Cooper is really quite isolated in the family. A neighbor took the two older boys to see *Hans Christian Andersen*. No one invites Cooper because he causes trouble. We talked about his grandmother or someone he likes taking him to see it. He has always wanted the baby to sleep up in his room. Perhaps she can eventually work that out.

She experienced a heart palpitation in the waiting room. Had to lie down. Mrs. H has not had one for a long time but had pills in her purse to take. Her doctor says there is nothing seriously wrong; when she gets too tired or upset, she has a spell.
JRS:bl

5/11/53 Cooper being seen by Mrs. Ackerman; see report.
BWL

5/18/53 Cooper seen again by Mrs. Ackerman.
BWL

5/18/53 Mrs. H was very upset when she came in—tears very near the surface. She said, "This past week was the worst of all. I hope we can see Dr. Palmer soon." She recited all the bad episodes.

1. They had guests, and when Cooper could not have his favorite program on the TV, he cried, went to the kitchen, threw the chairs around, broke two dishes, only came back to watch TV when his father "gave him the business."

Heartbreak Hill

2. He flew into a rage when he found his young brother (2½) had upset his airport in the sandbox. He threw and broke the toys. Mrs. H called her husband home from the store to punish him.

3. He fished all day Saturday, brought his fish home, cleaned and cooked them, and shared them with a friend. Then cried and was mad because someone broke the good luck feather in his cap.

4. He cries all the time when Stephen teases him and calls him "Fatty."

5. Mrs. H dreads every meal because someone says the wrong thing and there is a big quarrel.

6. Saturday the neighbors took the two older boys to a movie. Cooper stormed and cried, settled down when she told him he could go alone Monday. He said "It was a wonderful movie" when they came home.

Because Cooper is "such a problem," Mrs. H asked what I would think of sending him to live with her aunt in St. Paul, Minn. (the one she stayed with when she went to college). "There is a school for problem children right there," she said. Mrs. M. has corresponded with her about this plan, and she even suggested it to Cooper on his way up this morning. "He said he would go for the summer but not to stay."
JRS:bl

5/25/53 Hayneses in to see Dr. Palmer. See report.
BWL

6/8/53 Terse note received from Hayneses canceling their appointment for tonight.

BWL

Mission Impossible

AUGUST 1966

It was just past 5 a.m. when Cooper and a friend, Craig Handley, arrived at the municipal dock in Kingston. Awaiting them were the boats—a cabin cruiser and an outboard—that would accompany Cooper across Lake Ontario to Cape Vincent, specifically to his father's marina, which Cooper took great pleasure in having helped build.

Stripping down to a red nylon bathing suit, Cooper proceeded to lather himself up with a gooey mixture of lanoline and Vaseline, in equal parts, to help retain body heat and minimize drag. Early on in his ad hoc training regimen, he had opted not to use a wetsuit because of the threat of chafing.

Once Cooper had been thoroughly greased—top of head to tip of toe—there could be no turning back. The "grease job" committed him.

Two uniformed officers arrived in a squad car. One look at Cooper was apparently enough to assure them that the commotion presented no threat. "Good luck!" one of them bid.

Despite all the insulation, Cooper was well aware of the chill of the early morning air. He descended the boat launch next to the public pier, bid his crew adieu—"See you in the Cape"—and waded into water that was noticeably cooler.

Hypothermia was Cooper's greatest risk. If he failed to reach his goal, it would largely be a result of being immersed in relatively cold water for too long. To minimize the risk of being defeated by hypothermia, Cooper had made exposure to cold water part of his daily training regimen. Once a day, he would fill a bathtub full of cold water and immerse himself in it until he was numb. Sometimes he would do this twice a day.

The primary component of Cooper's ad hoc training program, though, consisted of swimming around the Cape Vincent breakwater several times a day, covering 2 to 3 miles. A second component consisted of Cooper running from his father's marina to the Tibbetts Point Lighthouse, a round-trip distance of 6 miles.

Ahead of Cooper lay 21 miles of open water that no one had ever swum before.

By launching himself at dawn, Cooper hoped to reach his father's marina in Cape Vincent between 9 and 10 p.m. Best case, he would be exposed to 69- to 70-degree water for 16 hours.

Cooper's stroke of choice was a modified breaststroke of his own invention. It consisted of extending his arms overhead, then sweeping them rearward while executing a frog kick. He would glide a few inches, then recock his limbs for another stroke.

His diet consisted of tea and broth.

His route would take him from Kingston, Ontario, around the head of Wolfe Island, the largest of the Thousand Islands, and downriver to Cape Vincent. Individual milestones included Simcoe Island, Grimshaw Bay, Reeds Bay, and Big Sandy Bay.

Noontime. Cooper was feeling good—strong and comfortable—but was behind schedule, by about an hour.

In freshwater, Cooper could swim forever, but he could not go fast. About two-thirds the way up the Simcoe cut, Cooper bore left, and entering Grimshaw Bay, soon found himself swimming through long strings of seaweed. He was in shallow water. He recalibrated his course until he could no longer feel seaweed pulling at his arms and legs—he was back in deeper water.

Family lore had it that Cooper's mother had caught a large bass in this bay.

The next milestone was Reeds Bay. The work of traversing it, however, seemed like it would take an eternity. The problem being the presence of a "minor bay" located between Grimshaw Bay and Reeds. At water level, this bay seemed much larger than it was. So when Cooper thought he was seeing Reeds Bay, he was actually seeing this minor bay he had missed on his scouting mission. When he realized his mistake, he could feel his morale slip. And morale was everything.

In just about every endurance situation Cooper was familiar with, morale was the difference between success and failure.

Finally reaching the far side of Reeds Bay, Cooper could feel an insidious coldness creeping into where he needed warmth. Worse, he was finding it increasingly difficult to interrupt his momentum to ask for tea or broth.

To reach the next milestone—Big Sandy Bay—Cooper had to swim around an underwater shoal that extended lakeward from the point separating Reeds Bay from Big Sandy Bay. Cooper could see, even touch, the boulders lurking in the darkness beneath him. These behemoths represented a clear and present danger to the escort boat's propeller. Following the escort boat's lead, Cooper reversed course and headed back to Big Sandy Bay and on to Cape Vincent.

It was 5:30 p.m. when Cooper crossed the imaginary line separating Lake Ontario from the St. Lawrence River. He searched the eastern horizon for any sign of the Tibbetts Point Lighthouse. It had been nonoperational for several years, so there were no flashes of light or booms of foghorn to discover or home in on. At first, Cooper didn't see anything distinctive, but then, with help from his crew, he was finally able to discern the distinctive tower. His heart sank. It was what seemed like a million miles away—lodged somewhere in the Orion Nebula, perhaps.

He was shivering. He had been in the water now for 12 hours.

He only infrequently paused to ask for hot tea or broth.

To make it to his father's marina, Cooper figured he had at least four to five hours to go. In cold water.

In an effort to boost Cooper's morale, one of his crewmembers, Fred Wiley, jumped into the water and began to swim beside him. Cooper resumed his requests for tea and broth.

When he had swum about 2 miles farther, Cooper saw, while taking tea, flashes of lightning on the western horizon.

He thought he could hear rumbles of thunder. The skipper of the escort boat told Cooper he had just gotten an updated weather report from Kingston Radio. It was not good: Severe thunderstorms were likely to strike the local area within the next two hours. High winds and heavy rain could be expected. The skipper ordered Fred extracted from the water.

Cooper hoped the storm would either quickly subside, as was often the case with thunderstorms, or bypass them altogether. In any case, he had to play it safe.

He changed course and headed toward the lighthouse. He swam as fast as he could, hoping to get out of harm's way.

The sky darkened until almost black. Chains of lightning illuminated the western sky.

Booms of thunder chastised the audacity of heaven and earth. The wind stiffened.

The two boats—one big, one small—flailed against each other.

"Get him out!" the skipper ordered.

The crew tried to board Cooper but could not do it. He was deadweight and still heavily greased. Cooper had trouble hanging onto the boat ladder. It was useless; it had not been made for this kind of situation.

At one point, the escort boat swung violently counterclockwise and nearly struck Cooper.

Cooper dodged out of harm's way, but then, looking back, he could not see the escort boat. He listened for voices calling his name but did not hear any; he looked for boat lights but did not see any.

The rain and wind continued. Cooper began to choke on aspirated water.

He treaded water while scanning 360 degrees around him, over and over, but he was too exhausted—and hypothermic—to last much longer.

Lights!

Cooper knew immediately what he was seeing. Several vehicles were flashing their headlights from the Tibbetts Point promontory! In essence, they had made themselves into a lighthouse! The escort boat would be close by, looking for him.

To his infinite joy, Cooper was now headed downriver, going with the surface current—

Could he still do it?

Mercy Hospital

NAME: J. COOPER HAYNES   **DOCTOR:** B. MECKLIN, MD

Patient attempted to swim 21 miles between Kingston and Cape Vincent. Patient was pulled from the water unconscious and acutely hypothermic after being immersed in frigid water for over 18 hours. Patient was warmed to extent possible and transported here. Patient was responsive to painful stimuli but not to verbal command. Reflexes were diminished but symmetrical. Core body temperature was 86.7 degrees, with a systolic BP of 40. The family priest was summoned.

21

Extreme Duress

Every cell in his body was screaming for mercy. The merest incline was Mount Washington—two times over.

So weak and wobbly had his legs become that Cooper could not avoid bumping into other laggards. He could no longer marshal enough energy to apologize. He could not so much as issue a grunt of acknowledgment. He was beyond giving a good goddamn.

Fuck 'em. Fuck 'em all. Fuck everybody!

Why were they looking at him like that? Why didn't they just mind their own goddamn business?

Father Driscoll

MAY 1953

Cooper and several of his fellow fifth graders had just arrived at the rectory for their weekly release-time class.

Cooper was ready. He had memorized his catechism lesson on the way home from his weekly Monday morning appointment in Watertown. His mother had been taking him there since March because he had been gaining a lot of weight. She wouldn't be taking him much longer, though, Cooper could tell, because his mother didn't like going there. It made her even more nervous than usual.

Cooper had long wondered why just one priest and one housekeeper needed such a large house. It was about twice as big as the Methodist minister's house, and he had a whole family, and probably four times bigger than the Episcopal minister's house, and he also had a whole family.

As usual, everyone waited for Jack LaVerdiere to ring the doorbell. Jack planned to become a priest one day. His parents intended to send him to Wadhams Hall in Ogdensburg.

Cooper liked how Jack's parents looked whenever they talked about Jack becoming a priest. It made him think about becoming a priest himself. Surely, the church would never let him enter the priesthood, though, because he was always doing bad things, sooting up his soul.

As usual, Miss Philbeam answered Jack's ring. Father Driscoll never answered the door himself. Priests didn't do things like that. Priests were like Jesus on Earth, and Jesus would *never* answer a doorbell. He would send one of his apostles to do it. Not Judas.

Instead of inviting them in and holding the door open, Miss Philbeam remained in the doorway, filling the space with her considerable self, which was very considerable indeed. Especially up top.

There was something odd about the look on her face—something Cooper had not seen there before.

"I'm sorry," she said, "but Father is ill and won't be able to hold class today."

A cherry bomb of joy exploded in the deep, dark depths of Cooper's secret-most self. *Woo-hoo!*

Cooper paused his celebration, realizing that it was fear that he was seeing in Miss Philbeam's face. *Maybe Father Driscoll is seriously ill. Maybe he's dying!*

He wouldn't think about that.

He liked Father. And he knew Father liked him. He could tell by the way Father was always reminiscing about the time Cooper had taken Father and a priest friend from Wadhams Hall fishing. There was a twinkle in Father's eye all the while he was telling people about it, as if he were telling stories about his own son rather than someone else's.

Cooper had invited Father Driscoll fishing because he knew how much Father liked to fish. He hadn't done it just because Father happened to mention after confessions one Saturday evening that a friend of his, who would be visiting him the following weekend, was an avid fisherman.

He had taken the two priests to a spot almost directly out from the end of Remington's Dock, leaving Tex, his fishing buddy, behind.

In the next few hours, Cooper had caught 11 bass, including a two-pounder, while the two priests had caught, between them, 2 rock bass—a species that tended to commit suicide at the mere sight of a hook—and a perch that had swallowed the hook seemingly down to its tail. As Father put it whenever he told the story, "Three fish caught two priests."

Cooper could tell that neither priest was a fisherman—the way they held their fishing rods or reeled in, creating a rat's nest of a snarl Cooper would then have to unsnarl (priests didn't unsnarl their own fishing reels). However, not being a fisherman had not been at the root of their ill luck in catching black bass that day.

The root of their problem had been that they had been so busy gabbing and giggling that they did not notice the telltale signs of their bait being stripped from their hook, minnow after minnow after minnow, until there were no more minnows to be stripped. Cooper had never in his life witnessed two men gab and giggle the way they did.

He considered interrupting them each time he saw the end of either fishing rod stutter—"I think you've got a bite, Father!"—but he just couldn't imagine himself interrupting a priest any more than he could imagine himself interrupting Jesus.

Both priests had told him that day that they thought he was the greatest fisherman they'd ever seen. What was his secret? Later, in his father's store, Father Driscoll had even said so to Cooper's father. "This son of yours is the greatest fisherman I've ever known," he had said, his round Celtic face flushed, his blue eyes sparkling.

Of course, it wasn't true. Cooper's father was the best fisherman ever. Every time Cooper's father spit on his bait, he would catch a fish!

Cooper was about to celebrate an unexpected reprieve from catechism class with an Almond Joy wrangled from his father when he heard an ominous crash and the sound of shattering glass. The fear on Miss Philbeam's face turned almost instantaneously into terror.

She shut the door.

Cooper could hear voices from within, Father's over Miss Philbeam's, as if Cooper were kneeling in the confessional on a Saturday evening feeling himself melt into a puddle of dread, alternately straining to make out the words coming from the other side of the confessional and trying not to—hoping Father would lower his whisper when it came Cooper's turn and vowing he would never do another bad thing as long as he lived. Not ever!

The door opened, and Father Driscoll appeared wearing a pair of black trousers and a paunch-inflated sleeveless shirt half untucked, so that his fully exposed Roman collar, attached like a bib, took on the shocking aspect of something indecent.

Father's full-moon face was even pinker than usual, and his thinning white hair looked as if he had just been driving his black Chrysler around town with all the windows down. He swayed unsteadily as he stood in the doorway.

Cooper could hear Miss Philbeam talking from behind in that tone of whisper the nuns used in church during summer school—the kind you could hear about five blocks away.

"Father," she whispered, "you're not well. Come in here."

Cooper could see Miss Philbeam grip Father by the arm and urge him away from the door.

Father tried to wrench himself free by torquing himself, like a naughty boy trying to escape his mother's grasp, but in doing so lost his balance and began to stumble backward. Miss Philbeam reached for him while at the same time Father's desperate grasps, like those of a drowning man, found purchase on the front of Miss Philbeam's pillowy blouse.

In a flash, Father disappeared from view, amid a terrible clatter—the front of Miss Philbeam's blouse in hand.

Cooper stood frozen in time, like a pillar of salt, then turned and ran a full block before slowing to a walk. By the time he reached his father's store, his only thought was about how hungry he was. Inside the store, he grabbed a package of Hostess cupcakes from his favorite fresh-baked-smelling aisle and asked his father, who was working behind the meat counter, if he could have it.

His father—using a wooden thingamajig to push chunks of raw meat through a hamburger grinder—glanced at the package of cupcakes and nodded.

Cooper exited the store through the back room and headed home. He couldn't wait to climb up to his tree fort, with his two chocolaty cupcakes tucked under his shirt, and pull up the ladder.

A Benevolent Barter

NOVEMBER 1982

Cooper was six minutes late for his appointment at the law offices of Pritchard & Fraley. He couldn't remember the last time he had been late for an appointment.

If thouest be rudely late, willst heaven kindly wait?

He was late because he had decided to run 5 miles instead of his usual 3 to 4. At this point in his training, he was feeling increasing pressure to push himself as much as he dared. Big mistake.

Because he was already going to be late for his appointment, he had decided not to take the time to put on his protective pads. Also a big mistake.

On his way home from his halfway point, Cooper's legs had suddenly cramped up on him, both of them, and he had lurched onto the pavement, banging himself up a bit—quite a bit, actually.

He had tried running 7 miles on a previous occasion, and that effort had not gone well either—so what in hell had made him think that now would be a good time to try again?

The bumps and bruises on his hands and knees were throbbing despite the ointment Julie, Will's secretary, had applied.

Cooper pulled a checkbook and a pen from his shirt pocket. "What do I owe you?"

Will Fraley smiled. "It's your lucky day. It just so happens we're running a special this week. You have a choice: You can write a big, fat check, or you can agree to speak to my guys in Concord at some point."

My guys? Concord?

"I'm not sure what you're asking."

"When I'm not drawing up wills and POAs for good people like you and Tessa, I'm doing pro bono work at the state prison. I try to provide as many indigent offenders as I can with competent representation. Mostly, though, I try to get them to recognize the root cause of the behavior that got them into trouble in the first place so they might control it."

Why me? "What would you want me to say?"

"Whatever comes to mind would do to start."

"Start?"

"They need role models."

The last thing Cooper needed was to get involved in a project to rescue the unrescuable.

Will smiled. "I'm sure they'd like to hear about your evening in jail."

Cooper stopped at Julie's desk on his way out.

Julie inquired about his bumps and bruises and handed him an invoice for $940. She grinned. "I see Mr. Fraley has mentioned this week's special to you? When would be the best day of the week for you to speak in Concord?"

22

Survival of the Fittest

Cooper felt the infinitesimal smallness of his insignificance, the utter meaninglessness of his struggle.

All he had been through, the totality of his effort, the depth of his agony, would leave not the tiniest stain on the canvas of an infinite universe.

He imagined the winners standing on the winner's podium receiving the adulation of the world.

Survival of the fittest.

He found himself staring at the desiccated carcass of a squirrel—and closed his eyes.

Sorry.

So very sorry.

Competitive Commuting

JULY 1981

Cooper was paused at the intersection of Route 125 and Route 27, a few cars back, waiting for the light to change. He was wondering how many of the cars stopped ahead of him would turn right when the light changed and crawl all the way to Raymond.

In the whole of the 10-mile stretch between Epping and Raymond, there were only two places one could pass. The first was just outside Epping; the other, farther down the present stretch of road. If he started out with more than three or four drivers ahead of him, he was doomed to being trapped in a seemingly endless line of traffic.

The green eye winked off; the red eye winked on. Nothing moved.

As Cooper expected would happen, a car intending to make a left turn was holding up two lanes of traffic, while the car immediately behind it sat in place, immobile, instead of bearing right onto the shoulder and maneuvering around the blocking car.

"C'mon, asshole, go around!" Cooper felt his stomach tighten as he anticipated the stoplight changing back to red before anybody had a chance to move more than a few inches. Finally, the car was able to turn, and traffic began to move.

One, two, three, four cars turned right, meaning Cooper would have at least four "snail cars" to deal with.

New Hampshire had turned out to be anything but the utopia perpetuated—perpetrated?—by Currier and Ives's idealizations, of which there was no shortage. No east-west highways. No shoulders. No public kindergartens. No spring. No jobs. No universal concern for the environment. No state support for public schools. No class.

Live free or die!

As the light changed from amber to red, Cooper turned right slowly behind a line of snail cars into tawdry little Epping—the "Home of Three Governors"—which reminded him a lot of jaded little Cape Vincent, which, whenever he visited his mother, always seemed to have progressed further into decay. In both cases, the only structure that looked as if it were receiving sustenance on a regular basis was the post office—which, of course, wasn't really an integral part of the local economy.

Checking his gas gauge, Cooper was relieved to find it registering over half full. He hated to stop for gas; it was "one more thing."

As he approached the western outskirts of Epping, Cooper determined he was fifth in a line of snail cars crawling in lockstep. He would keep left in order to get as early a look ahead as possible, and then, just as soon as he was able to verify there was no oncoming traffic, he would swerve into the left lane and, pressing the accelerator to the floor, pass all four snail cars at once. *Four in a row—Woo-hoo!*

He hugged the yellow center line around the gradual curve until he was able to see the entirety of the open road ahead. The only traffic was a car coming down a hill at the far end—too far away at the moment to be of concern.

Cooper swerved into the left lane and slammed the accelerator to the floor, slowly beginning to pull ahead of the other cars. There was no surge of power, only a sluggish acceleration.

Someday he would own a *real* car! He passed one car, a second, a third—

A squirrel had stopped on the road! Cooper was going to run over it!

If he hit the brakes, he would be trapped in the left lane with a car coming right at him.

Thump.

Cooper passed the fourth car and, swerving back into the right lane, steered onto the shoulder and stopped. After the last of the four cars he had whooshed by, Cooper stole a glance in the rearview mirror.

He slumped in his seat. *Who had cut down the last tree on Easter Island? Who would run over the last squirrel on Earth?*

Returning to the scene of the crime, Cooper removed the squirrel from the pavement, holding it by its tail, and laid it to rest at the foot of a second-growth oak tree. He assured himself the carcass would not go to waste.

He sat in his car, feeling physically ill, until a trooper stopped and asked if everything was all right.

Everything was fine, thank you.

Survival of the Fittest

A Walk in the Woods

DECEMBER 1969

Cooper smiled at a mob of screeching jays. What a racket!

"Look at me!" one seemed to screech.

"No, look at me!" a second screeched.

"No, look at me!" screeched a third.

"I screeched first!"

"I screeched loudest!"

On and on.

Cooper unzipped his jacket and pulled a small pad and a pen from his shirt pocket:

The only legitimate reason humankind has to judge itself superior to all other species is its ability to puff up feathers it does not have.

He walked on, leaving the jays to fight it out, but soon stopped to a rustling of dry leaves to his left. The sound seemed to be coming from behind a wall of ancient fieldstones, not far from an oak tree still bearing a surprising number of desiccated leaves. The previous season seemed to be having trouble giving way to the next.

A diminutive gray head popped into view from behind the stone wall. The head remained motionless while the only eye visible refused to blink. *Do squirrels blink?*

Cooper continued to stare, blinking several times, then began to kiss-call as if to summon a house pet.

The squirrel sprang onto the oak in one fluid motion and disappeared behind the trunk. When it reappeared, about 12 feet farther up the tree, it was well out of harm's way.

Cooper kiss-called to it again. *Can we be friends, you and I, do you think? Can I meet you here now and then to see how you're doing—and maybe chew the fat for a bit? I want to be a writer. I take long walks hoping for little bolts out of the blue, as they say.*

The squirrel remained motionless. *I do not trust you, human. How can you expect me to? You maim and slaughter my kind with your instruments of death, wholly for the amusement of it. You run over us on your highways and give the carnage no notice. I would like to come down and greet you, for we are cousins, you and I. Our separate selves share the same miracle of being; our separate souls flow from the same deep well. But I dare not. Indeed, what would you do if the situation were in reverse?*

The squirrel vanished.

Cooper paused a moment, then, shuddering to an insinuation of chill air, wrote,

When all else fails, try laughing.

He returned the pad and pen to his shirt pocket, looked over his shoulder at the squirrel, and smiled. "Thank you."

9-Mile Run

JANUARY 1983

He had not run on Old Stage Road before. A week earlier, he had decided he would try to run 13 miles—half a marathon—on the sly, to see if he could actually make it that far.

He had just passed the 9-mile mark on the course he had laid out the previous week when the kids were at school and Tessa was at work.

His footing had deteriorated over the last half mile or so because Old Stage was not heavily used and had not been salted since a storm three days earlier. The snowpack had melted only enough under the afternoon sun to form a layer of sand-laden slush. Cooper had assumed that, after three days, the pavement would be bare. He should have driven out to surveil the situation.

He had tried to run 13 miles before he was ready, fearing he had started to lose ground, even though his last checkup at Mass General had indicated he had neither gained nor lost any ground.

Starting up a relatively steep grade, 12 to 15 degrees maybe, Cooper began to have trouble finding traction. And as was typical of roads in New Hampshire—except for the main north-south thoroughfares used by cash-laden skiers—there were no shoulders to speak of.

Running in his usual manner, head down, senses turned inward, Cooper did not see it coming—even sense it—until it was too late. A large black-and-chestnut Doberman was on him before he could do anything more than raise an arm to ward off an attack. It had not barked.

Cooper slipped on the snow-packed pavement and fell backward. Rolling onto his stomach then, he shielded his face with his arms. He did not have the strength to do anything more.

It seemed an eternity before he heard a whistle and "Here, Satan! Come, boy!" A woman's voice. Her clapping was like applause.

Cooper struggled to his feet and took inventory. Nothing seemed to be broken, and he seemed not to have been bitten. Cooper walked to the end of Old Stage, where it intersected with Route 9, then broke into a jog on bare pavement and headed home.

Days later, Cooper had felt a surge of adrenaline as he approached a ranch-style house on his right. A black pickup truck was parked in the driveway; an NRA sticker was conspicuously attached to the rear window.

Cooper pulled two well-rounded stones, about the size of a baseball, from the pouch in his sweatshirt. He would wait until the son of a bitch was charging—the last possible moment—then let him have it. *Wham! Wham!*

Starting up the grade that began just before Satan's house, Cooper kept his head positioned to appear like he was looking straight ahead while keeping his eyes cocked askance, to Cooper's right.

He didn't immediately see his quarry. Satan was in the side yard to the left of the house, chewing on something. Even from a distance, the dog seemed huge. It lifted its head and perked up its ears.

Cooper stopped in the middle of the road and adjusted his grip on the stone he was holding in his right hand. He took a defiant step toward the fire-breathing dragon he had come to slay. And another.

The dragon rose to all fours. It lowered its head and began to breathe fire.

"C'mon, you son of a bitch," Cooper whispered. "Come to Daddy."

C'mon, you son of a bitch, Satan seemed to echo. *Let me turn you into me.*

Cooper opened his hands and looked at the stones. *Which is it going to be?*

Cooper took a deep breath and lowered himself onto one knee.

He beckoned, "Here, Satan. C'mon boy! C'mon!"

Satan looked confused. He began to wag his tail. He extended himself into a deep stretch and plopped onto his belly. He yawned.

Cooper continued to beckon. "C'mon, Satan!"

Finally, tail wagging, Satan made his approach—tentatively at first, then with greater confidence.

Cooper sat back on his haunches. When Satan was within reach, Cooper slowly moved his hand toward its muzzle. The dog sniffed at Cooper's fingers, keeping its coal-black eyes fixed on him.

"Git in here, Satan!"

A woman was standing in an open doorway—it was the same voice Cooper heard last time.

"Git in here right now!"

Chest Cold

FEBRUARY 1983

Cooper had been running longer distances for several weeks when the boys were at school and Tessa was at work. He confined himself to rural roads to minimize the possibility of being recognized.

It had been four days since his last run as a result of an unshakable cold. It had begun in his head about a week ago and settled then into his chest. Lungs. Despite the tightness in his lungs and unending congestion, he knew he *had* to get outside and run. He couldn't wait any longer.

The sliding door was frozen shut. Planting both feet and using both hands, Cooper managed to jerk it open. Closing it was a little easier. The speed at which he was losing function was increasingly scary. It was a race to the finish in more ways than one.

Cooper spit phlegm beyond the deck railing.

He had decided not to bother stretching today. Because he wasn't going to be starting out very hard, he didn't see the need. It was distance he was after, not speed. He had to keep reminding himself of that. Distance over speed. He would warm up gradually.

Pausing at the top of the driveway, Cooper looked up at a leaden sky and took a deep breath. The chill air smelled of snow.

He loved snowstorms—the drama of them, of course, but also the feeling of coziness they engendered if you were someplace warm, safe, and well stocked.

At the bottom of the driveway, Cooper was greeted by a gust of wind and promptly lapsed into another coughing fit. He knew he should go back into the house right then and there, but of course he did not. *There is no tomorrow!*

He propped his arms on his knees until the coughing quieted, then launched into a slow jog. Though stiff from his four-day hiatus, Cooper savored a rush of well-being. He should have gotten back into running years ago!

He could tell from his first step, though, that his body was distracted with other matters—which was another reason for him to go back into the house. Then again, the more adversity he ran against in the present, the better. *No pain, no gain.*

Just past the half-mile mark, near the top of Evans Road, Cooper found himself sidelined by another coughing jag. No matter how hard he tried, however, he couldn't seem to clear his throat.

When finally he was able to continue, he noticed he was already sweating despite the massive cooling effect of the gale-force wind blowing out of the northeast. He decided to stay on Pudding Hill Road rather than proceed on his normal route on Evans Road. If it started to snow, the footing would be better on paved roads.

He would head out on Route 155 and go as far as Town Hall Road. That would be 2 miles out and 2 back—just enough to get him back into his routine.

The long, gradually curving hill on 155, stretching from the railroad tracks to the intersection with Madbury Road, seemed even steeper than usual, despite the wind being more or less at his back the entire distance. By the time Cooper reached the top of the incline, he was drenched in sweat, and his breathing suggested he had sprinted the entire way instead of merely jogging.

His right side felt as if it were incubating a side stitch—about a 9-pound, 4-ouncer! But the good news was there were no signs of leg cramping.

He toyed with the notion of stopping for a bit anyway so as not to overtax himself early on but decided to keep going instead, for fear he might get more chilled than he already was.

Bearing onto Town Hall Road, Cooper realized he had erred in taking this route instead of Evans Road. He was running almost directly against the wind now. The wind chill had to be about 10 degrees below zero, and he was not dressed for it. Had he taken Evans Road, he would have been more protected. Then again, *No pain, no gain!*

One more mile would give him a total of six. He simply *had* to make up at least part of the mileage he had lost to being sick. He continued.

The remaining distance to the Town Hall—300 yards maybe—was generally uphill, but after that, the going got a little easier. Stands of trees on either side of the road helped protect him from the wind, which had stiffened since he had left the house.

Reaching the 3-mile mark, Cooper decided he would try to run 1 more mile, for a total of 8. What the hell. He was out there anyway, so why not make the most of it! It would go a long way toward making up for all the time he had lost—at least psychologically. And if the forecast was right, the snowfall might prevent him from running tomorrow or the day after.

Just past the 3-mile mark, Cooper began to cough so violently that he came close to losing his balance. He propped his arms on his knees. When his breach finally quieted, he thought he caught a glimpse of something red where he had last spat but decided whatever he had seen, if anything, was probably just a remnant of something cast from a car window—a candy Valentine's heart maybe. Or a jelly bean.

Cooper continued on, his lungs now feeling sore with each breath.

A silvery film of water was sheeting down the reservoir spillway as Cooper thumped down a steep incline to where the water from the spillway passed under the road. For a few euphoric moments, Cooper savored a sense of omnipotence—he could run forever!—but by the time he was halfway up the mirror-image incline, he had to slow to no more than a shuffle.

He did not have the strength to do any better.

A little farther on, Cooper started to cough again. Instead of stopping, however, he forced himself to keep moving. When he reached the top of the incline, he considered heading for home, but the 4-mile mark was now less than a mile away. Every little bit helped!

There were no stands of wind-breaking trees on this stretch, and although the grade was only about 10 degrees, on average, it felt at least twice that—and it seemed to go on and on.

By the time Cooper reached the 4-mile mark, the wind was gusting to what felt like 35 to 40 miles an hour. Shuddering, he began to cough again. And once again, he spotted specks of red on the shoulder of the road. A chill ran up his spine. He turned 180 degrees and started to retrace his steps, but his legs had become stiff and leaden. He thought of Captain Scott in the Antarctic—freezing to death after having overextended himself.

When he got home, he would take a hot shower. No, a hot bath—so he wouldn't have to stand up. He would soak for an hour, then he would turn up the heat in the bedroom, curl up under the covers, and by morning, he would feel better.

He started to cough again. He had to get home. Then he would dose himself up with half a bottle of NyQuil and sleep for 12 hours straight—maybe 24! That's what he *really* needed—

What he did *not* really need was to make up for any of that lost time!

How stupid could he possibly get?

A snowflake streaked across his field of vision. Then another—and another. He had to get home before the snow began to accumulate. If he ended up having to walk, it would take him over an hour to get all the way home. By then his lungs would be shot.

He increased his pace a little, but even with the wind at his back now, he was only able to sustain it for a few hundred yards. By the time he reached the reservoir spillway, snow had begun to accumulate on the pavement. He was in trouble.

To guard against slipping, Cooper shortened his stride and stayed on what little shoulder there was. At the bottom of the incline, he paused to clear his throat. The white snow served to highlight the red stains Cooper left behind almost every time he coughed.

He couldn't remember when he had last seen a car. Everybody with at least half a brain was at home snuggled up to their woodstove. *Let it snow, let it snow...*

As he leaned into the ascending incline, Cooper's sweat-soaked T-shirt was now chafing his nipples. He winced—why in God's name did men have nipples?

Copying error? Symmetry imperative? It made no sense!

Then again, a lot of things didn't make any sense...

Cooper tried to maneuver his sodden T-shirt with little success.

About halfway to the top of the incline, he tripped over an errant stone and fell. He could feel snow melting on his upturned face—and then light, headlights.

A man with a scruffy, gray-streaked beard was peering down at him. He was wearing a Patriots cap.

"You OK?"

Cooper felt woozy. "I think so."

"Do you think you can stand up?"

"Yes."

"Any pain? Anything broken?"

"No. I'm fine."

The man helped Cooper to his feet and held him steady. His grip suggested he had pursued something more valuable than three academic degrees.

Cooper wobbled.

"How about I take you home? You don't want to be out in this. People can't see you. I almost ran over you myself."

"I don't want to trouble you."

"It's no trouble. Where do you live?"

"Garrison Lane. Not far from the sand pits on Mast Road."

The man nodded. "I know right where you are."

He led Cooper by the arm to the passenger side of his truck and held the door open. "Don't mind my dog."

Cooper climbed into the front seat and found himself side by side with a large black-and-chestnut Doberman.

"Satan?"

"You know my dog?"

"We've met."

Tipping Point

MARCH 1983

He had just passed the 2-mile mark on Perkins Road, not far from where Perkins Road became Canney, and was now trudging up a modest rise that stretched ahead for about 200 yards.

Noah was running beside him.

It was one of those unseasonably warm days in late winter that tease of spring. At the beginning of the run, Cooper had expected to be juiced up with hope and optimism, but the opposite had proven to be the case, and he was pretty sure he knew why.

He could feel that he had passed the tipping point. He was starting to lose ground. Up until recently—no more than a few days' time—Cooper had still been gaining ground thanks to all the running and strengthening he had been doing, not to mention all the supplements Tessa had insisted he take. He could sense the progress. However, over the last few days, there was a growing unease, sort of like the shift that is felt when a roller coaster is about to take a steep plunge.

The only systemic recourse he had now was to remain defiant—in charge of his body.

"Let's go an extra mile today," Cooper invited.

"How are you feeling?" Noah asked, dubious.

"Good," Cooper lied.

"You look like you might be struggling a bit," said Noah, suddenly the adult in the room. "It's a bit warm today."

"No pain, no gain."

"Don't push it. OK, Pop?"

"OK."

Cooper picked up his pace—just enough to ratchet up his defiance. He was stronger than ever, he told himself. Stronger today than yesterday and stronger tomorrow than today.

Tomorrow he would run 8 miles when Noah was at school—as compensation for the poor performance he had turned in so far today. He wasn't going to take any shit from those little God-created monsters eating him alive.

As he continued up the rise, Cooper felt a growing sluggishness, as if he were running through deepening water. If his legs and lungs began to beg for mercy, he told himself, he would not give in to them. He would refuse even to hear their plea.

At the top of the rise, Cooper paused to catch his breath. He braced his arms on his knees. All of a sudden, he lunged at a nearby mailbox hanging on chains, attempting to kick it into oblivion. Missing the mark, he fell backward onto the ground.

When he opened his eyes, Noah's face was looming over him. "Are you all right, Pop?"

Cooper could taste blood on his lip. "What happened to my helmet?" he asked.

"It popped off." Noah laughed. "You looked pretty funny going after that mailbox, Pop."

"Do you know who Don Quixote is?"

Noah grinned.

Cooper remained on his back.

"One might think I would've learned a thing or two about kicking things, wouldn't one? Once an idiot, always an idiot," Cooper said, struggling to rise.

"You're not an idiot, Pop."

"We'll see."

Noah helped Cooper to his feet, then retrieved his helmet.

Cooper tightened the chin strap and pulled on his helmet. "Let's keep it at 4 miles today. Four is plenty." Forcing a smile, he added, "I really appreciate your being here with me, Noah. It helps me a lot. It's always good to have an adult along."

Noah grinned. "You're doing great, Pop."

"So, you want to have a beer with me when we get home?"

"Sure!"

"Are you old enough?"

"Almost 15."

"Close enough!"

23

Citgo or Bust

Cooper turned onto Beacon Street and felt his heart sink. The famous Citgo sign—marking the beginning of the end of the Boston Marathon—seemed to be at least five times farther away than he had expected it to be.

Sinking to his knees, Cooper heard a familiar sound coming from behind and to Cooper's left. Opening his eyes, he found the Wheezer extending a hand toward him, palm up.

Cooper squeezed his eyes shut several times in an effort to clear them.

He was surprised to see onlookers on the sidelines, a significant number. The race had been over for several hours.

Cooper slapped the Wheezer's extended hand. "See you at the finish," the Wheezer said.

Fixing his eyes on the Citgo sign, Cooper managed to rise from the pavement and fought then to keep his balance. Peering downstream, he thought he caught a glimpse of the Wheezer.

If *this guy* could stay in the race no matter what, Cooper said to himself, so could he!

Cooper sensed another presence—*Richardson. He was going to force him to quit!*

"On your feet, puke, or I'm gonna muster that fat, fuckin' ass o' yers the fuck outa this program. Who the fuck ever told you you could be a real man anyway? Yer mommy tell ya that, did she? You're the goddamnedest sorriest excuse for manhood I've seen in my entire 23 years of puttin' up with pukes like you."

A stream of tobacco just missed the mark.

"I'm sorrier than I can say to hafta stand here and look at you. You're a goddamned fucking disgrace. They really had t'reach down to the bottom of the barrel to come up with the likes o' you, didn't they, college boy? That's the trouble with wartime—they'll take anybody and everybody."

Richardson began to make exaggerated sniffing sounds. "You don't even smell right, for fuck's sake. You smell like a goddamn queer. Get the fuck up here right now and look me in the eye, college boy. Can you do that, fuck face?"

Richardson squirted another stream of tobacco juice at Cooper. "Get up, puke!"

Cooper struggled to get up.

He collapsed.

He spat sand out of his mouth.

Richardson grabbed ahold of his right arm, Stovers ahold of his left arm.

They were going to take him to the truck!

Cooper tried to wrest himself free.

"Let me finish!

"I can do it!"

He struggled to get to his feet.

He fell back.

A flash.

A rumble of thunder.

A burst of wind.

A flash, a rumble.

A deluge.

Cooper lifted his head.

He closed his eyes.

He held his mouth open.

He struggled to get to his feet.

He collapsed.

He struggled to get to his feet.

He collapsed.

He struggled to get to his feet.

You're done!

Easter Sunday

EARLY 1950S

Cooper was kneeling in front of the statue of Mary at St. Vincent de Paul's, his knees throbbing. Not once over the past three hours had Cooper allowed himself to take the pressure off his knees. *No pain, no gain.*

He had outlasted Jack LaVerdiere, who was going to become a priest someday.

A few candles were flickering in the votive bank to Cooper's right, as if to the breath of something present but unseen—like the creature in *Forbidden Planet*. The scent of incense lingered in air grown chilly.

About an hour earlier, just after Jack had left for home, Cooper thought he had seen Mary's eyes move. After about 10 minutes of blank staring, he attributed it to the dancing light of the votive candles.

He had lost count of the number of rosaries he had said. If he had to, he would say them all night. There was no way he was going to let his Bad Voice talk his Good Voice out of it.

Shuddering in response to a deepening chill, Cooper pulled the collar of his ill-fitting sports jacket up and folded his arms against his chest. He should have worn a warmer coat.

She moved!

Cooper fixed his eyes on Mary's face, her eyes, her lips. Again, he forced himself not to blink.

Hail Mary, full of grace, blessed art thou among women—

Lifting his eyes, he peered into the emptiness of the vaulted ceiling. Tears scudded down his cheeks.

24

Daffodil Dreams

Cooper was lying on a windswept knoll, eyes closed, head on Tessa's lap. He could hear snippets of joyful voices. They would be fine. The world was a hard place, especially for the gentle of spirit, but it was not an impossible place.

People like George would always be there for them. He did not have to be there himself. He felt Tessa lift his hand to her lips.

"Sleep, my love," she whispered. "I will always be with you."

Cooper smiled. He was the luckiest man in the world.

25

Awakening

Rhythmic beeping.

Something foreign in his nose.

A bad case of dry mouth.

Cooper opened his eyes.

Someone was sitting in a chair, a recliner, close by.

Tessa.

Asleep.

He would never forgive himself for what he had put her through.

He tried to wipe his cheeks.

An IV was in the way.

He tried to speak Tessa's name.

He could not.

Tears welled.

He tried again.

He could not form the word.

He touched the railing on the left side of his bed but could not grasp it.

He coughed.

Tessa shrieked and leaped from the recliner.

A nurse rushed into the room.

"He's awake!" Tessa shrieked.

"Hallelujah!" the nurse replied.

Tessa dragged a chair to the side of Cooper's bed and sat down in it. "George said you'd be back. He told me you two had more work to finish."

Cooper winced as Tessa calmly explained that six weeks had passed and, in the process of being airlifted to Mass General, his heart had twice stopped.

"Are you in pain?" the nurse asked.

Cooper struggled to speak, but he couldn't form the words.

Tessa put a finger to Cooper's lips. "Give it time. Your brain was so badly swollen when you got here, they had to relieve the pressure. Dr. Parag warned me there might be some lasting damage from all the trauma, but you're still here, and as far as I'm concerned, that's all that matters."

Cooper felt a lump at the back of his throat.

I'm sorry, he wanted to say. *I'm so very sorry.* But he could not form the words.

Tessa brightened. "I have something to show you."

She snapped the ceiling lights on, removed something from a metal table on the far side of the recliner, and quickly returned. Tessa oriented a newspaper clipping so Cooper could see it. "This is from *The Boston Globe*. The same photo appeared in hundreds of other newspapers around the country. What you're looking at, Cooper, is a man—a very large man, as you can see—carrying you across the finish line. Your body gave out just short of the finish line, and you were unconscious. He carried you the rest of the way to the finish line and disappeared."

Cooper smiled.

The Wheezer.

26

Making Peace

AUGUST 24, 1983

Tessa lowered the lift on the van, and Cooper backed his wheelchair down it.

The boys had painted the chair red and printed "The Little Engine That Could" on the back. The angled, superscripted letters *-ld* served as testimony to the fact the artists had not correctly calculated the amount of space that would be needed to accommodate all five words. The problem, of course, had been the inescapable fact that all three boys had inherited their visual art abilities from their father.

Looking across the intersection of Point and Lake Streets in Cape Vincent, Cooper took a quick measure of the homestead he had grown up in. It had obviously slipped further into decline since he had last seen it. The paint on the clapboards had continued to peel unabated, especially around the window sills. The once-perky picket fence now had dental problems. The fence along Lake Street was entirely missing. Some of the window shutters—the real-wood kind—appeared loosely held together, perhaps more by habit than anything else. The roof, badly discolored, was in need of replacing. An unsightly stovepipe was protruding from the sunporch roof. What shrubbery was visible seemed badly in need of a good trimming. The term *benign neglect* came to mind.

As they say, you can't go home again—unless, of course, it's to say goodbye.

Cooper looked to the once-vacant lot that had made up his brother Stephen's Royal Republic of Brainia. It was now taken up with prefab homes and house trailers. The mammoth elm that had once stood near the intersection was gone. When he was 9 or 10, Cooper had buried a small treasure chest at the foot of that tree and had not been able to find it again. He had wondered over the years if someone had discovered it and what Cooper had considered "treasure" back then—a stack of Monopoly money, likely.

He felt a lump form in his throat. His fort was gone, as was its host. Chestnut trees tended not to live very long. Cooper suspected it had something to do with the demands of producing large quantities of chestnuts every year, year after year. It would seem likely that the more fruitful a species was, in size as well as quantity, the shorter its life.

Cooper shuddered.

Get your ass down here—right now!

Tessa crouched beside the wheelchair and grasped Cooper's hand with both of hers. "You OK?"

Cooper nodded.

"Rough stuff."

Cooper nodded.

Cooper motored to where he thought the tree holding his fort had stood.

He was holding a trowel and a Ziploc bag on his lap. He gestured toward the ground.

Tessa took the trowel from Cooper's lap and touched the ground. "Here?"

Cooper nodded.

Tessa dug a hole in the soft earth. When it was about a foot deep, she looked to Cooper.

"How's that?"

Cooper nodded.

Tessa picked up the plastic bag from Cooper's lap and placed it in the hole. "I forgive you," Cooper whispered.

Tessa kissed Cooper's hand, filled in the hole she had made, and looked at Cooper. "You ended it, Cooper. Not only does Noah know what it's like to be loved by his father; he knows what it's like to be cherished by his father. For that reason alone, J. Cooper Haynes, I will love you until the end of time. It is an honor and a joy to be your wife."

Cooper bowed his head.

Prisoners Alike

SEPTEMBER 1983

Cooper and Tessa followed Will Fraley into a large room lit almost entirely by a wall of windows on the far side. About two dozen men, ranging from early 20s to perhaps mid-60s, all of them wearing bright-orange jumpsuits, were sitting in rows of chairs facing a whiteboard and a lectern.

Cooper and Tessa followed Will to the front of the room. Tessa sat down in a chair to the right of Cooper's wheelchair.

Will introduced Cooper as the Little Engine That Could, adding, "Most of you have seen the news clips," to nods and smiles.

"I have invited Cooper here today to share with us his experience."

Tessa quickly stood up to interject. "Cooper has trouble speaking. If you miss anything or don't understand something, please raise your hand. If need be, I will interpret for you."

She sat down.

Cooper bowed his head, acknowledging his audience, and began. "Thank you for honoring me with your presence. Like you, I'm a prisoner. In my case, I'm confined to this wheelchair. There is no escape. What are my options? Do I have any? Do *you* have any?

"One of my options would be, of course, to allow myself to be angry about my situation. After all, it wasn't my fault. It was inflicted on me. Or maybe I could dedicate some part of myself to creating something beautiful. Something that expresses who I really am as a human being. Something that brings some measure of happiness to other people and, through them, to me.

"I've spent most of my life in a rage. I was angry at my parents and at my eldest brother. My father pretended I didn't exist. My mother loathed my very presence. My eldest brother wanted me dead.

"Later in life, I took my anger out on my oldest son. I did a lot of damage, all of which, thank God, has been repairable. Do you all have something to write with?"

Nods.

"If you would, please complete the following statement: *The purpose of my life is...*"

He paused, scanning the men's faces for feedback.

"There are other ways of saying the same thing. For example, *I was put on this Earth to...*"

Pause.

"Has anyone ever asked you this question before?"

Cooper noticed a few heads nodding, and plenty of the others seemed less sure but engaged.

"If someone had asked you when you were 10 years old to complete the statement *The purpose of my life is*, and you answered with *to create something beautiful*, do you think you would be sitting in this room at this moment?"

Mystery Missive

SEPTEMBER 20, 1983

Cooper woke to find a folded sheet of paper lying on his lap, bound up in a bright-red bow. He had slept in his downstairs bedroom, formerly the dining room, because it was increasingly a hassle for Tessa and the boys to get him up and down the stairs.

Cooper sensed he was supposed to read this missive in private, so he got right to it. Fortunately, he was wearing his glasses and had been, day and night now, so as not to have to keep asking for them. There was just enough ambient light in the room for him to be able to read the handwriting, which was Tessa's:

Dearest Father and Husband,

We don't want you to suffer. We know things are going to get bad for you. When the time comes, tell us what you need us to do. We will do it. Rest assured.

With deepest love—

Cooper smiled at the thought of slipping into a benign oblivion. He closed his eyes.

New Routine

JANUARY 17, 1984

A chickadee fluttered from one of the feeders to a nearby fir tree, and Cooper wondered anew how anything so fragile could survive a single subfreezing night, much less an entire winter.

Although Zak had replenished Cooper's feeders before rushing off to catch the bus—just in the nick of time, presumably—the larger of Cooper's tube feeders was already empty at the top, most likely the result of near-continuous pilfering at the "hands" of the usual gang of suspects.

Cooper couldn't be mad at them—at least not for long—because they served as entertainment for anyone whose physical world had shrunk to little more than his own cadaverous dimensions. Besides, justice on a universal scale would seem to require that any creature clever enough to foil every human effort to squirrel-proof their bird feeders should be allowed to reap whatever bounty their considerable cleverness could avail to them. Within limits, of course!

As Cooper watched, a squirrel jumped to the top of the larger tube feeder and, finding purchase where seemingly there was none, stretched down the length of the tube and proceeded to lift one seed at a time from one of the access apertures.

Voices now—from the kitchen. Tessa greeting George.

Hooray!

Cooper took several short breaths. He was in a hurry. There was still a lot to be done, and the sand in the upper part of his hourglass was getting precariously low. It was plain for all to see. He could resume hoping for something to come along that would slow the progression of his disease, of course—a new drug—but hope was not what he needed at this late point. *Time* was.

You're late, George! Get in here!

Cooper could hear claws clicking on the kitchen floor. Satan.

A light tap at the door, and George appeared, preceded by a rambunctious black-and-chestnut dog.

"Ah, so there you are," George teased, showing Cooper a mischievous grin.

George patted one of Cooper's pencil-thin legs. "How's our fabulous fabulist this fine morning?"

Cooper used Morse code via eye blinks: *dot-dash-dot* (R), *dot-dash* (A), *dot-dash-dot* (R), *dash-dot* (N), *dash* (T), *dash-dash-dot* (G), *dash-dash-dash* (O).

"Raring to go," George translated. "OK." He explained his tardiness with an accident on Route 108 and quickly shed his down vest.

The room was stifling. Tessa kept the temperature at 80 degrees.

Satan had trotted to the far side of Cooper's bed, his tail striking everything within range. He greeted Cooper with the usual slathering of saliva.

Emily, who was lying against Cooper's side, took no notice. Being "top dog" meant she could do, or not do, whatever the hell she pleased, and Satan had to live with it. Typically, she would remain at Cooper's side, while

Satan slept on an outsized dog bed on the floor nearby, until the kids returned from school. There were two notable exceptions: Emily would leave Cooper's bed now and then, jump onto a small table positioned in front of the north-facing window, and watch the activity at the bird feeders.

Once the kids arrived in the afternoon, everyone—kids and pets alike—would head outdoors for a round of street hockey, with Satan being happy to fetch errant pucks and Emily observing the drama from a safe distance.

Tessa entered the room and asked George and Cooper if she could get them anything before she left for work.

"I'm good," George replied.

Dot-dash-dash (W), Cooper blinked.

Taking Cooper's cue, Tessa eased a tube attached to a plastic water bottle into Cooper's mouth and squeezed the bottle lightly. Even so, most of the water backed out of Cooper's throat and dribbled down the front of him.

Tessa waited for Cooper to recover from the effort, rubbing his back; then, turning her head so only George could see her eyes, she placed an oxygen mask over Cooper's nose and mouth. She held it there until Cooper had managed to take a few breaths.

George looked to Cooper. "I have to leave at around 10 today."

Dash-dot-dash (K), Cooper replied.

George moved an accountant's chair closer to Cooper's bed and lifted himself into it. Provisioning himself with a yellow pad and a pocket protector stuffed with no. 2 pencils, George turned the sheets to a near-blank one and read what had most recently been written on it—in Luke's hand, George could tell:

Humility is the...

George and Cooper continued on from where Cooper and Luke had left off:

...last lesson learned and the first...

They worked slowly to accommodate Cooper's tendency to become easily fatigued.

Making Peace

At one point, Cooper glanced out the window and caught two squirrels in the act of hanging upside down on two of his feeders. Fortunately, Satan's master, Ted Beardsley, had a daughter who worked in a local tack shop. She could get birdseed for Cooper's feeders at half price.

Satan groaned. Emily purred.

Cooper continued to blink.

27

Unchained Melody

JULY 13, 1984

There is a time to live and a time to die. It was time.

When Tessa next entered Cooper's room, Cooper closed his eyes and held them shut for a count of four. He paused, repeated in kind, then blinked: *dash-dot-dash-dash.*

"Are you sure, my love?"

Cooper repeated the request.

Tessa kissed him on the forehead and switched off his ventilator. She crawled onto his bed and laid her head alongside his. She could feel him struggle to breathe.

"Dance with me, my love," she whispered, "one last time—

"Around and around—

"Around and around—"

> *Lonely rivers cry*
> *Wait for me, wait for me*
> *I'll be coming home*
> *Wait for me...*

Noah found Tessa in Cooper's downstairs bedroom. Her gaze was fixed on Cooper's feeders outside. Noah knelt down beside her and rubbed her back.

"Your father has gone for a run," she said. "His feathered friends miss him already."

Acknowledgments

An early draft of this work languished in limbo for 50 years, until the author's middle son, Matthew, suggested it might be a good time to take a fresh look at it. The author is grateful for Matthew's poke. The author is grateful also for the contributions of his early mentors, Marston LaFrance and Will Jumper; ALS patient Alan (Smoky) Sherman; medical experts Theodore Munsat, Thomas Decker, and William Stone; and readers Dori Hale, Ray Goodwin, Melissa Osborne, Laurie Fitzgerald, Betty and Tom Gidley, Darlene Padura, Paul Cooper, Michael Holmes, Tina Butler, Susana Gustavson, Dave Adelman, Pete Thompson, David Sundberg, the Fitzgerald boys, and Renee Jardine.

An extra special thank-you to Digital Equipment Corporation, Sanders Associates, the Wang Institute of Graduate Studies, AT&T Bell Laboratories, Boston University, Wellfleet Communications, and Convergent Networks.

In the author's youth, the attentions and kindnesses of several teachers were a lifesaver. Among these were Winnie Sullivan Blum, Vera Hollenbeck, Kathryn Pillmore, Bessie Tanner, Betty Ellsworth Morrison, Eileen Chambers, Jim "Pop" Garvin, and Blanche Webster. Also Edna Edsall, Alexander Sundberg Sr., William Carruthers, Jack Hanlin, Don Youmans, Betty Kelleher, Jim Gosier, Bill Mein, Doris Countryman, Marion McKenzie, Dorothy Mannigan, and Hannah Dashley.

All deceased; none forgotten.

About the Author

Raised in the tiny village of Cape Vincent, New York, on the St. Lawrence River, Tom Fitzgerald did not grow up with the knowledge that it was possible for a farm boy like him to make a living as a writer, and it took him a while to find his true calling. After graduating from high school as class valedictorian, he studied engineering at Clarkson College, an experience that taught him he did not want to be an engineer.

A subsequent stint in law school and a master's program in mathematics taught him that he also didn't want to be a lawyer or a mathematician. But when a mentor encouraged him to pursue an advanced degree in English, Fitzgerald was on his way. His first novel, *Chocolate Charlie*, was published in 1973, achieving great commercial success and personal praise from the legendary actress Elizabeth Taylor. This was followed by three more novels, including the critically acclaimed *Poor Richard's Lament*, a popular fitness manual called *Get Tough!*, a children's fable, several nonfiction titles, and two collections of aphorisms.

A lifelong athlete, Fitzgerald completed a series of solo open-water swims in his late teens and early 20s and later became a Navy SEAL, serving in Vietnam. He ran the Boston Marathon three times in the 1980s, while researching and writing *Road to Redemption* (originally titled *A Private*

Agony). He later abandoned the novel, but returned to it thirty years later at the urging of the second of his three sons, Matt Fitzgerald, himself an author of many books on running.

In 2023, Fitzgerald lost his wife of 56 years, Laurie, to Alzheimer's disease. He currently resides in Vancouver, Washington, near his sons Joshua and Sean and their families. Now in his 80s, he still writes and exercises every day.